Stories of Sicily

Also by Alfred Alexander:
Giovanni Verga (1972)
Operanatomy (1971, revised edition 1974)

Stories of Sicily

Edited and translated with an
Introduction by

ALFRED ALEXANDER

Schocken Books · New York

First published by SCHOCKEN BOOKS 1975

Library of Congress Cataloging in Publication Data
Alexander, Alfred.
Stories of Sicily.
1. Short stories, English—Translations from Italian. 2. Short stories,
Italian—Translations into English. 3. Sicily—Fiction. I. Title.
PZ1. A395.St [PQ4254] 853'.01 75-9843

Photoset, Printed and Bound in Great Britain by Weatherby Wool-
nough, Sanders Road, Wellingborough, Northamptonshire NN8 4BX.

Contents

Acknowledgements

'The Bond of San Giovanni' is a translation of 'Comparàtico' (see also Alfred Alexander's *Luigi Capuana's Comparàtico - A Story which Made Literary History*, Ciranna, Rome, 1970), which was contained in Capuana's *Homo!*, Milan, Brigola, 1883. The same volume contains 'La Mula' ('The Mule') and 'Povero Dottore' ('The Doctor's Torment'); the latter story, under the name 'Il Tormento' ('The Torment'), is also contained in the volume *Ribrezzo e Fascino*, Sandron, Palermo, 1921. 'Il Mulo di Rosa' ('Rosa's Mule') was published in Capuana's *Nuove paesane*, 1898, and the text was made available to me by the kindness of my friend Professor Gino Raya.

Verga's three stories, 'La Lupa' ('The Wolf'), 'Cavalleria Rusticana' and 'Libertà' ('Liberty') were translated from the Mondadori edition of Verga's collected stories, seventh edition, 1967.

Luigi Pirandello's 'Ciàula scopre la luna' ('Ciàula Discovers the Moon'), a story included in the volume *Tu ridi* (1919), is translated from the text as contained in *Luigi Pirandello: Novelle*, edited by Giuseppe Morpurgo, Edizione Scolastiche Mondadori, 1947. I thank Mr Giorgio Moscon for his kind permission to translate it.

Vitaliano Brancati's 'Storia di Mila' ('The Story of Mila') and 'Storia di un uomo che per due volte non rise' ('Story of a Man Who Twice Failed to Laugh') are contained in *Il vecchio con gli stivali*, Bompiani, 1949; Giuseppe di Lampedusa's 'La goia e la legge' ('Joy and the Law') in *I racconti*, Feltrinelli, 1972; Virgilio Titone's 'La zolfara' ('The Sulphur Mine') in *Storie della vecchia Sicilia*, Mondadori, Milan, 1971; and Leonardo Sciascia's 'L'antimonio' ('Antimony') in *Gli zii di Sicilia*, Einaudi, 1958, Turin. Gino Raya's 'Filippa' appeared in the journal *Narrativa*, Rome, March 1957; Carmelo Ciccia's 'Passato Remoto' ('Remote Past') in the journal *Italscambi,* Ivrea, 1968; and the two Dolci sketches were translated from the text of *Racconti siciliani,* Einaudi, 1963.

Those difficulties bound to present themselves in dealing with copyright arrangements across frontiers were solved in the most friendly and efficient manner by Peter Halban for the stories by Sciascia and Dolci, and by Elizabeth Stevenson for that by Titone.

I should like to express my gratitude and appreciation to Hazel Wood, whose acute sense of taste and discernment have substantially assisted in the selection of the stories, and to Antony Wood, who has carried out the laborious and often insufficiently appreciated task of the publisher's editor, putting his exceptional gift for expression, as well as his tenacity, to the best of uses.

Bronwynne Farman and Diane Service have helped me in countless different ways: to both I am very grateful.

Alfred Alexander

Introduction

Folk songs, it is generally agreed, reflect the spirit of their country. 'D'ye ken John Peel?' and 'The Ash Grove' are said to represent England, with 'Auld Lang Syne', 'Yankee Doodle' and 'Frère Jacques' standing for Scotland, America and France. Sicily's most popular song is *Vitti na crozza* ('I Saw a Skull'): the words address a skull lying on a cannon, and the skull itself replies. Sicily's second most popular song, *Ciuri, Ciuri* ('Flowers') is less macabre, but its gaiety is veiled by the sad inflection of a minor tonality. Sayings and proverbs, too, mirror the people who coin them. In Sicily, the brief though very acute and numbing pain caused by knocking one's 'funny bone' is called a 'widow's pain'; and the proverb 'A father will look after a hundred children – but a hundred children won't look after one father' typifies the cynical humour of the island.

From outside their island, Sicilians have popularly been regarded as either aristocrats or mafiosi, or possibly both. Only lately have visitors, who previously congregated almost exclusively in a few resorts, ventured to explore the interior, increased their contact with the island's inhabitants, and become curious about the 'ordinary' Sicilian; and it is at least part of the Editor's purpose, in presenting this volume, to illuminate the habits, attitudes and ways of thought of the people of the island. Virgilio Titone, Professor of Modern History at Palermo University, explains that a Sicilian nation does not really exist: 'The different races which for centuries superimposed themselves upon one another not only failed to fuse, but did not even succeed in getting closer to one another.'

The major purpose of this selection of stories is to further the English-speaking public's appreciation of the Sicilians' abundant literary gifts. Over the last century, Sicilians have played so disproportionately large a role in Italy's literary life that it has sometimes constituted a source of irritation to the Italians of the mainland. When once almost half of Rome's theatres were presenting plays by Sicilians, a newspaper suggested that Sicilians 'seem to be either writers or illiterates'. From an enormous output, inevitably only a very small number of examples could be selected for this volume. With the exception of the stories by Verga and 'E. A.' by Dolci, this selection contains only work that has not been translated into English before.

The absence of English translations is perhaps in no case more surprising than in that of Luigi Capuana (1839–1915). Capuana, a remarkable man and an exceedingly versatile writer, was one of the most important figures in Italy's literary *ottocento*. He is so neglected in English-speaking countries that the standard histories of Italian literature do not even mention the existence of his short stories – many of which can stand comparison with those of Guy de Maupassant.

From his early youth to his old age, Capuana was a close friend of Giovanni Verga, and the two are regarded as the co-founders of *Verismo,* a literary movement that later extended its influence into music and inspired some of the best tunes in opera. Although it was essentially an Italian literary movement, the roots of *Verismo* lay in French Realism and Naturalism. In nineteenth-century Italy, French prose-writers had a large public. Little good prose was being written in Italian, and any Italian not wishing for a steady diet of poetry had to turn to prose in French, a language understood by all educated people. In the first half of the nineteenth century, the French novel had undergone great expansion, rather more in the sense of development than of revolution. Stendhal, George Sand and Balzac had turned to a strict observation of reality. Earlier writers had not ignored reality, but they had only permitted themselves a partial view of it. The Realists wished to reproduce it *in toto,* and every aspect of human nature, pleasant or unpleasant, was to be shown.

In 1857 Flaubert's *Madame Bovary* dealt Romanticism its final blow, and opened the way for the Realist novel. Emile Zola (born in 1840) at first followed Flaubert, but soon branched out into Naturalism, whose theory he expressed in 1880 in his famous

Roman expérimental. The intention of Realism was to give a documented picture of reality; Naturalism now claimed a scientific basis. For the Realist writers it had been sufficient to observe and to document: Zola claimed that 'the novelist is both observer and experimenter'. Zola had arrived at this view as the result of the new trends in physiology, particularly Claude Bernard's *Introduction à la médecine expérimentale* (1865), a guide to the assessment of the results of medical experiments which had important literary side-effects. 'I shall only have to adapt,' wrote Zola, 'as the experimental method itself has been established by Claude Bernard. The scientist provides me with a solid basis . . . and I can confine myself to quoting his irrefutable arguments . . . more often than not, it will be sufficient to substitute the word "novelist" for "doctor" to make my thoughts clearer, and to give them the power of scientific truth.'

Verga as well as Capuana found the new French literary trends much to his taste. The part-Italian Zola was naturally beloved by all francophile Italians as a symbol of Italo-French friendship. Italy's cultural, social and political structures, however, led Italian writers to apply Naturalist principles rather differently. The most significant difference, perhaps, was that French writers concentrated their attention mostly upon the bourgeoisie and town-dwellers, while the Italian *Veristi* highlighted the lowest rung of the social ladder, the poor peasants of country regions.

Luigi Capuana, born in Mineo (the ancient Manae) in the province of Catania, was the first of the *Veristi*. At the time of his youth, Sicily, according to Federico de Roberto, was still an island 'morally close to the feudal period, and geographically isolated from the centres of real culture. Without railways, without schools, without newspapers and almost without books, most men of Capuana's background wrote poorly, and read little and badly: the women could not even match that. Ships – sailing ships rather than steamers – formed the only communication with the outside world.' Capuana soon realised that he would have to go to the mainland of Italy to find the background and the stimulus that his literary interests required. He went to Florence, since 1864 the capital; his gifts were appreciated, and he became theatre critic of the *Nazione,* the leading newspaper. This important post, however,

11

brought such meagre financial rewards that, unable to maintain himself, he was forced to return to Sicily a few years later and became mayor of his home town.

Capuana's literary output was enormous – he wrote nearly a hundred books, including novels, short stories, poetry, plays and children's stories, in Italian as well as in the dialect of Sicily; but his income almost throughout his life was pitiful. A man of many parts, he was an outstanding amateur photographer, interested himself in hypnosis and spiritualism, and was a keen student of female psychology. While he was living in Rome, a newspaper report about the attempted suicide of a young teacher tempted him to pay her a visit in hospital. Shortly afterwards they were living together, and eventually married – a chain of events preserved for posterity by his old friend Pirandello in the play *To Clothe the Naked*.

Capuana's greatest importance lies in his short stories. Verga acknowledges him as the true founder of *Verismo* in a letter written to him in 1882, in which he refers to the story 'Comparàtico' ('The Bond of San Giovanni'): '. . . Never, never can I forget that story. . . that perfect little masterpiece, and I must confess that I owe entirely to you the basic inspiration for that straightforward, popular style which I have tried to give my own stories. . . '

'Comparàtico' has a curious history. The Sicilian poet Lionardo Vigo wished to publish an authentic selection of the stories which the wandering story-tellers of the time recited, and requested his friends to send him good examples of popular poetry from their own districts. Capuana contributed the ballad 'Lu Cumpari' ('The Godfather'), claiming that it originated from the district of Mineo. Vigo accepted it as genuine, and included it in his extensive *Collection of Sicilian Popular Poetry*, which appeared in 1870–74. Several years later, Capuana published a volume of stories under the title *Homo!*, which contained *Comparàtico*, telling the same story. In a note at the end of the book, Capuana admitted that the inclusion of this story might at first appear to be an act of doubtful propriety: he assured his readers, however, that he had only appropriated what was really his own, and confessed to having played a deliberate trick on Vigo when he submitted his own work as folklore.

12

The title 'Comparàtico' requires explanation. *Compare* means literally 'co-father', a term originally used for two relationships: the *compare d'anello* or 'ring co-father', i.e. the marriage-witness who signs the church register, and the *compare di battesimo* or 'baptismal co-father', the child's godfather *in his relationship to the parents* (though not in his relationship to his godchild, to whom he is *padrino* or 'godfather'). The English language has no word for this relationship between father and godfather.* Gradually the word lost its specific meaning and assumed a vastly amplified one; it became merely a word of esteem, indicating that the person thus addressed was worthy of being made a child's godfather. Eventually the term *compare* became a general mode of address vaguely indicating respect and approbation. In Sicily it is no longer used in this way, but the term survives, rather surprisingly, in Peru, introduced by settlers from Sicily. In Capuana's story the word *comparàtico* is used in its original meaning. 'Godfathership' is a holy bond, protected by St John the Baptist himself (for this reason referred to as the Sangiovanni), and must not be violated. Owing to its beginnings as a hoax, the story lacks, perhaps, the psychological refinement of some of Capuana's other stories, but its stark realism and new, 'direct' style fully justify the special place that it holds in Italian literature.

With 'The Mule', we are in the range of Capuana's true masterpieces, in which psychology and motivation of the characters emerge with exceptional clarity. This psychological insight is even more marked in 'Rosa's Mule', a story which deals with the problems of adoption. The perfect shading of the different attitudes and reactions involved supports the claim that this may well be the finest literary treatment of adoption's problems. In 'The Doctor's Torment', medical case history plays a leading role, reflecting the literary interest of the time in experimental psychology aroused by Zola's *Roman expérimental*. The English title of this story is a combination of the two titles under which it was published: 'The Poor Doctor' and 'The Torment'. Many of Capuana's stories were published in several versions and at least two versions of the story 'The Doctor's Torment' exist. The one selected here is the original one, though

* Bar the archaic 'gossip'.

some amendments of the revised edition have been incorporated in this translation.

Capuana did not think that a good story need be based on an actual incident; he held that the incident and its psychological implications were best invented. Giovanni Verga (1840—1922), on the other hand, regarded the actual happening as an essential ingredient of the story. Capuana's junior by one year, Verga was born in Catania, and the two writers were from early youth linked by a firm and lasting friendship. Their home towns, Vizzini and Mineo, were only some twenty miles apart; their social background – impecunious gentry – was similar. Their careers too showed similarity: neither managed to achieve success in his lifetime.

At the beginning of his adult life, Verga too left Sicily and visited the cultural centres of Florence and Milan. His novels of the erotic-sentimental type had some success, but he changed his style when he was approaching forty to write his famous short stories as well as his greatest work, the novel *I Malavoglia,* the first volume of the projected series of five novels *Ciclo dei Vinti* ('Cycle of the Doomed'), which was never completed. None of his major works made any impact on his contemporaries. While some critics appreciated his stories, they disliked the way in which they were told, disapproving not only of Verga's choice of language, but also of his pessimism and the harshness of the reality he described. Manzoni, too, had described harsh situations, but there was a fundamental difference in their attitudes: Manzoni's harshness was always mitigated by a deep religious feeling; Verga was an atheist – he wrote to his great friend, Dina di Sordevolo, 'God does not exist, or is cruel: that's all there is to be said about it.'

Verga died in Catania in 1922 at the age of eighty-two, and only towards his eightieth year did his contemporaries begin to appreciate his work. By then he had been suffering for almost thirty years from a depression that had sapped his literary powers and his creative desire; he had become a disenchanted and silent old man, disappointed and disgusted with the literary world which had treated him so shabbily. He even declined to attend the celebrations in honour of his own eightieth birthday, where his young friend and admirer Pirandello was to be the official speaker. When the chairman of the celebration committee attributed this refusal to Verga's well-known shyness, the latter asked him how he knew it was shyness that made him disinclined to attend.

'What else could it be?'

'Contempt,' said Verga, 'because all of you left it too late.'

The celebrations had to take place without him. Pirandello, who had travelled all the way across Sicily from Agrigento to Catania in order to deliver his address, spent the night in Catania; late at night, tired and disappointed – Verga's absence had cast a shadow over the festivities – he returned to his hotel. When he opened the door of his room he saw, to his surprise, Verga sitting quietly in a chair. Pirandello walked towards him. Verga rose slowly, and came to meet him with outstretched hand. He gripped Pirandello's right hand and, with tears of sadness in his eyes, looked into his friend's face. For a few moments they stood in silence – and then Verga left, without saying a word.

Verga's literary ambition was 'natural and true' story-telling. He believed that 'true' writing (he preferred the expression *Verità* to *Verismo*, which means 'akin to truth') rested on two conditions: that the author must 'disappear' in order to enable the story to 'tell itself', and convey the impression of actual happenings without evidence of the author's hand; and that the language used must fit the individual – a requirement that led to Verga's most important stylistic innovation. Without resorting to dialect, but not insisting on syntactical correctness, he distinguished his characters by the *cantilena* of the spoken words of ordinary people. By these stylistic means, and generally within the boundaries of correct Italian, he made his writing echo their words and their mannerisms.

The critic Benedetto Croce, the first to recognise Verga's genius, nevertheless regarded impersonality as a 'confused concept for asserting a true need, i.e. that a work of art must have an inner logic or necessity, and can tolerate neither arbitrariness nor whims. However erroneous these *Veristic* formulas may be, they undoubtedly acted beneficial for Verga – as well as for others – because they served as a stimulus to great scrupulousness in artistic workmanship'. This 'scrupulousness', together with the rules of *Verismo,* brought Verga into conflict with those who did not adhere to such norms, particularly the enormously successful Gabriele D'Annunzio, whose gift for poetical expression Verga appreciated, but whom he thoroughly disliked as a person and thought a hoaxer and a cheat; true to his principles, Verga wrote to his friend Dina: 'Accurate background details are as indispensible to me as roses are for D'Annunzio's stuff.'

The three of Verga's short stories selected here show his high 'artistic workmanship' and masterly depiction of the Sicilian character. 'Cavalleria Rusticana' was first published in 1880, and is based on an incident in Vizzini's 'black chronicle', the town's criminal record. It is a classic example of *Verismo,* and loyal to its principles, written in strictly factual, almost sketchy style; not only is the author's hand concealed, but a good deal of the background information is missing and must be supplied by the reader. The story was originally intended for *I Malavoglia,* but was discarded and published on its own, still retaining names (e.g. Alfio) and characteristics from its original *Malavoglia* setting. Its fortunes – or misfortunes – are the reason for Verga's disillusionment with the literary world and his long depression.

Verga adapted 'Cavalleria Rusticana' for the theatre, and his play of the same name was first performed, with the greatest success, in Turin in 1884, and subsequently all over Italy. In 1889 Mascagni used it, adapted by two librettists, for his one-act work which won the important Sonzogno prize for 1890 and became one of the world's most successful operas. However, Mascagni's failure to obtain Verga's consent to the use of his literary property, followed by the publisher Sonzogno's remarkably high-handed attitude, led to friction. Both parties agreed to submit the dispute to the Italian Society of Authors for an 'opinion', but when this turned out in Verga's favour, Sonzogno refused to implement the Society's recommendations for a settlement, and Verga had to resort to court action. The court found that a serious breach of copyright had occurred, and the judgement in favour of Verga was upheld by the Court of Appeal, and again confirmed by the Corte di Cassazione, the Italian equivalent of the House of Lords. Although Verga was declared to be the opera's co-author, and entitled to twenty-five per cent of all its proceeds, he was unable to make the powerful Sonzogno declare the true profit figures, and in 1893 finally felt compelled to accept a 'once and for all' settlement. A substantial sum was paid to him, but this was not to be the end of the affair. One of the longest court actions in history ensued, and it was conducted with a bitterness and hostility without parallel in the history of the relationship between writer, publisher and musician. Only now, after eighty years of litigation, does the case appear to be nearing its conclusion. A court verdict of September 1973 has, 'in view of the changed conditions created by the new media of dissemination', declared the old agreement null and void, and Verga's heirs may therefore still see their rightful part of the royalties allotted to them – until the fiftieth anniversary of Mascagni's death, in 1995, frees the work from all such obligations. For many years, Verga's name did not even appear as the author of the story on the programmes when the opera was performed. This has now been remedied, but Verga's name is still omitted from the score.

'The Wolf' dates from the same period as 'Cavalleria Rusticana' (it was first published in 1880), and is based on an incident in Mineo which Capuana had mentioned to Verga. Its subsequent history is not unlike that of 'Cavalleria Rusticana'. The story was reworked by Verga into a play, which was first performed in Turin in 1896. With a libretto arranged by Verga's 'Boswell', Federico De Roberto, Puccini later decided to set it to music, but eventually abandoned the project and incorporated the music he had written for it into *La Bohème*. De Roberto's libretto was finally used by the Sicilian composer Pierantonio Tasca for his opera *La Lupa,* which was first performed in 1933. Thirty years later the original play too was revived, and successfully performed with Anna Magnani in the title role.

The literary achievement of the story lies in the crystal-clear and dispassionate rendering of the protagonists: real people who do wrong, and whose wrong-doing is the result, almost the inevitable result, of their character and circumstances. They are true *vinti,* doomed ones, whom Verga always portrays so well in that dry and matter-of-fact style which strengthens his power to convince. The theme of 'The Wolf', incest, has been much sounded in literature from the earliest times. While Greek dramatists dealt with the subject among kings and deities, and later literature among illustrious personages, Verga treats it in peasant setting, without any loss of dramatic power. Using – as Luigi Russo has said – the technique of the sculptor rather than of the painter, he gives the female protagonist of the story true tragic stature.

The ending of 'The Wolf' is not really conclusive. At the time of the story's publication its readers took it for granted – and so would most readers today – that the end is a violent death, as in so many of the other stories from the volume *Vita dei campi* ('Life in the Fields') in which 'Cavalleria Rusticana' and 'La Lupa' were included. Now Verga never hesitated to describe gruesome details, but he says nothing to indicate the Wolf's death: the axe, gleaming in the sun, is held high, but not every axe that is held high necessarily chops off a head.

'Liberty' is a concentrated political story, devoid of any secondary interest. What Disraeli critically observed in England in his novel *Sybil, or The Two Nations* was far more evident in Sicily, and even now persists to some extent. The story was written in 1881, and deals with events that had taken place in Bronte, a township two thousand feet up in the Etna range barely twenty miles from Catania, during the 'massacres of the gentry' in 1860. At that time, the Risorgimento was in full swing, and *Libertà!* was one of its war-cries. But the Risorgimento, as Matteo Gaudioso has recently stressed, was a movement within the traditional ruling strata of aristocracy and upper middle class: the poor, particularly the landless peasants, saw liberty in one direction only, i.e. possession of a little land and money. For them, liberty was a *feeling,* not an idea; a feeling that could not to be shown by words, but had to be proved by facts; and the most important of these was ownership of a plot of land. Verga, twenty years old at the time, had no doubt received accurate reports of what had happened, and the story may be taken as substantially true in incident. It displays Verga's 'impersonal' style in the description of the horror, together with his sympathy for all the victims and understanding of the rights and wrongs on both sides.

The rural Sicily of Verga and Capuana is now gradually disappearing, but it is still reflected in the writings of Virgilio Titone. Born at Trapani in 1904, Titone was eighteen years old at the time of Verga's death, and his stories maintain features of *Verismo,* though, noticeably, not the writer's self-effacement: the final paragraph of 'The Sulphur Mine' would have been anathema to true *Veristi.* When asked to comment on the publication of this story in English, Titone replied that even if it was not his favourite story, it revealed aspects of Sicily's soul and civilisation that are little known abroad, such as its sexual customs, 'a subject about which, even today, one generally reads only the usual commonplaces, from which originated the myth of the fiery Sicilian soul and such-like nonsense'.

'The Sulphur Mine' illustrates the belief in murder as the only honourable way of righting a wrong that still persists in Sicily, rooted in the inadequacy or absence of the executive forces, and the shortcomings of and delays in legal procedure. The references to various types of mafia may surprise those who believe that the mafia is engaged only in violent gang activities; the old pedlar's remark about the mine, 'No policeman has ever been seen there, and it isn't likely one ever will be,' points to the vacuum that has to be filled with some sort of 'order'. If honour demands murder, then murder must and will be committed by essentially decent people. The status of the honest prostitute, as well as the 'mid-week' homosexual relations of the miners with their *carusi* (which recalls the homosexual activities of ancient Greece), are other points of background detail that emerge in Titone's story.

The world-wide fame that Luigi Pirandello (1867–1936), the best-known Sicilian writer, has achieved as a playwright, should not be allowed to obscure his importance as a short story writer. Pirandello actually began by writing poetry, and on Capuana's advice he took up prose writing; like his friends and mentors Capuana and Verga, he too from time to time adapted a suitable prose piece into a play, until at the age of fifty-four *Six Characters in Search of an Author* earned him world-wide fame as a dramatist.

Pirandello's father and father-in-law were connected with sulphur mines, and Pirandello himself worked for a time in the administration of such a mine. 'Ciàula Discovers the Moon' has the same background as Titone's story, but out of this material Pirandello has hewn a very different type of story. It is a moving story of the underdog's underdog, which shows Verga's compassion for the doomed, but sublimated on a different level, and exhibits Pirandellian features that are closely related to Verga and to *Verismo*. But Pirandello's *Verismo* begins where Verga's has left off, and Verga's *Verismo* of facts becomes in Pirandello the *Verismo* of thought.

'Ciàula Discovers the Moon' dates from 1912. Olga Ragusa in her *Pirandello* (Columbia University Press) refers to it as the most powerful of Pirandello's many works with a sulphur mine setting. Pirandello collected all his stories (he wrote well over two hundred, but did not achieve his ambition to bring them to 365 under the title *Short Stories for a Year*. He craved his readers' indulgence if these 'numerous little mirrors which reflect my conception of life and the world fill the reader with too much bitterness and give him too little joy'.

In 'Antimony' by Leonardo Sciascia, the leading figure is again a sulphur miner. Sciascia was born in Roccalmuto, near Agrigento, in 1921. His novels are read all over the world, and his plays too have been highly successful. 'Antimony' was first published in 1960. The French literary critic Claude Ambrose sees the significance of this novella set in the Spanish Civil War in the fact that it is 'the story of a literary vocation', and Sciascia accepts this as the explanation for why it came so naturally to him to write the story in the first person.

In a letter to the Editor, Sciascia writes: 'This story is true twice over. It is true in the facts, because those were related to me by two people who fought in the War on the Fascist side. These two have entered into the story for what they were: the young undesirable expelled from the United States who wanted to get back there [no reader is likely to forget the brilliantly endearing rogue Ventura], and the young officer who let the two prisoners escape instead of executing them. The story is also true in the protagonist, the narrator, inasmuch as it deals with myself and my conscience regarding the Spanish Civil War, that "world raped by Fascism" in which I found myself living. I did not take part in that war, nor could I have taken part on account of my age; but I lived through it as the fundamental experience of my life, and a few years later I wrote it all down: it came perfectly naturally to me to write it in the first person. To start with, I used as a title a line from Dante: "De l'onore di Sicilia e d'Aragona". Afterwards, I gave the story a title which is less solemn, but I believe more significant.'

One of the most important literary achievements that the Spanish Civil War has stimulated, 'Antimony' illuminates that war from a viewpoint hitherto unknown in this country. Among the facets of Sicilian life of absorbing interest that are highlighted in 'Antimony' are courtship, ties within the family, and the relationship of the islanders to the people of the mainland of Italy, 'the Continent' – a relationship which Sciascia compares to that between Spaniard and Moor. This comparison may seem exaggerated, but the Sicilian is, in fact, always aware of his 'Trinacricity', his difference from mainland (especially Northern) Italians, and prone to sense contempt and suspicion even where they barely exist. This defensive attitude is the result of an inferiority complex which goes hand in hand with what Sciascia calls the Sicilian's 'sensual pleasure' in abasement and self-denigration; caused by Sicily's poverty, lack of industrial activity, lack of water, and the feeling of her inhabitants that they live in a backward and neglected island, much of the Sicilian's bravado must be interpreted as a mechanism of overcompensation.

A special type of Sicilian and southern Italian bravado is the so-called *gallismo* ('cockiness'), the preoccupation with sex generally ascribed to all southern Italian males. *Gallismo* has drawn Vitaliano Brancati (1907–54) to a sarcastic irony that has been compared to Gogol. Characterised by a particularly readable and flowing style, Brancati's work encompasses novels – notably *Don Giovanni in Sicilia* – short stories, plays, essays, journalism and literary criticism. He deserves to be much better known in English-speaking countries, where he has been rejected rather out of hand on account of his quick-changing political affiliations: at the beginning of his career he indulged in the *Palazzo Venezia* type of writing (promoting the Fascist cause), and upon Mussolini's downfall his attitude changed to violent anti-Fascism. Whatever the rights and wrongs of his political views Brancati's gentle 'existential realism' makes his prose most attractive to read, and gives even his bitterest moralistic satire a sympathetic resonance. In the words of Emilio Cecchi, Brancati, 'with his prose of the greatest agility, instinct with healthy and wholesome sensuality, raised the jollity and mockery of the journalistic tradition of his time to a high literary level – and made it all the more palatable with the sauce of his capacity to shock innocently'. Both 'The Story of Mila' and 'Story of a Man who Twice Failed to Laugh' are characteristic examples of his entertaining satirical style, as well as his powers of observation.

Similar in some respects to Brancati's gentle irony is Lampedusa's elegant and subtle mockery. Giuseppe Tomasi, Prince of Lampedusa (1896—1957) and his novel *The Leopard* are the subjects of one of the most intriguing chapters in literary history. In 1959 Giorgio Bassani, author of *The Garden of the Finzi-Contini,* was editing a new fiction series when 'a Neapolitan friend who lives in Rome' sent him the typescript of an unsigned novel. Later he learned the identity of the author, and the fact that he had died just over a year previously. A vist to Palermo produced the original manuscript of the novel, more complete and correct than the typescript, and revealed the existence of some other work, including four short stories. 'Joy and the Law', here translated into English for the first time, has been referred to as 'an allegorical story, perfect in its tone as well as in its measure'. It was probably written in 1955 or 1956, and is a fine example of Lampedusa's sensitive and eloquent treatment of Sicilian life.

Carmelo Ciccia's prize-winning 'Remote Past' features romantic Sicilian love, and a character sketch which is depicted with considerable virtuosity. Ciccia, born in Paternò in 1934, is now headmaster of a secondary school near Conegliano in the Veneto, but his literary interests have for the most part remained linked to Sicilian topics.

Gino Raya is one of Italy's best prose-writers, a pungent chronicler of the cultural scene, and a philosopher-teacher whose history of Italian literature is in its fifth edition. He is little known to the English-speaking world, but his writings are certainly important enough to be translated. He was born in Mineo, Capuana's home town, in 1906. In a typically Sicilian way, he feels himself excluded from the mainstream of editorial, academic and journalistic circles in Italy, and attributes this isolation to the severity and frankness of his literary criticism, expressed in his literary journal which began its existence as *Narrativa* in 1956. A change of its name was connected with Raya's movement towards a philosophy of his own, *famismo,* a philosophy that pledges itself against reverence towards the 'metaphysical capital letter words' that he sees as characterising Western society – words denoting generally respected concepts that are abhorrent to him, such as Reason, Thought and Honour. According to Raya, the driving force of the human race is and will remain *fame,* hunger. Adhering to the idea of *famismo,* Raya's literary periodical was renamed *Biologia Culturale;* his literary criticism is couched in physiological terms.

Raya is the unsurpassed expert on Italy's literary *ottocento,* and an outstanding Verga scholar. His strong links with Sicily have never prevented him from pillorying the more despicable traits of his fellow-islanders. Some of his most severe criticism is contained in dry, factual accounts of true incidents, thoroughly researched, and reported in the best tradition of responsible journalism. 'How Filippa Died' is a true story, and happened only a few years ago in the town of Gela, the first Sicilian town liberated by British troops during the last war. The name of the victim was even changed by the author at proof stage in order to avoid possible legal consequences; and a photograph of the victim actually appeared in *The Times* on 27 August 1973. To Raya, Filippa is another deplorable victim of the capital letter word 'Honour', a word of particularly tragic associations in Sicily.

It remains to introduce the two *racconti* by Danilo Dolci. Dolci is not a Sicilian; he is a North Italian. But this sociologist and politically active social reformer has identified himself with Sicily to such an extent that it seemed natural to include examples of his work in this volume. These sketches could be viewed as the apotheosis of *Verismo:* the hand of the writer is completely invisible. The poor of the island talk to Dolci with a freedom of expression that results from meeting an extraordinary and fascinating personality, and their stories, in the tellers' ungrammatical and often repetitive style, can be compared to those that form the basis of a sociologist's analysis. Partinico, mentioned in 'E.A.', is the pitiably poor township in the vicinity of Palermo where Dolci has established his headquarters.

Finally, a word of comment on the work of translation.

Translations do not last for ever. Writing and translating are quite different kinds of activity. Good writing remains, as true art invariably does, timeless forever. Translating is not art but expert craftmanship, and for that reason it does not remain timeless. All translations noticeably 'date' and echo their own period; they are bound to lose their flavour when the character of the language has sufficiently changed to make modes of expression appear antiquated, a situation that arises every forty or fifty years.

Translations must, furthermore, fulfil two different requirements: they must render the original author's words and meaning clearly and correctly, and they must be readable. Translations that deserve admiration for accuracy may be uninspiring to read, and some lines written by Lessing in another context can justly be applied to this conflict inherent in translation:

'For Klopstock all show admiration

But do you ever read him? No!

We do not look for approbation;

We hope that you will read us, though.'

The translator did not wish to sacrifice accuracy in order to improve the flow of his translated prose, and trusts that his resolve to adhere as closely as possible to the original texts will enhance rather than detract from from the enjoyment of reading these little masterpieces.

Alfred Alexander

The Bond of San Giovanni

LUIGI CAPUANA

One day Uncle Peppe Cipolletta had taken him aside and mentioned the matter – just a whisper in his ear, as a mere suspicion, a slander put about by evil tongues, for he didn't want to risk damnation by saying it was true.

'Still, if people are gossiping they've certainly got good reason. Godfather Pietro's always in your house, morning till night – of course there's the Godfather relationship between you, but you can't rely on that too much. Women can be kindled!'

Janu* had looked calmly into his face and replied:

'Yes, I know, it's my father who's spreading these lies. I wish he'd stop it – he can eat his way through everything my mother left me and I'll never ask him for a soldo, he can rest assured!† Why does he want to stir up so much trouble in our house? All because I went and married Filomena instead of that dark-haired daughter of farmer Pino's he wanted to foist on me?'

Uncle Peppe insisted: 'No, your father has absolutely nothing to do with it, I swear to you.'

'Well,' Janu went on, 'you just tell people to see to the horns on their *own* heads. Mine I can look after myself.'

He was so blindfold he couldn't even see the sun. Godfather Pietro was in his house morning noon and night, and it was always 'Godfather, can I do this for you . . . can I do that for you?' He simply could not credit such villainy, such great treachery.

After all, if it had been true the blessed Saint John the Baptist would already have punished the crime. No one could break the bond of San Giovanni, the Godfathership,‡ and get away with it.'

* Diminutive of Sebastianu.
† The property of the mother has passed automatically to her son upon her death.
‡ See Introduction.

Still, bit by bit he started to have his doubts. At first he crossed himself to drive out this temptation of the devil – it was impossible to believe!

One night they were toasting beans on the fire with Godfather Pietro, and when Filomena went down to draw a drop of new wine he said to him:

'Godfather Pietro, let me tell you how far people's slander can go. They're daring to say –'

But he got no further, for Filomena returned just then with a jug in one hand, a lamp in the other, and little Pietro, christened after his godfather, clinging to her skirt.

Godfather Pietro behaved as if he didn't understand; he took the beans out of the hot cinders with the fire shovel and put them one by one on the table, while Filomena rinsed the glasses and took a handful of roasted chick peas from the big walnut chest – they made the wine taste better.

'No – it isn't possible,' said Janu to himself.

But that night he lay restless for a long time before he could sleep. His wife heard him tossing and turning.

'What's wrong with you?'

'Nothing.'

'You looked so gloomy tonight. Pietro noticed it!'

'Did he tell you?'

'He was on the doorstep to go while you were giving the donkey his barley, and he asked me: "What's up with Janu?"'

'Nothing,' replied Janu. He turned over. But for a long time he lay in the dark with his eyes wide open; he saw rings of fire.

'You've been talking to your father!'

Janu was silent.

'He went past today, and he gave me a very nasty look!'

'Leave my father out of it,' grumbled Janu.

'What's wrong with you tonight?'

But when Janu felt his wife's hand fondling his chest under the bedclothes, and felt her warm body drawing near his own, he felt a lump in his throat: no, no – it wasn't possible!

However, the affair had been going on for over four years, and even a blind man could have seen it; the two of them took his goodness of heart far too much for granted. While he walked behind the plough on the piece of land he rented at Pudditreddi and the sun beat down on his head, they were having a snack and laughing at him behind his back – 'Friend Billygoat', Godfather Pietro would call him when the two of them were alone together.

She would often say to her little boy:

'Who's this?'

'Godfather,' the child would reply.

'Call him Daddy, call him Daddy!'

The child would look at them puzzled:

'But what about the other Daddy? No, he's *Godfather.'*

Pietro would make a face and start to swear worse than a Turk: to have a son and not be able to call him his proper name – on his word of honour, it made him boil! He would give the boy a soldo to go to the market square and get himself some sugared carrots.

Yet some days, without knowing why, he felt pangs of conscience. 'What we're doing isn't right. Staining the Sangiovanni. It's not good.'

She would start laughing and say teasingly:

'You're a man, aren't you?'

'Well, last night at the Quartino, when Nino the poet told us the story of the Godfather from Comiso, it sent shivers down my spine.'

'So that's why you didn't come and see me last night?'

'Yes.'

'And you're supposed to be a man? Ha, ha, ha!'

Godfather Pietro didn't like hearing her talk and laugh like that.

'Be quiet, woman. You scare me.'

But she kept on: What had they done wrong? It had been fate.

'Yes, just fate . . . Still, it would have been better if we had got married instead of you marrying Janu. Do you remember the nights I used to come and talk to you from the street under your window, when Janu's father bolted the door and wouldn't let his son out? Janu used to say – "You go in my place, Pietro!" '

'In those days,' she observed, 'I didn't think . . .'

'I did, though!'

'You see then, it was just fate. Still, we were mad to get tied with the Sangiovanni. But for that blessed Godfathership there wouldn't be anything to worry about!'

Janu seemed more and more immersed in his thoughts, and spoke very little. He often stood still, with his arms folded and looking as if he were daydreaming.

'What's wrong with you?' asked Filomena. 'What a face!'

He didn't answer, and she began to nag him about his father. 'It's all the work of that nasty old man, he's always hated me! Why can't he ease his conscience by letting you have what your mother left you rather than inventing all those nasty things about me?'

'Be quiet,' said Janu softly.

'I won't!'

And hands on hips she planted herself in front of him, furious.

'Your father threw you out because he didn't want you to have anything . . . You should have obeyed him! You should have married the baroness, the princess, the dark-haired woman with the slimy nose!'

'Hold your tongue!'

'I wish I'd broken my leg that night I tiptoed down the ladder to run away with you! But there's a God up there and he'll grant my wish, and before I die I'll see that wicked old man carried past my door on a ladder* with a knife sticking in him!'

'Will you stop?'

'And all the tears I shed because of him will mean so many drops of his own blood, I swear to you!'

'Will you stop?'

But she raised her arms, her hands outstretched, and screamed even more loudly:

'Lord, give him the deadly shivers.† Lord, let him die accursed with no confession and no sacrament!'

---

* Ordinary household ladders, eight to nine feet long, were used as stretchers for emergencies and also for the transport of the dead.

† A malignant type of malaria that was a frequent cause of death in Capuana's time.

'Will you stop?'

But Filomena wouldn't stop all day. She went on screaming and tearing her hair; finally she threw herself on a chair in the corner, hid her face in her apron and bewailed her misfortunes.

Janu was moved.

'Silly ass, silly ass,' he said in a voice that had become friendly again. He kept on walking around the room as if looking for something he couldn't find; in fact he was terrified by all the curses hurled at his father's head. 'Silly ass, silly ass, what's it all about?'

'Why were you looking like that? It *was* your father who put you against me, you can't deny that! It *was* your father!'

'Do me *one* favour,' said Janu sharply. 'Don't mention my father any more. Don't mention him again.'

Filomena, who had taken her apron away from her eyes, looked at him in surprise, and he walked away with the curses still ringing in his ears.

The night Uncle Peppe Cipolletta came to awaken him to tell him his father lay dying, Janu felt cold shudders going up and down his spine; he remembered those curses and felt more frightened than ever.

'Now see what you've done!' he said, dressing hurriedly in the light of Uncle Peppe's lamp. 'Holy Mary! Now see!'

Filomena sat in her nightdress on the bed, half-dazed with sleep.

'Is he very bad?' she asked at length.

'He's got the deadly shivers,' Uncle Peppe replied.

A gasp of terror escaped from Janu's throat. He felt his hair standing on end, and the curses his wife had uttered a month ago resounded in his head:

'Lord, give him the deadly shivers. Lord, let him die accursed with no confession and no sacrament!'

He staggered along the street, his feet stumbling over the stones. On the steps of his home, steps he had not trodden for five years, Uncle Peppe had to steady him to prevent him from falling over.

A woman who had come in from next door to help stopped him from entering the sick-room. 'The Father Confessor is with him,' she said.

In the silence the voice of the Father Confessor could be heard through the door, speaking rather loudly so that the dying man could hear:

'Farmer Croce, farmer Croce, hear the Father of Forgiveness. We must forgive our enemies just as He forgave all those who crucified him. You must know that any moment you may find yourself before the tribunal of His everlasting justice. You must know that I, His unworthy minister, cannot grant you absolution if you persist in your hatred. But you don't hate him, do you? No, you forgive him! Why don't you wish to see him then? He is your son after all! Give him your blessing, farmer Croce, give him your blessing, it is Jesus Christ's command.'

Janu strained his ears, tears running down his cheeks so that he could hardly control his sobbing, his fingers clasped together. When after a short silence he saw the door open, he rushed to the bed of the dying man, fell on his knees and covered his father's hands with kisses.

The priest left the room, closing the door behind him so that father and son might be alone together.

'I am dying,' said the old man with a great effort, and very short of breath. 'I'm dying, and I don't want to bring a curse on myself. But you ought to know – that whore – carries on with Godfather Pietro . . . she carries on with Godfather Pietro!'

Janu felt a sledge-hammer fall in his head.

'Ah! What a blow you deal me at the end, father – what a blow!'

So it was true! It was true! There are no lies in the face of death. Still, he would have to make sure with his own eyes . . . Once he had seen with his own eyes . . .

Bending over his heavy tilling-hoe, Janu kept looking at the upturned soil without seeing it, his head going round like a spinning-wheel, while the little boy, who had insisted on going with his father to the fields, splashed about in the muddy water of a stagnant pool nearby.

'It must be true, it must be true,' he kept repeating to himself. There are no lies in the face of death. Still, he would have to make sure with his own eyes ... Once he had seen with his own eyes ...

But what he was going to do once he had seen with those eyes of his he didn't know himself, though he had thought and dreamt of nothing else for weeks.

He felt he was going mad, and on Carnival Thursday he had to get away to the fields and try to assuage the fire that burnt in him by striking the tilling-hoe against the hard soil.

Useless!

The thought of the nights he had spent standing under her window, in wind and rain, went round and round in his empty head; and the night he had taken her into his arms like a child from the end of the ladder, after his father had refused his consent and they had run away together, seemed only yesterday.

He had worn himself out so that he could keep her in luxury. He would have thrown himself in the path of the Mammadraga monster* if she had so ordered him. What a fool he had been! What a poor fool!

His arms went slack and his eyes hazy with the tears that wouldn't come; his throat felt tight with the lump that had been nearly choking him for a month.

They were betraying the Sangiovanni! And Saint John the Baptist up there didn't seem to have eyes or ears either, if he wouldn't bring them to justice!

At that moment the little boy came running up with a grasshopper in his hand.

'Daddy, Daddy, keep him for me. I want to take him to Godfather!'

Furiously Janu tore the grasshopper out of his hand.

'Don't mention Godfather to me!'

'Tonight I'm going to tell him – I'm going to tell him ... and Mummy too ...' screamed the weeping child, holding his fists in his eyes.

Janu started to tremble like a leaf, and firmly held his head with

* A beast of the Ichthyosaurus type, conjured up to frighten naughty children.

31

both hands to stop it from bursting. Was it the devil that put that thought into his head? The temptation of hell? O Lord, O Lord, how could it not have occurred to him before – what if this was not his son at all, but the son of . . .

The child kept on.

Tonight – he was – going to tell Godfather – and Mummy too . . .

'Be quiet! Don't talk about them! Be quiet!'

Janu tried to frighten the boy by shaking him by the arms, and felt the blood rushing to his head.

'Be quiet, be quiet!'

The defiant child raised his ruffled little head and mud-stained face and threatened:

'I *shall* call my Godfather Daddy, like Mummy wants me to.'

'Ah . .' cried Janu, 'is *that* what she's told you? Is that what she's told you to do?'

'No, Daddy – no, Daddy!'

But Janu no longer saw or heard; he brandished the heavy hoe . . .

When he became aware of the monstrous deed he had done he looked all about him, white as a corpse, his mouth parched, his chest heaving.

What if someone had seen him!

But in the vast field stretching in the sunshine, on the roads, along the winding paths, amidst the fresh green of the corn, not a living soul was to be seen. Only his donkey was staring at him, head erect and ears pricked, chewing a mouthful of straw under a sheltering roof by a cactus hedge.

Thank heaven that one couldn't talk!

Godfather Pietro was already in the kitchen, putting the firewood under the large copper pot for boiling the water to cook the macaroni. Filomena, her face flushed, a turquoise kerchief wrapped around her head, was grating the cheese in the kneading trough onto a plate. She giggled every time Godfather Pietro – just to pass the time, he said – took her round the waist from behind.

'Keep cool – if you can. Go and see to the fire.'

She continued her grating, with a swaying movement of the hips, without turning round.

'Why don't you go off and dance?' she asked, hearing the *tam-tam* of a cembolo* from Aunt Maricchia's house next door; her daughter had been married that morning, and all the relatives had been invited.

'The real dance is for Mangiapicca – he's picked that nice plump little quail Josephine all for himself. Let's hope it'll do him good!'

'Your mouth's watering, you old sinner!'

Pietro burst out laughing.

'What now?' demanded Filomena. 'Let's hear it.'

'Well . . . Shall we try to sleep like a newly-wed couple too tonight?'

'Are you crazy?'

'Of course not. We'll just make friend Billygoat drunk, that's all.'

'Are you crazy?'

Suddenly Filomena was convulsed with laughter even louder than his.

'What an idea!'

'Let me arrange it. Splendid . . . just wait!'

They laughed and laughed so much that he had to hold his belly with his hands, and she put her apron over her mouth, looking even more flushed than before. Her eyes sparkled, and all over her body she felt the tingling of pleasant anticipation.

Suddenly they stopped laughing, embarrassed to see Janu standing in the kitchen doorway, standing quite still and looking at them with a face as white as a real billygoat's.

'Welcome, friend Janu,' said Pietro. 'We were just laughing at . . . at . . .'

'Let's make a really good fire,' said Janu quietly.

The sausages were smoking away on the grid, and Filomena, trying to appear unconcerned, hastened to draw his attention to them.

* An instrument comparable to a large tambourine, made to sound by the knuckles or palms of the hands.

'Look what friend Pietro kindly brought us!'

'He shouldn't have bothered – let's make a good fire, friend Pietro.'

The two of them looked each other in the face, reassured. When the pot started to boil Pietro chopped one last piece of olivewood.

'On with the macaroni.'

And the boiling pot seemed to gurgle in time with the sound of Aunt Maricchia's cembolo, which went on with its jangling *tam-tam,* while all the relatives hopped about like a herd of goats let loose and made the ceiling of the kitchen dance as well, and Mangiapicca could be heard shouting the old French commands of the Quadrille: 'Balanzé! Turdumé!'

All three ate in silence, Filomena and Pietro sulky because of the absence of the child who had insisted on staying behind in the country with Aunt Nela's other children. To the mother and godfather this didn't seem to be a proper Carnival Thursday at all; Pietro kept saying:

'I can't forgive you, Janu.'

'You should have made him come back,' said Filomena. 'Are you going to let the child do as he likes?'

Janu made no excuses, letting them give vent to their feelings, and tried to swallow a few forkfuls of macaroni. But his mouth felt as bitter as poison, the food stuck in his throat. He kept having to take a sip of water or wine. When he lifted the glass of wine to his lips, it made him blink: its redness brought back to his mind that other red he had seen sprinkled on the green clods of Pudditreddi under his iron tilling-hoe, and he tried not to think of it.

That innocent little creature hadn't been guilty of anything, and had paid with his life for the antics of that wretched couple who were now trying to make friend Billygoat drunk . . . But blessed Saint John the Baptist had dimmed their lights and placed them in his hands so that he could cut both their throats as if they were pigs in a slaughterhouse. If he had to go to prison, at least he would go contentedly, with his mind at rest.

That was why he forced himself to eat up the plateful of macaroni in front of him; that was why he had drunk and drunk again. After every gulp of wine he felt a wave of strength running from his stomach into his veins.

The stewed pork and Godfather Pietro's sausages helped to break the ice. With the smell of the stew and the roast sausages, the clatter of plates, forks and glasses, neither Filomena nor Pietro mentioned the child again. When Pietro saw that Janu never stopped drinking, one glass after the other, he pressed his leg against his lady friend's under the table, and she responded with a smile as she filled the dishes, keeping her eyes well down.

Pietro dug his fork into a juicy piece of sausage, held it to Janu's mouth and said:

'For my sake, Janu, eat this.'

And he poured some wine and filled Janu's glass to the brim. 'And this, for my sake.'

Janu took the piece of sausage with his fingers and placed it on his wife's plate.

'I can't eat any more,' he said, 'I'm full up to the ears, all that grape juice has knocked my head off.'

'Go on! You've hardly drunk anything!'

Pietro filled his glass again. But the more Janu drank the clearer his head felt; the turmoil of bitterness seemed to have died down in his heart, and it its place rose a dark, wild joy, the joy of the wolf about to leap into the fold of sleeping sheep.

Aunt Maricchia's cembelo started up again. 'They won't fill their bellies up with that tam-tam of theirs, Godfather,' said Janu.

When the music stopped, they could hear the noise of thunder and a torrential downpour like the Flood.

'That's the real tam-tam,' he added with a wink. 'Our Lord's enjoying himself, trundling the barrels about in paradise. It must be Carnival up there as well. Let's have another drink!'

He yawned, stretched his arms, and with half-closed eyes grumbled about the wine which had made him drunk. The other two looked at each other full of longing, and pressed their feet even closer together.

'You're sleepy, Godfather. And that downpour isn't going to stop!'

Janu, more sober than the other, saw him open the window and heard the rush of water in the gutters which were running like streams.

'Where are you off to?' he said. "Do you want to be carried away by the flood? For mercy's sake, this bed's as broad as a field, it's large enough for four! I'd give up my place for my brother in Saint John!" '

Janu spoke slowly, in a husky voice, and slurred his words; the other two thought it was the wine.

'In this infernal weather the best place to be is under bedclothes. Where else is there for Godfather Pietro to go? Does he really want to be carried away by the flood? We'll place *her* between the two of us. Can't we trust him? Our brother in Saint John?

'Don't you know you're dead drunk? Don't take any notice of him, Godfather.'

Filomena had to turn away and force herself not to laugh.

'Don't you know you're dead drunk?'

When it was heard that Janu Pedi had killed his wife and Godfather Pietro that night and afterwards given himself up to the police sergeant, no one could believe it. But there were the two lovers, still naked iħ bed and clutching one another: the two could hardly have had time to say 'Holy Jesus and Mary!' People thronged the streeets, everyone in sympathy with Janu, that poor fellow who had done the right thing and couldn't possibly be condemned by any court of justice.

Only Peppe Nasca, a distant relative of the dead man, couldn't refrain from shouting 'Murderer!' when he saw Janu pass, handcuffed between two carabinieri, his head erect and a smile on his face. 'So you've just begun to feel your horns – after four years!'

'Sooner than you, anyway!' replied Janu looking straight into his face; 'You haven't noticed yours yet – your sister's carrying on with the baker!'*

* In the Sicilian code, the honour of a sister is as important to her brother as the honour of a wife to her husband.

Rosa's Mule

LUIGI CAPUANA

'Shall we have a foundling?' the wife had asked with tears in her eyes. 'All right,' her husband had answered with resignation.

And so husband and wife climbed one morning onto one of the carts that carry those heavy terracotta urns – a speciality of Mineo – to the town of Caltagirone, and presented themselves at the offices of the Committee for Foundlings.

'We want a weaned child; we'll care for him better than we would our own son.'

The sister took them to a large ward which was full of cots and cradles, and showed them two children who were both fast asleep:

'This one is fourteen months old; his name is Angelo and he's as pretty as his name. The other one is twenty-two months, and he's called Nino.'

'Like you,' she said to her husband. 'Let's take him, and may it be God's will!'

Roused from deep slumber, the child began to cry. The wife kissed him and caressed him, and made her husband kiss him as well; almost at once she succeeded in quietening him.

After six years of marriage, the poor girl had given up every hope of one day having a baby of her own. She now held the child tightly in her arms, while members of the Committee made endless entries in their enormous books, as large as church missals: Christian name and family name of the husband... her own Christian name and family name... Fortunately the papers they had received from the mayor's office were all in order, and towards midday, radiant with joy, husband and wife walked down the steps of the ancient, prison-like place that housed poor abandoned creatures breastfed by wet nurses and cared for by nuns who were incapable of understanding the maternity they had voluntarily renounced.

'My son, I am your mother! And here is your father!' said the wife to the baby, who looked at her in bewilderment, as if mistrustful of the new faces.

They became his father and mother indeed, and their quiet little house re-echoed with the child's gay squeals and shrieks.

The poor woman, who had never felt the quickening of her own child in her womb, seemed mad with joy at the sight of that baby of unknown origin, with his fine features, blond hair, large eyes of such deep blue that they appeared almost black, and delicate but well-proportioned body. Sometimes she believed that he had come straight down from heaven, a true gift from God, in return for all the prayers she had said, and the many alms she had given to the poor so that they would beseech the Lord with prayers perhaps more effective than her own. It had surely been inspiration from the Blessed Virgin that had made her say to her husband: 'Let's have a foundling!'

On summer evenings, after the husband's return from his work in the fields, he and his wife sat outside their front door with the baby on their knees. They were more proud of this frail, beautiful child than if he had been their own son.

'Isn't he an angel, Uncle Cola?'

But Uncle Cola, sitting outside the door opposite, shook his head, a sulky frown on his face.

'Don't you think so?' persisted the wife.

Uncle Cola replied pointedly: 'All children of loose women are lucky!'

'Why should he be the child of a loose woman? How do you know?'

'Because otherwise he wouldn't be loved so much! If you'd really wanted to do an act of charity you'd have taken one of Stella's children, she hardly knows how to keep them from starving. Looking after mules is the King's job!'

'What do you mean, mules? Don't mules belong to God too, unfortunate abandoned creatures that they are?'

'Looking after mules is the King's job!'

Uncle Cola rested his chin on his hands, clasping his cherrywood stick; his eyes were half-shut, and he frowned. He was thinking of the old days. To him, foundlings were mules and only the King, in other words the Government, should provide for them.

But Rosa replied, giving her baby a big kiss:

'He's a baron, a prince, the king of my house!'

Her husband sat seriously with his hands on his knees; he looked at her and the child and said nothing.

In malice and envy the women of the neighbourhood, seeing the foundling dressed up like a child of the gentry, began calling him 'Rosa's mule'. When Rosa heard this she left off kneading the bread, appeared at the door with her bare arms covered in dough, and shouted:

'You ignorant, heartless women! Your own brood will be mules if you have no charity for a poor creature who hasn't done you any harm!'

'Who are you talking to, you hussy?'

'All of you! One of you is going to get a slap in the face!'

When the boy grew older and got into scuffles with the other boys, they would shout at him: 'Mule! Mule!'

It made him cry when they used that word his mother hated, and Rosa would become furious and run after the young urchins, shoving them violently and clouting them about the head.

'As true as I am Rosa Zoccu, I'm going to mangle one of you!'

When her husband came home from the fields he would find her in tears and he would comfort her:

'Let them say what they want – it won't take the bread out of his mouth. He's going to have a better life than their children! It's just envy – let them talk. Soon we'll send him to school!'

When the boy came home from school with his wax-cloth satchel slung over his shoulder, Rosa would beam with delight; and when he sat scribbling in his exercise books at the little desk that had been made for him, she looked at him in awe.

She saw him already grown up, a good-looking, serious young man. A solicitor? A doctor? A priest? She could not make up her mind which profession she would like him to choose. She would be pleased to see him a priest, a parish priest. She would go to hear him say mass and preach.

'He should be a doctor,' the husband said.

'He is going to be what God wishes,' she said finally. It amused her to ask the boy himself:

'And what do you want to be? A solicitor? A doctor?'

'I want to be a sergeant, Mama, with a sabre and a plumed hat!' replied the boy.

Rosa was a little shocked. A soldier? No! The King could take a lot of mothers' sons, but her own son would stay with her forever. He would become the support of her old age, the pillar of her house, the palm tree of her garden, her own banner: all the imagery of the folk songs came to her mind, and stirred her imagination. The poor woman had practically forgotten that the boy was a foundling, though she loved him all the more for it; she wanted to be his mother twice over, in order to make up for the ill luck that had put him into an orphanage all alone in the world, and handed him to strangers like a little animal.

So she was heartbroken, and cried a whole day afterwards, when the boy came home from school and asked her:

'Is it true you're not my real mother?'

'Who told you that?'

'De Marco, the pasta-maker's son.'

'Tell him . . . '

But she stopped, and all day long muttered to herself the vicious words of her intended response, swallowing her tears and biting her lips in rage. Then she went to the pasta-maker to create a scene, and make him teach his son how to behave.

'Let him say it!' said the husband. 'It's just envy. Soon he shall be dressed as an angel for the Feast of the Shepherd, the first Sunday in May. Don Antonio the poet has told me he's going to give him a beautiful piece to recite.'

And that day husband and wife truly thought they were touching the heavens with their own hands. The boy was dressed in his armour of silver paper, splendid wings of painted cardboard were fitted on his shoulders, and don Carmine the sacristan put a golden helmet on his head.

'Look at him now, Uncle Cola!'

Holding the boy by the arm, Rosa showed him to the grumbling old peasant who spent his days sitting outside the door of his house. He was nicknamed 'Uncle Talk-Talk' because he couldn't keep quiet for a single moment, and always said spiteful things about all and sundry.

'Look at him, Uncle Cola!'

'All the children of loose women are lucky!' the old man replied again.

'And you're a stupid fellow! said Rosa, turning her back on him.

The day they had gone to Caltagirone to get the child, the day they had first sent him to school, the day they had seen him act the angel at the Feast of the Shepherd with the children of the gentry, remained unforgettable for Rosa and her husband; they frequently talked about those days, and they thanked God and the Blessed Virgin.

'Do you see? Everything turned out well for us from that year onwards. Good luck came to our house with that child. Tomorrow I'm going to buy another ox; we're going to have two ploughs, and I'm going to get another piece of land for crop-sharing.'

'And that good linen – the hen with her chicks – the fat pig we're going to sell at Christmas – it's all through him! He hardly seems a child any more, he's so clever!'

'The teacher told me he's going to get first prize, and we ought to try our hardest to send him to Caltagirone to continue his education.'

'All by himself?'

'Just like the others.'

'I'll go with him. What would he do without me? He'd feel lost.'

'He's thirteen, he'll manage like the others,' concluded the husband. 'My godson's father lives in Caltagirone and he can keep an eye on him.'

They dreamed of the happiness that the future held in store, of the prizegiving soon to come. Rosa was going to prepare a special meal for the occasion, and invite some neighbours. She would also send bread, wine and meat to poor Stella who was nearly starving with all her children; it wouldn't be right if they were happy alone.

But that very day the postman called and told her:

'A registered letter has come for your husband. As he can't write you must come to the post office with someone who can sign for him.'

'A letter? Who from?'

'How should I know?'

It was all so unusual that the poor woman at once thought it must be something bad. She threw a shawl round her shoulders and ran wild-eyed to the post office. A letter! Who could it be from? They had no relatives close or distant!

The post office official handed the letter to her, and she turned it over and over in her hand; the five red seals suggested sorcery to her mind.

'Open it and read it please,' she said to the official.

Her hand and voice trembled as she handed him the letter. She devoured him with anxious eyes while he read through the four pages of the folded sheet. He kept shaking his head as if he were reading something extraordinary, and without knowing why, she felt a lump in her throat.

'It's from the father,' said the post official at last, expecting her to understand at once.

'From what father?'

'The father of your foundling. He says he's coming to take him back. He's going to acknowledge the child and marry the mother. He is a magistrate. He's going to pay you back all your expenses. He's going to be here in a week's time!'

Rosa stared at him, pale as a washed-out rag, incredulous – he was surely playing her a vile joke. But he repeated:

'He's going to pay you back all your expenses.'

She was dumbfounded. Her heart beat in her chest so violently that it seemed about to burst. Was such a thing possible? Take the child back? In a week's time? And the law? And justice? No, it was impossible!

'Have you read it properly, sir?' she stammered.

'You can get someone else to read it for you!'

She staggered away with the fatal letter in her pocket. On the road home she began to understand, but it all seemed so outrageous that she wouldn't believe it. What, a child could be simply thrown away, and afterwards, when others had brought him up, watched him grow and educated him with so much more love than those who had got rid of him as soon as he was born, those same wretched parents could come forward and say: 'Give us that child back – he's ours!' And the law allowed that sort of thing? Ah, she would see about that! She would see! Surely there was no God in heaven, no Blessed Virgin, no saints, if such a monstrous thing was permitted to happen. She would see whether the carabinieri came and tore the child from her arms, the child who was now hers!

Tears streamed down her face, and she didn't think of drying them; she didn't notice that her shawl had fallen from her shoulders and was trailing behind her; she waved her arms and clenched her fist at the man who was going to come in a week's time.

'What's the matter, Rosa?' everyone asked.

'Nothing! Nothing!'

She was practically running, and when she saw Nino romping with some other boys in front of her house, she caught him by the arm, dragged him inside, and closed and barred the door behind her.

'What is it, Mama?'

'Nothing! Nothing!'

She knelt down and kissed him, holding him tightly in her arms as if the man who wanted to take him away were already at the front door. She kept him indoors until the evening, and when her husband knocked at the door and called 'Rosa! Rosa!' she said to the boy:

'Don't move!'

Going down the steps she looked back several times, afraid that the boy might follow her.

'They want to take our son away from us!' she said to her husband, and burst into a flood of tears.

'Who?'

'His father! He's written a letter!'

The poor man at first thought his wife had gone off her head.

He shrugged his shoulders.

'You silly girl! Do you think it's so easy?'

He too looked with suspicion and irritation at the letter that his wife took from her pocket. His mouth gaping like an idiot's, he listened to Rosa's account, interrupted by her sobbing as she tore her hair.

'He's going to be here in a week's time . . . a magistrate . . . He has married the mother!'

'Do be quiet! Be quiet for the boy's sake! Give me that letter. I'm going to Mastro Simone the blacksmith. He knows more than a solicitor.'

'No, you can't oppose it. According to the law, children belong to the father.' This was what Mastro Simone said, and he knew more than a solicitor.

It was a death sentence for those two poor people.

'I'm going to kill him, even if he is a judge! I'd rather go to prison than give the child back to him!'

'For Jesus Christ, take back what you said.'

For the first few days the husband considered all kinds of violent plans. His wife, in the fury of a disappointed mother, preferred the death of the child, who was as dear to her as her own blood, to knowing him to be alive with someone else. Both of them tormented the boy with questions he couldn't understand and couldn't answer:

'If they wanted you to have another father . . .'

'If they wanted to give you another mother . . .'

' . . . Would you go with them?'

' . . . Would you have the heart to leave us?'

The boy only answered:

'I want to stay here! Why do you keep me locked up?'

They were afraid he would be taken away unexpectedly in order to avoid trouble. A judge, they imagined, could give orders to the carabinieri, and might take the law into his own hands. In vain did the solicitor to whom they had gone for advice and protection assure them that everything had to proceed legally, and that once a child had been a foundling, the father could not possibly claim him back without first complying with all the necessary regulations. They kept the boy locked up at home, not even allowing him to go near the window. Several times a day they ran to the solicitor, the husband no longer having the heart to work, his wife completely unable to swallow the bitter pill.

'Try *something,* sir, some objection!'

'But what? What objection? The father has a right to take his own child back.'

'Can't we make a law case, and drag it out for a long time? Doesn't one court action lead to another? What the law should say to this man is this: "You didn't want the child when he was born, did you? You made him a foundling, without bothering whether he would die of cold or hunger in the hands of the hags paid to feed him. For thirteen years you didn't give a thought to whether your son was alive or dead, whether he was being loved or maltreated. And now, when it suits you, you want to claim him back? Nothing doing. On the contrary, now we know of the infamy you have committed, we'll seize you and put you into prison!" That's what the law *should* say! Who made the present laws? They're heathen laws, not Christian. Who made them? The King? Has the King no children?"'

Th poor woman became more and more eloquent; she was amazed that the solicitor could find no pretext for a long case that would go to the District Court, then the High Court, and in the end the Court of Appeal. Who had made that heathen law?

'I certainly haven't made it myself!' laughed the solicitor.

'How can it be? We have given him our very blood, we have brought him up with so much care, so much hardship to ourselves! We have sent him to school. If he had been our own son, I would have taken him with me to hoe and plough, I would have made him into a peasant just like I am. But he had his text-books, and his exercise books, and his pens to write with, and everything! What wouldn't we have done for him ... And now?'

'And now the father will pay you back all your expenses – don't you understand?' insisted the solicitor, vexed that this hard-headed peasant kept repeating the same argument.

At home, his wife started to tear her hair once more in desperation. He sat slumped in a chair, his elbows on the table, and held his head in his hands.

'By God, I'm going to kill that scoundrel!' he murmured. 'The child is ours now!'

On the evening before the man who had destroyed all their happiness with a piece of paper was due to arrive, the two felt so discouraged and helpless before the power of the law that they thought of throwing themselves at the feet of the magistrate as soon as he arrived, begging him and beseeching him. Who knew? Once he realised that the boy had found such a good home, they might be able to soften his heart. Anyway, how much love could he feel for a child he'd never seen?

'What if the boy doesn't want to go with the father he has never known? What if he wants to stay with us at all costs?'

For a moment they thought this was the fairest solution. They must ask the boy: he must choose! They spoke with deliberation, as if the magistrate were already standing before them. Rosa held the boy between her legs and asked him, stroking his hair and holding him by the chin: 'Who do you want as father and mother? Us or ... some other people?'

'He doesn't understand. I'll explain it to him!'

With some astonishment, now locked between the legs of the man he believed to be his father, the boy listened intently.

'If someone came and said to you: "I am your father, your true father. Come with me and leave these people!" ... what would you do?'

'I would stay here with you! But who's going to come?'

'No one! Holy Angel, Jesus Christ speaks through your mouth!'

Rosa covered him with her kisses.

'There, that's how it is. The boy has got to be asked: it's the boy who must choose!' And the next morning they went to tell the solicitor their plan.

But who should be at the solicitor's? The man, the magistrate, dressed in a dark suit, tall, lean, with a short red beard and spectacles. What treachery! But what else could you expect from judges or solicitors? They were all flour out of the same sack!

But Rosa did not lose heart and burst out:

'So he's *your* son? Who says so? For thirteen years you haven't given him a thought. You've come by yourself because you're even more brazen than your wife! Why hasn't she come – beast of a mother who abandons her own children? Only now she's got married, only now she remembers there's a little child in this world that she's left to its fate . . .'

The solicitor tried to calm her and make her keep quiet.

'Well, the answer's No! I don't want to give you the boy! What can you do to me? Send me to prison? That's just where you should be, and should have been for some time. Instead it's him who sends people to prison. That's what justice is all about! No, I don't want to give the boy to him. It's no use, Mr Solicitor!'

'But can't you see he's crying?' asked the solicitor.

And truly the fair-haired man in the dark suit was crying, his face covered with both hands. Between sobs he said:

'Yes, you are right. You are right. But . . . circumstances . . . if you only knew the circumstances!'

Rosa was bewildered by the sight, and she glanced sideways at her husband.

'Let the Lord's will be done, Rosa! Let the Lord's will be done!'

And he took her by the hand and led her away, more dead than alive. She did not sob, her eyes were dry, and he kept repeating to her gravely:

'Let the Lord's will be done, Rosa! Let the Lord's will be done!'

Their own grief enabled them to fathom the sorrow of that father who had come for his son after thirteen years. They somehow felt equal to him now, and recognised at last that it was justice for the son to return to his father.

What happened to them in the end?

It was God's will! If the boy had died, wouldn't it have been much worse?

'They were wonderful . . . wonderful,' said the solicitor, recounting the scene. 'They brought him along, they pressed him in their arms. "You will think of us every now and again, won't you?" They didn't ask for anything else, those poor people, and they looked as if their hearts had been torn out of their breasts.

47

"Oh!" said husband and wife. I have never seen a more vivid expression of gratitude in the eyes of human beings in my whole life. They were wonderful . . . wonderful.'

The Doctor's Torment

LUIGI CAPUANA

'Very well, then,' Lorenzo had replied, 'find her for me.'

And barely a month later his father, with the help of a clergyman friend, had located the very girl in the nearby town of Niscemi.*

'An only daughter, well-educated, pretty, and with a considerable dowry . . . you'll see! You'll be pleased with her!'

Overjoyed, the dear old man walked briskly around the room rubbing his hands together and looking at his son with eyes full of tenderness. The very thought of Lorenzo's marriage seemed to have taken years off his shoulders, and he held himself much more erect than before. Lorenzo had previously always shown hesitation about the marriage plan: that 'You'll see! You'll be pleased with her!' – spoken with such obvious emotion – pushed him over the brink now.

To Lorenzo, bachelorhood had never seemed objectionable. He was immersed in his studies and his work as a young doctor, and was content to lead a sequestered life, without domestic ties. Their home never appeared as cold and empty to him as it did to his father.

Don Giacomo, on the other hand, after the death of his wife, and later that of his sister who had come to live with them, felt as if he had been cut to pieces. He depended upon the services of a simple soul of a woman who produced dried-up food for lunch, and didn't know how to dust properly or keep the house clear of cobwebs. He couldn't bring himself to replace her, he said to his friend the priest, because she had grown up in his household, and

* The main action of the story takes place in Caltagirone in the province of Catania. With 35,000 inhabitants it was, acording to the Baedeker of the period (1882), the most civilised provincial town in Sicily. Niscemi, the antique Nisemum, fifteen miles from Caltagirone on the road to the port of Gela, had 20,000 inhabitants.

he had become used to her; a new face would have bothered him.

'I know, I know! That's why we're going to Niscemi,' replied the priest, as the carriage sped along the wide road, bouncing up and down in a cloud of dust. 'Isn't that so, Doctor?'

Silent and deep in thought, Lorenzo nodded his head in agreement. He was smoking, and gazed out of the carriage window at the hills which sped by, with their little wild plants and trees white with dust suffocating in the sun.

The strange, sombre countryside made him restless and sad. 'Why did I let myself in for all this?' he asked himself.

But he felt reassured as soon as he saw the girl. For an hour he sat on the settee in a sitting-room obviously refurbished for the occasion, with her on one side of him and her father, don Paolino, on the other.

His first reaction to his future father-in-law was unfavourable. He was tall and thin, with hair as black as pepper, and the face and eyes of a ferret. But his diminutive, fair-haired daughter made an unexpected impression on Lorenzo. She looked at him with unaffected curiosity, smiling and asking questions, and replying to his as if she had known him for a long time, though she blushed a deeper red each time he spoke to her.

'Is this the first time you've been to Niscemi?'

'Yes.'

'What do you think of it? You're used to bigger towns, aren't you? How does it appeal to you?'

'I like it – it's a pleasant place.'

She spoke gently, with sweetness and simplicity, and seemed to have a thoroughly sensible outlook on life. Every now and again she would toss a lock of hair that kept falling over her forehead out of the way, and she frequently moistened her little lips with a rapid movement of the tongue. When her natural colour returned, the daintiness of her white complexion emerged and made her look even prettier.

Don Paolino asked his daughter to sing something for them: 'Casta Diva – the greatest piece of music ever written, isn't it? The greatest piece of music ever written!'

'What an idea!' Concettina replied. 'The gentlemen will run away!'

But don Paolino insisted, shaking his pepper-black head: 'The gentlemen will make allowances. They know you're not Patti!'

That blessed father of hers – he *would* have to make her look silly!

To his surprise Lorenzo heard Concettina sing quite exquisitely Perrota's charming romance 'The Gentle Dream', a song she adored.

'Bravo, bravo!' shouted Lorenzo when she had finished.

'Don't make fun of me into the bargain!' was Concettina's answer.

The clergyman and don Paolino had begun to discuss business matters:

'The young couple can only count on Concettina's maternal inheritance,' said her father. 'For the time being I cannot part with my own property – it's a mere trifle, barely enough to keep me alive. But, after my death, if there's anything left . . .'

The priest shook his head.

'Always the same, you lady-killer,' he sighed. 'Can't you see that you're getting old?'

Don Giacomo was secretly and lovingly eyeing his own fledgling while he watched Concettina. They were talking about music, and the College of the Sisters of Charity where she had been educated. The old man missed not a single word or movement of the two young people. To him they seemed made for each other. Had it not been improper, he would have said to his son: 'Go on, give her a kiss!'

He could hardly contain himself for joy. Now it only remained for him to await a grandson who would play on his knee and say for each other. Had it not been improper, he would have said to his son: 'Go on, give her a kiss!'

Don Giacomo couldn't stop talking about his future daughter-in-law: 'What an angel she is! So gay and so full of chatter! I can't wait to have her around the house!'

'I'm not sure that she isn't *too* full of life!' replied Lorenzo seriously. He had paid further visits to Niscemi, and spent whole days with his betrothed.

'All the better! All the better!' maintained his father.

Lorenzo didn't contradict him. Yet Concettina's boldness of manner, unusual in a girl from a small provincial town, puzzled him. And when he heard her say things to her father that a daughter should never have said, he was perturbed.

Was it her innocence? Light-hearted coquettishness, trying to impress? Was it . . . He could not explain it. At times he suspected that a rather perverse and wilful character lay behind the façade of a good-hearted, sincere and gentle girl, and he began to worry about what was in store for him – particularly when the charming little figure gained the upper hand, and he found himself becoming tied to her in a way he would not have believed possible, when a quick quiver ran from his head to his toes as he thought that before long this delicate, fair little creature, with her wonderful deep blue eyes and little lips so crimson that they seemed painted with red-lead, would be truly and wholly his.

When he was away from her, bent over his books in the silence of his room, thinking things over, he regarded the approaching wedding date with a kind of dismay. Concettina seemed to become more and more impassioned at every visit he paid her, and he could not convince himself that all this emotion was sincere. He began to wonder, and he regretted that he might have been too compliant with his father's wishes. He remembered how one day she had utterly disconcerted him – though he had forced himself to smile – when she had taken his hand and, squeezing it with all the strength of her slender fingers, said to him: 'How I love you – oh, how I love you!'

Another time, one evening, had been even worse. He had been about to say good-bye to her on the terrace in the dark; it would be a few weeks before he saw her again, because of his patients.

'Oh,' Concettina had said softly. Suddenly she threw her arms around his neck. 'Why have you never given me a proper kiss?' she asked; and trembling all over, she kissed him.

Lorenzo had returned to Caltagirone half-dazed by the kiss and by what she had said amid the tears which almost choked her flute-like little voice.

'What a strange girl she is!' he had thought. 'Not really the wife for me – far too excitable!'

It was not surprising, therefore, that he felt sad on the last night of his bachelorhood. As he sat in the little room where he had slept since he had been a boy, he sensed that something within him was dying, something that had intimately belonged to him and had perhaps been the best part of himself: the cherished freedom of an unattached young man and serious-minded doctor. His narrow bed, the little table piled with his textbooks, the pictures on the walls – everything seemed to bid him a sad farewell; and he knew that their memories would soon fade, chased away by the new life that was about to begin for him. When he opened the window which gave onto a town deep in slumber in the dark of a starless night, with the flickering light of lanterns faint in the mist, he felt a sudden pang in his heart. 'Why did I let myself in for all this? Why?' he asked himself reproachfully.

Before the guests arrived on the wedding morning, don Giacomo noticed that his son was silent and gloomy. While Concettina was getting dressed he asked the young man, astonished, 'Don't you feel well?'

'Perfectly well.'

'What is it, then?'

'Excitement, perhaps.'

And Lorenzo tried his best to look cheerful.

On this their wedding day Concettina seemed to him less pretty than usual, less graceful – almost awkward in her trailing white dress with the veil and garland of orange blossom.

But later, when he saw her fair little head lying on the white pillow, veiled by the curtains of the big double bed; when he saw her sparkling eyes, her smiling, half-opened lips, and her cheeks of such vivid pink that her white skin seemed stained, he looked at her for a lingering moment – and threw himself on top of her.

Distressed by a last maidenly perturbation, Concettina let out a little scream and covered her face with her hands. Lorenzo put them gently aside without finding any resistance. He too felt agitated: yet he had believed that he did not love her at all, and had married her only in order to please his father. Kissing her half-opened lips again and again, he said softly: 'I love you, I love you!'

'It's taken some doing to get those words out of you, you awful man!' she reproved him tenderley, and Lorenzo smiled. He felt satisfied and proud, stirred by a deep, sweet commotion.

Kissing her, he said gently, 'You forgive me?'

'Oh yes, yes!'

She caressed his head with her girlish little hands, and ran her fingers through his hair.

'Yes, my Lorenzo. You were right to be mistrustful. After all, we knew so little of each other. And besides, you were quite happy as a bachelor. You had a great deal to lose by marrying me, and nothing to gain. Yes, let me say it – it's true! I, on the other hand, loved you before I even met you: I loved you from the moment I knew that you might become my liberator. I suffered a great deal from my father – immensely – you can't imagine how much I suffered. And then, when I saw you for the first time . . .'

Concettina stopped suddenly, aware that Lorenzo was not kissing her any more; on the contrary, he seemed to be trying to free himself from her embrace.

'What's wrong?' she demanded, quickly withdrawing her arms.

'Nothing. Go on, go on talking,' replied Lorenzo huskily, finding it difficult to control his voice.

While she had been speaking, he had been lying with his cheek pressed against her nightdress, his ear on her breast as it rose and fell with the rhythm of her breathing; to his horror he had become aware of an ominous murmur inside her chest.

'Go on talking, go on,' he encouraged her. 'I want to hear the beating of your heart . . . let me hear it . . . let me hear it while you say how much you love me . . . Let me listen to it . . .'

'Oh, Lorenzo,' she replied, and closed her eyes in sweet abandon, as if her whole life lay becalmed on a sea of indescribable tenderness.

Lorenzo continued to listen, holding his breath.

'O God, it is possible?' he thought. 'That rumbling sound, that gurgling in her lungs! No, it can't be!'

Terrified by his discovery, unable to believe his own senses, he sat up.

Concettina opened her eyes again and moved her arms a little, as if awakening from a long sleep.

'Have you had your answer? Are you happy now?' she asked him with a smile. Lorenzo felt his legs go weak: the bed, the bed-curtains and her fair head were all spinning around him in a sudden attack of giddiness.

Away with such thoughts! It couldn't be true! Surely he would have noticed it before!

Pulling himself together, he once more bent passionately over her and covered her with short, repeated kisses. He held her little face with its soft skin tightly in his hands, a face somewhat thin and lean, but which became beautiful when she smiled, as she did now, lying half-submerged in the pillows. Her deep blue eyes were shining like stars, and her little teeth were barely visible between the ruby-red lips of a mouth that seemed smaller than a ring.

'Have you had your answer?' she asked him again. 'Are you pleased now?'

He began to wonder if it had all been a nightmare. It seemed so now, but he was too frightened to make sure: not now, when he knew that he loved her, when he was convinced of her love for him, after the intimacy of their embraces had made him realise what a treasure he had come to own.

When he saw her on the terrace, coming towards him on the arm of her new father – who also wanted his share of his dear little daughter-in-law – when he saw her so fresh, so rosy and so gay, Lorenzo was filled with joy.

'It must have been one of those stupid doctor's hallucinations!' he thought, and he took her by the hands.

'Are you jealous?' asked his father, gently pushing the young wife towards her husband.

Laughing like a child and jumping with delight, Concettina turned round and hugged her father-in-law.

'We'll make him green!' she said to don Giacomo with a happy smile.

In his cold, empty house in Caltagirone, don Giacomo had been going round and round for years like a fly without a head. Now, at a single stroke, it seemed to have been brought to life again by the arrival of his daughter-in-law. The house felt warm once more, warmed by the love of these two children who behaved like lovebirds rather than a married couple.

The bleak and barren little balconies blossomed with greenery and flowers. A few months ago, the row of rooms had looked dismal and untidy, trapped in desolate, uninterrupted silence; the furniture had been covered in dust, and the windows had looked as if they were coated with batter: now everything began to look gay and cared-for again, and more so than ever before. It was all due to the little swallow who flew nimbly about the house, noticing every detail and taking care of everything. She even seemed to have rejuvenated the old maidservant, who no longer served shrivelled remains for lunch, and loudly proclaimed that her new mistress had the touch of a little princess.

The piano in the drawing-room was played frequently, especially after Lorenzo returned from his round of calls and, smoking a cigarette, spread himself out in an easy chair, one leg across the other, with his eyes half-closed. Concettina would sing softly, turning her fair little head every now and again to look at him and smile, completely intoxicated by the music. Lorenzo's old suspicions, and the fears he had felt for the future, came back to his mind every now and then, though his quiet, home-centred life of work and study had hardly changed: it had actually become sweeter, more intimate, and taken on a religious, elevated aura of true poetry. At times he could hardly believe his good fortune; and Concettina, too, was blissfully happy: she had entered paradise.

Her mind went back to her suffering at home, where her father had shown a complete lack of respect for the dignity of her young womanhood, dragging into the house a succession of women he had dug up from heaven knew where, sluts who left everything in a mess and cost him no end of money into the bargain – she shook her head violently to drive away the memories of those painful scenes, and in her sadness about the past, she felt relieved that her father had been to see her only once or twice since her marriage. Now he was free to take home any woman he fancied, and to desecrate the room where her saint of a mother had died. She had no wish to think of it all again . . .

Her health seemed to flourish rather than deteriorate, and when Lorenzo, prompted by the suspicion that haunted him every now and again, asked her how she felt, she would reply: Excellent – she had never felt better!

But it was not true. For some time she had had an indefinable sensation of being unwell which she did not want to admit to her husband, partly out of shyness and partly because she did not wish to worry him. It was a feeling of exhaustion, difficulty in breathing, disturbed digestion and pains; a feeling of constricting pressure about her chest with palpitations, particularly at night, which prevented her from sleeping. She tried to comfort herself with the thought that it was nothing serious, and whenever Lorenzo's suspicion was reawakened, and he began to scrutinise her intently, she would do everything she could to appear more lively and gay.

'It's nothing, nothing,' she repeated to herself.

One morning, however, after several sleepless nights, she was unable to get out of bed. Lorenzo had already left to visit his patients. On his return don Giacomo said to him with smiling eyes, 'Concettino doesn't feel well': he felt sure this meant that a grandchild was on the way. When he saw his son turn white and run his fingers nervously through his hair, he was dumbfounded. What could be wrong?

Don Giacomo didn't dare enter his daughter-in-law's bedroom: he walked to and fro outside her door, waiting for Lorenzo to come out.

'What's wrong?'

Lorenzo let himself fall onto the chair standing next to the bedroom-room table, and holding his head in his hands he began to sob; 'It's all my fault. What an egotist I've been! Yes, it's my own fault!'

He could say nothing else to this poor old man who didn't understand what he meant, and suffered with him without knowing why. At last, with frequent interruptions and wringing of hands, Lorenzo managed to give him some idea. Don Giacomo tried to reassure him.

'Oh, you're exaggerating ... We could go to Catania for a consultation with a specialist, or even to Naples ... Why upset yourself like this? Do you want to scare me to death?'

Concettina herself was quite unaware of the gravity of her illness: to her it was nothing. The drugs prescribed by Lorenzo afforded her some relief, and soon she was darting about the house again, gay and light-hearted, suspicious of all the medicines and the special attention offered to her. However, sometimes she felt nervous, and she suffered from short bouts of depression that seemed strange even to herself.

For diversion she played the piano more frequently than ever. But the romance by Perrotta, which she loved so much, that memory of Lorenzo's first visit, now moved her unusually, and gave her the feeling that she heard it being sung by someone else. Its sound had changed, its character, its expression and significance: it seemed to have become a lament, the sigh of a soul in distress. One day she simply couldn't finish singing it.

'That song upsets me,' she said to Lorenzo in a shaky voice. 'It makes me cry.'

'Don't sing it any more, then,' he said soothingly. 'Why let it worry you? Anyhow, you really ought to relax: you mustn't let things upset you so much. The way you're always bustling about the house ...'

Concettina was still trembling with agitation. She sat on his knee, softly stroking his cheek, and looked deeply into his eyes while he continued: 'You're so delicate, you see! For anyone else this would have been just a little indisposition, but for you – don't you understand? – it becomes almost serious. Can't you see that?'

Concettina threw back her head. 'No, I can't!' she exclaimed. 'Do you think I'm a weakling – or worn out?'

'I didn't mean that, but – '

'Do you want to know what you can do with your medicines? You can keep them for your patients! I won't take them any longer! I'll get well by myself. I can be a doctor too, you know, and this is what my remedy will be!' and she kissed him again and again.

All of a sudden she gave way to the frenzied love that had been tormenting her for the last week.

'I want you always at my side, just as you are now! I hate all those nasty patients of yours who never get any better, who just steal you away from me from morning till night. You hardly belong to me any more!'

In the balmy days of spring they often went walking together in the grounds of the Villa.* Concettina would press Lorenzo's arm to feel their closeness, and to make him feel it too. They walked slowly and talked little. Every now and then they stopped to admire a small plant in flower, or to watch a tiny goldfinch and listen to its trilling as it swung to and fro on the branch of a bush. They looked at the relief figurines on Vaccaro's lovely terracotta vases.

'I want to walk across that green,' she said, 'and fill myself up with sunshine and clean air, and wander up and down those winding paths. They look so deserted you almost feel sorry for them!'

They reached the hill with the view across the open countryside: the green plain spread out ahead, Mount Etna in the background and a chain of hillocks, dark with olive trees, on the right. Although deep breathing hurt her, Concettina filled her lungs.

'How beautiful! I never want to leave here! But what are you thinking about, Lorenzo? Why are you looking so worried?'

How could he possibly tell her his thoughts? How could he tell her of the torment he felt as his doctor's eye followed the terrible progress of her malady? Day by day, hour by hour, the illness was wearing down the delicate organism that was unable to offer any resistance to it. How could he tell her of the incessant remorse that tore him to pieces because he, a doctor, had neglected the disease from the day he had first noticed its presence? And all out

* A feature of Caltagirone, containing large public gardens with fine views, and permanent exhibitions of terracotta objects by local artists.

of sheer selfishness! It was unforgivable! It was nothing less than a crime!

Carelessly and joyfully they had yielded to the caresses, the kisses, the embraces, all the intense joys of love, as if – egotist! – he had not known that these excitements would break the poor creature all the sooner. His thoughts and his memories turned into anguished remorse, and tore him apart. He had deserved it. In fact, he had deserved even worse... Weary of endlessly disguising the dreadful truth, he attempted to deceive himself with the thought that nature could produce miracles that took even science by surprise. Who could tell?

He dared to hope again. But one night she woke him up with a cry: 'Lorenzo, Lorenzo!' He saw her sitting up in bed, with her hair loose, terrified by the sight of the blood that flowed from her mouth and stained her pillow. That night Lorenzo gave up hope. She was doomed. And that night Concettina too realised for the first time what was happening. With terror in her eyes she clung to him in tears, crying, 'Lorenzo, my Lorenzo, help me! I don't want to die!'

'It's nothing, my silly little girl,' he said soothingly, 'nothing.'

But in his look of desolation and the expression of horror that his agony had frozen on his face she could read her death sentence.

'My mother died of the same illness. Have I got to die too? I don't want to die! I'm so happy with you – with you, my Lorenzo! I don't want to die!' she sobbed heart-rendingly.

Sadness, almost the sadness of mourning, was spreading through the house. Lorenzo, his poor old father and the servant all seemed stunned by the fearful silence, and wandered about like three shadows, three souls in purgatory walking round and round in their place of punishment.

'Who could have suspected it? She looked the flower of health!' Don Giacomo, like his son, felt overwhelmed by remorse. 'I was the one who forced him to marry her,' he thought. 'But who could have foreseen this? She looked the flower of health!'

Concettina remained confined to her room. Huddled in an

armchair, her eyes half-closed, coughing and short of breath, she burned with the fever that never left her. Ice-cold sweats exhausted her, and made beads of perspiration stand on her brow like drops of wax. Her little hands had grown so thin that the blue veins could be seen under the transparent skin. She wanted him here, she wanted her Lorenzo, and she was consumed by a terrible jealousy about the future – a future when she would not be here any more, just like her poor mother. She wanted to take him with her, to continue to love and to be loved even in the grave, in the next life, for ever and ever.

At every opportunity she implored him, 'Kiss me, kiss me!'

And when Lorenzo hesitated because these frequent excitements only made her worse, she added in a voice choked with tears, 'Are you frightened, or do I disgust you?'

'Are you trying to make yourself worse on purpose?' Lorenzo demanded.

In reply she would press her colourless, feverish lips onto his, and hug his neck tightly with her thin little arms. With her kisses, her hot, violent, never-ending kisses, she was trying to impart her own fearful illness to her husband. At night she held him closely in her arms, breathing in his face, so as to permeate his body completely with the fever that was consuming her with its icy, deadly sweats, the fever that she had decided should be Lorenzo's end as well as her own. If he resisted her invalid's whims she would scream, weep and fall into a state of nerves that terrified him; it seemed to him as if she might die in his arms.

At such moments she was implacable. 'Ah, so you don't love me any more! You're tired of me! I know – you can't deceive me!'

Lorenzo beseeched her, with his hands clasped, to be silent; tears stood in his eyes.

'Oh yes, I've noticed – you can't stand me any more. Will it be too long for you before you can get rid of this corpse? Perhaps you hate me!'

'Concettina! Concettina!'

'Yes, yes, you can't fool me. I can read your mind. And to think that I adored you, that you were my God! I gave you my life! And now I am dying, dying of love for you. How ungrateful, how thankless you are!'

She would put her emaciated hands over her white, sunken face and shake her head desolately; fits of coughing made her lose her breath and left her exhausted and faint between the pillows that propped her up on all sides, while Lorenzo on his knees before her, his face streaked with tears, silent and even paler than she was, tried to make her swallow spoonfuls of sedative.

'For the sake of my love for you, for the sake of your love for yourself!' he implored her. 'Do you want to kill yourself with these scenes?'

The sight of him at her feet and the sound of his anguished voice would melt her heart. She would sit up and look at him, and, overcome by the compassion of a woman in love, feel for a moment capable of any sacrifice.

'Forgive me,' she would say. 'Forgive me. No, don't touch me – don't kiss me. I'm dying of a plague. Forget me! It's enough for me just to see you, just to hear your voice. But before you go, tell me that you still love me as much as you did before. Tell me that you love me as much as you ever did.'

'Even more!'

'Well, then. Swear that when I'm dead you will never love another woman.'

'I swear it.'

'And that you will always sleep in this room, in this bed, in these sheets . . .'

'I swear it to you.'

'But what if you're lying? What if you don't mean to keep your promise? Come, come nearer to me. Give me a kiss, just one little kiss. I know I'm ugly now, I know, I don't even need to look in the mirror . . . But I love you so much! You are mine, aren't you, Lorenzo?'

'All yours, body and soul.'

'Say it again!'

'All, all, body and soul.'

'Thank you, Lorenzo. Those words do me so much good. Oh, if I could only get well again . . . ! If only I could go on living, even as I am now, even if I had to suffer twice or twenty or a hundred times as much!'

'You'll get well again. We have every reason to hope! Without these terrors, without these scenes – '

'I'll be good. I'll be quiet – you'll see. I'm going to obey you like a little girl. Let me kiss you. I don't disgust you, do I? Press me to your heart. Tightly, tightly, Lorenzo!'

But these truces would last barely a day. Sometimes it took only a few hours before her obsessions returned.

It was a pitiful spectacle to see her imprisoned within the four walls of her bedroom while the May sunlight poured in through the big windows in its full splendour, to see her in silence lasting for hours, broken only by a subdued moan or by the tearing cough that every now and again seemed almost to suffocate her; that pathetic figure, nothing but skin and bones, with sunken eyes that appeared bigger than ever in her shrivelled face, her un-combed hair still with its gleam of spun gold, sitting up in her easy chair supported by pillows as she would not stay in bed.

Lorenzo was never permitted to leave her room; she did not want to see anyone else's face, not even her father-in-law's, except for very brief periods. During these terrible months Lorenzo aged a great deal. His hair turned almost completely grey, and he hardly recognised himself. Concettina fixed him with a silent gaze; occasionally she would flash a lightning glance towards him as if trying to place him under a deadly spell.

She wanted to take him with her, snatch him away from that other woman who was perhaps only waiting for Concettina's death to throw herself into his arms, so full of health, beautiful, loving and triumphant that she would erase every trace of poor Concettina from Lorenzo's memory. No, this woman should not have him! She should not have him! Concettina and Lorenzo would always stay together, arm in arm in death as well as in life. He was hers! That other woman was not going to have him. Never!

He must not be allowed to escape. And for fear that her disease had not sufficiently embedded itself within him, she kept kissing and kissing him, his mouth, his cheeks, his neck, his eyes, his hair. Sometimes she would bite him with the fury of a wild animal. 'Ah, have I hurt you?' she would ask, and to ease the pain she would immediately kiss the place where she had bitten him. Sometimes she made him wipe his face with a handkerchief soaked with her sweat; sometimes she made him drink out of her cup, placing his lips on the very spot where she had put hers ... No, she would not leave this dear prey of hers to anyone else!

And indeed, Lorenzo felt himself gradually dying too. He never approached her now without a feeling of indefinable, superstitious terror. His forebodings had come true, he thought. A dull fear of the inevitable catastrophe possessed him. So that when one day she told him she felt a little better, he believed her readily.

'Yes, I feel better,' she said. 'I feel as if I've suddenly recovered. Is it because of the lovely day and the sunshine?'

She had become gentle, sweet and affectionate, just as in the early days. She even referred jokingly to her illness. 'I'm winning after all! ... And it's only right that I should. I have a big source of strength on my side – love!'

'You have another as well – youth!' replied Lorenzo, and they smiled together.

Concettina even wished to see her father-in-law, and she asked him to forgive her for being so unloving towards him while she had been ill.

'When one is sick,' she explained, 'one doesn't always realise what one is doing. Today I feel so much better. You do understand, don't you?'

Don Giacomo was not deceived. 'Alas! The lamp is giving its last flicker,' he whispered to his son. 'You should call the priest – if there's still time.'

Suddenly Concettina grew faint: the thin thread that linked her with life was about to break. She fell back into her chair, gazing at Lorenzo with a wild look of envy.

'So you're not coming with me after all?' She made a sign with her head: 'I want you to carry me out onto the terrace, in this chair. I want to see the town, and the countryside, for the last time ... Hurry, hurry!'

Mechanically, Lorenzo did as he was told.

'Look at the clock-tower.'

Lorenzo looked towards it, stupefied.

'Remember that you saw it with me for the last time. Those hills, those trees . . . remember that before I died we looked at them together. Remember that I told you to look! Can you see the pine trees by the Church of Saint Mary of Jesus over there on the left, where we used to walk together? Remember . . . remember!'

'I will,' replied Lorenzo, with his voice and head, transfixed. He could feel the clock-tower, the tree-covered hills, the pine trees by the Church of Saint Mary of Jesus imprinting themselves on his eyes as if by bewitchment. This scene would always remain before his eyes . . . forever . . . forever . . .

With a supreme effort, Concettina drew him to her chest, searching blindly for the lips of the man for whom she had lived.

'Die with me, die with me!' she gasped.

The Mule

LUIGI CAPUANA

Don Michele got up as usual at seven, at dawn, and created havoc in the house. First he pulled the feet of the young housemaid who slept wrapped up in a miserable wool coverlet on a pallet in the little room next to the kitchen. Then he yelled from the top of the staircase to the boy who slept in the stable:

'Give the mule her barley, and draw some water from the rainwater tank. The animal wouldn't drink last night. I'm sure her bad habits are your fault, you son-of-a-bitch!'

He returned to the bedroom, treading heavily with the iron-ringed heels of his hobnailed field boots. Donna Carmela had just slipped into her petticoat, shivering and numb with cold. Her eyes were heavy with sleep, her hair dishevelled.

'What's the matter with you? Why does it have to take you years to put those two rags on? Am I made of such different stuff? And how about that other sleepy creature there – aren't ten hours of sleep enough for her?'

Presia, the maid, stretched herself and yawned. He couldn't convince *her* that her few hours of sleep could pass for ten! What did he want her to do?

'Don't you know ... By the blood of Christ, do you want to drive me to despair? Do you think I want to throw the seedcorn to the devil next year?'

'It's all ready,' said donna Carmela.

Don Michele didn't answer – vexed that the seedcorn had already been prepared, as it robbed him of an excuse to shout at the other two. He paced around the room muttering unintelligibly, pushed a chair out of his way and hung a key on its nail. Soon he found another cause for anger.

'Has my bottle been filled?'

the morning.'

'Why don't you get a move on? Why are you asleep on your feet? Do you think I'm going to the fields tomorrow?'

Donna Carmela and Presia went down to the cellar to fill the wine bottle from the special cask with two-year-old wine that was kept for don Michele alone. Meanwhile don Michele himself went to the stable, and found the boy in tears: the mule wouldn't drink, and the boy knew all too well that the hands and boots of his master would leave their marks on him for days if the animal refused the water again.

'Anyone would think I'd told the beast not to drink!'

The boy whistled coaxingly to the mule, and began to cry.

But the mule only sniffed listlessly at the water, and wearily shook her ears. Then she dipped the edge of her lips into the water bowl, shook her head, snorted, grimaced with her muzzle in the air, and bared her teeth.

Don Michele gave the boy a kick and tore the halter rope out of his hands.

'What are you doing? This mule is worth forty ounces* – do you think I'll stand by and let you make her sick? If I don't skin you with my own two hands my name isn't don Michele!'

He fondled the mule, patted her belly, adjusted her forelock, and passed his hand over her back.

'What's wrong, my beauty, my little beauty, why don't you drink? Come on, Bella, my lovely little Bella.'

But the mule stepped back, insensible to her master's fondling and whistling.

Then he noticed that there was something dripping out of her nostrils and her eyes were bleary; and he began to swear worse than a Turk. He invoked all the souls in purgatory, the Blessed Virgin, and Saint Eloi the patron saint of horses, asses and mules: for this was 'candle sickness',† capable of killing an animal in less than a week.

'Christ, what have you got against me? Are you trying to amuse yourself by robbing me of forty ounces' worth of mule?

---

* Highest unit of Sicilian currency of the time, originally representing an ounce of gold; the other units were *tarì* and *grani*.

† The nasal discharge in this sickness resembles dripping wax.

Do you think that's funny? Well, they did a good day's work when they nailed you to the cross. If I'd been among the Jews I'd have helped them ram in those nails, believe me!'

At the sound of his swearing, donna Carmela and Presia hurried up. Donna Carmela carried the funnel in her hand, while the servant held the light in one hand and the wine bottle in the other.

'Holy Virgin – what a disgrace, what a disgrace!'

Donna Carmela clasped her forehead, while don Michele stared at the mule which was tied to the manger, standing with his legs apart and his hands dangling by his side. The poor beast, her ears limp and her eyes full of suffering, wouldn't even smell the barley and straw, and she turned her head towards her master as if asking for his help.

'Forty ounces' worth of mule! What a bolt out of the blue! This year I'll have to go begging with a stick in my hands, and . . .'

'Why are you swearing like that?'

'I know when to swear and when not to swear! Look at her flanks heaving!'

Tears stood in donna Carmela's eyes; her teeth chattered.

This disgrace was all that was needed to complete the inferno of her house. Yes, the Lord had forgotten her in this world: now she would have fresh troubles to suffer.

Don Michele heard her teeth chattering, and whirled round in a rage: 'What's wrong with you, woman?'

'Nothing . . . perhaps I'm getting a touch of my malaria . . . just see to the mule!'

The poor woman could hardly hold herself up, and had to lean against the wall for support. She kept her hands hidden underneath her large apron. Although she was barely thirty years of age, she held herself bent like an old woman.

Don Michele went on gazing at the mule as if willing her with his eyes to get better, and with his own breath to breathe new life into her. To his wife he said: 'Are you trying to make yourself ill as well? That will just complete the party!'

But donna Carmela had become hardened to her husband's pleasantries. 'Attend to the mule,' she replied.

The stable boy had been sent to call Master Filippo the blacksmith and Uncle Deco. Uncle Deco understood such things not only better than Master Filippo, but even better than the doctor. Don Antonio the doctor killed quite a number of his sick patients; but when Uncle Deco laid his hands on an animal, there was no danger that it would fall down and roll its legs in the air. Don Michele had sent for Master Filippo as well because he thought four eyes would see more than two.

The consultation was a lengthy one. As soon as Master Filippo saw Uncle Deco, he began to feign ignorance in the hope of embarrassing his rival.

'Quite possibly it's a case of . . . I wouldn't say that it isn't a case of . . . ' the blacksmith said doubtfully.

'Yes, it's the glanders all right, and what a case!' exclaimed Uncle Deco. 'What we need is a seton* with knots. Otherwise, don Michele, you might as well make arrangements to have her skin tanned, because the mule will be gone.'

Don Michele lost his temper again, cursing the saints and the Blessed Virgin. He didn't notice his wife standing shivering in a corner, pale, her nose as sharp as a corpse's, unable to utter a single word.

O Lord, thy holy will be done!

For twelve years the poor woman had done the holy will of the Lord. Not a single joyful and quiet day had she had with the husband who never had a kind word for her: although she had brought him more than eight hundred ounces' worth of dowry, he begrudged her the very shoes on her feet.

All day donna Carmela stood with Presia in the kitchen, preparing bran drenches and making calamint potions for the mule to inhale, while don Michele held the animal by the collar and talked to her as if she were a human being. And the mule lifted her head and looked at him as if she understood his words.

The poor woman's back and legs felt totally worn out from trudging up and down the stairs from the kitchen to the stable. At meal-time she couldn't eat a mouthful; her husband sat down at the table and without even asking whether she wanted any,

* Piece of surgical thread drawn through a fold of skin to facilitate drainage of discharge. Nowadays cases of glanders are treated with antibiotics.

angrily gulped down two fried eggs and a portion of red pepper salad. But she wouldn't have been able to get so much as the skin of a bean between her teeth. Her stomach had closed up completely; the smell of the calamint which permeated the house gave her a deep nausea. During the meal don Michele argued all the time about the seton they had to insert into the mule's chest; he seemed to dip his bread into the incision they would make in the animal.

'It will cost me at least three lire – and the scar will remain forever – even if Saint Eloi himself blesses it!'

The possibility of calling the doctor for his wife didn't occur to don Michele. Far from it – whenever he saw her during the next week stumbling about like a corpse from the graveyard, worn out by all the running up and down the house looking after the mule, he would repeat to her:

'Are you trying to make yourself ill as well? That would just about complete the festivities!'

His voice was threatening.

All this made donna Carmela resign herself to the feeling that her own body was dying as she walked about. She hoped her husband wouldn't commit any further sins of blasphemy. She even helped in the stable, although the stench of the seton and the calamint took her breath away. And during the night, when don Michele – sleeping with his clothes on – got up to see to the poor beast, she followed half-dressed behind him, although she had to prop herself up against the stable wall so as not to fall over; the poor woman could hardly stay on her feet.

In the morning she no longer had the strength to get out of bed. Don Michele started to shout at her:

'Are you doing this on purpose? You enjoy seeing me ruined! You've never been any use – that's why everything in this house is going wrong. The Lord will see my mule from up there, but he won't see you!'

'Be quiet,' begged his poor wife, 'this time the Lord will surely hear you!'

Don Michele shrugged his shoulders and went to attend to the mule, his forty ounces' worth of mule, which had become a mere skeleton hovering between life and death. No one would give him more than a few grains for the beast now!

When Presia found the courage to tell him that while he was fussing about the mule his own wife was dying, don Michele yelled:

'You and your mistress can both go to hell!'

But Presia persisted:

'If I see don Antonio I shall tell him to come up to the house.'

'Hold your tongue!' And he made as if to hit her with the halter rope.

Presia raised her voice:

'The poor mistress is going to die before that mule does – and you will have her on your conscience! No one would even abandon a dog like that!'

'Hold your tongue!'

'The Lord will hold you to account for this in the next life! It's because of the way you behave he doesn't help you now.'

'Hold your tongue, I tell you!'

'The Lord is righteous – your mule will die – and you deserve even worse!'

Don Michele finally pretended not to hear her. With the rope in his hand he scratched the forehead of the poor mule, whose head hung so low that it seemed she wanted to kiss the floor.

Aunt Rosa, their neighbour, came and said to him:

'The doctor's here, he's gone into your house.'

But don Michele only went wild with rage, calling all the angels and saints and seraphim down from heaven – even the Blessed Virgin Mary herself.

'Your soul be damned!' he cursed the woman.

Aunt Rosa made the sign of the cross and scuttled away:

'That this house isn't sinking into the ground is a miracle if ever there was one!'

Don Michele went to find don Antonio, who had just written something on a piece of paper.

'But this is the first morning she has stayed in bed!'

He could not grasp that his wife was so ill that the last rites of the Holy Church had to be administered as quickly as possible.

When the priest came with the Eucharist and extreme unction, don Michele knelt at the foot of the bed. He held his head in his

71

hands, and leaned his elbows on the seat of a chair. The priest anointed the eyes and lips of the dying woman.

The women of the neighbourhood talked among themselves.

'There are no children, so all her belongings will go back to her own family!'

Don Michele, who was thinking exactly the same thing, sighed deeply.

The neighbours concluded:

'He's behaved like the crocodile who first kills and then cries for the victim. He has made that poor saint of a creature suffer for twelve years, and now he's getting her out of the way altogether!'

Donna Carmela was lying on her bed, her head sunk deeply in the pillows, her eyes hollow, her nose as black as soot. Her great difficulty in breathing made it impossible for her to find rest. As soon as the priest had left, she signalled to her husband and whispered almost inaudibly in his ear:

'Are you pleased now? May the Lord look after you and sustain you when I'm gone.'

Don Michele broke down and cried.

'Why do you say such things to me? Haven't I always loved you? Now look at the state I'm left in – I'll have to return the dowry. And if the mule dies too I might as well go and hang myself. I'm truly thinking of it. I'll make a running knot in the halter rope, fasten it to one of the roof beams, and I'll hang myself, so I will!'

'You wicked man! Only you could do such a thing!' his poor wife reproached him, and she looked at him with her compassionate eyes, eyes full of pity and forgiveness.

Tears rolled down don Michele's cheeks.

'Yes, yes! As sure as there's a God in heaven, I'll hang myself if this misfortune happens! But the good Mother of all the sick will work a miracle for me – I'm sure she will! And if she doesn't, I'll tie that running knot in the halter rope before all your relations can come and strip my house to get the dowry back. That will make them happier still!'

'Do you want to be damned forever, you wicked man?' asked his wife in a thread of a voice, raising her hand with difficulty.

Don Michele seemed to want to bang his head against the wall in his despair. His wife saw how he felt; and when her eye fell on Presia, who was drying her eyes in her apron and looked all dirty and dishevelled, donna Carmela called her and whispered something in her ear. Presia seemed not to understand what she had said, for she asked her to repeat it.

And later the notary and four witnesses too thought at first that they must have misunderstood the request they heard from her own mouth: she wished to leave all her belongings to her husband, on condition that as long as he lived he should have a mass said every year on each of the four Fridays of March, and one on All Souls' Day.

While the notary was busy writing down the last will and testament of donna Carmela, don Michele went to see his mule, unable to bear the torment any longer. He fondled her and bathed her nostrils in calamint water.

'If I don't look after her the poor animal will die of neglect, and who would care? Poor little beast! Do you know that your mistress will never come down to you again with your measure of barley?'

The animal shook her head as if replying that nothing and no one mattered to her any more: the calamint water had got up her nostrils.

Whenever don Michele was not in the stable, he would sit at the foot of his wife's bed, an expression of deep sorrow upon his face, his arms held crossed together, his head hung low.

The poor woman got neither better nor worse, and the shortness of breath that made her so restless continued.

If the good Mother of the sick wouldn't perform a miracle and make her well again, then why did she let this saintly creature suffer so long? What torment! She would be so much happier in paradise! Yes indeed, now that she had made her will, the Blessed Virgin should surely take her to heaven.

Presia fled to the kitchen. There were certain things she simply could not bear to hear – they made her boil inside. She had to bite her tongue hard to keep it in check.

The doctor came twice a day, but wouldn't say whether to expect better or worse.

73

Not Uncle Deco. One morning he clearly and bluntly stated that his patient, the mule, would not see the day out. 'Better,' he advised, 'let her walk on her own four feet behind the castle and leave her to the dogs than pay two men to drag her carcase there.'

Don Michele lamented:

'Forty ounces' worth of mule dead! It's plain the curse of God is on my house. I'll have to have the whole place reconsecrated from top to bottom! My wife who has made her will and had the last rites of the Holy Church – she stays alive. And my mule who should have got well again – she'll be eaten by the dogs behind the castle. It's obvious for all to see – someone up there doesn't like me!'

Cavalleria Rusticana

GIOVANNI VERGA

After his return from the army Nunzia Macca's son Turiddu liked to strut around the piazza on Sundays, wearing his regimental uniform with a red beret like the fez worn by an itinerant fortune-teller with his cage of prophetic canaries. The girls on their way to mass, faces tucked up to the nose in their mantillas, could hardly take their eyes off him. The boys swarmed around him like flies. He smoked a pipe decorated with a carving of the King on horseback, and when he struck a match on his trouser-seat he raised his foot as if aiming a kick at someone.

But Lola, daughter of the farm manager Angelo, showed herself neither at church nor on the stairway terrace; she had got engaged to a man from Licodia, a carter with four fine Sortino mules in his stable. When Turiddu heard of the engagement, holy smoke, he swore he was going to tear this Licodia fellow's guts out, he was! But he never did anything of the sort and only let off steam by singing all the songs of wrath he knew under his beauty's window.

The neighbours wondered: had Nunzia's Turiddu nothing better to do than spend his nights chirping like a solitary rock-thrush?

In the end he ran into Lola on her way back from a bare-foot pilgrimage to the Virgin of the Perils. When she saw him she neither blushed nor blanched, as if he were no concern of hers.

'How lucky I am to see you,' he said.

'Oh, Turiddu,' said she, 'I heard you'd got back at the beginning of the month.'

'I've heard a few things as well!' he replied. 'Is it true you're going to marry Alfio the carter?'

'Yes, God willing,' replied Lola, adjusting the ends of her headscarf over her chin.

'Do you think your chopping and changing is God's will? Is it God's will for me to come back all that way to hear this fine news, Miss Lola?'

The poor boy tried to keep up his stern act, but his voice failed him. He walked behind the girl sadly shaking his head, and the tassel of his red beret swayed from one shoulder to the other. She was sorry to see him with such a long face, but she hadn't the heart to lead him on with kind words.

'Listen, Turiddu,' she said at last, 'let me catch up with the other girls. What would people say if they saw me with you?'

'That's right,' answered Turiddu. 'Now you're going to marry Alfio, with all his mules and everything, you musn't cause gossip! When I was in the army, my poor mother had to sell our bay mule, as well as that little piece of vineyard by the road which we used to own. Times have changed – don't you remember how we used to talk to one another through the window in the yard, and how you gave me that handkerchief before I left? God knows how many tears I cried into it while I was so far away that even the name of our village sounded strange. Goodbye then, Lola. "Rains have come and rains have gone, our friendship's over." '

So Lola married the carter; on Sundays she would stand on the stairway terrace, holding her hands well up so that everyone could see the heavy gold rings her husband had given her. Turiddu went on walking nonchalantly up and down the street ogling the girls, pipe in mouth and hands in pockets; but within himself he was furious that Lola's husband was so rich, and that she pretended not to notice him when he passed by.

'How I'd love to teach the bitch a lesson!' he muttered.

Just over the way from Alfio lived Master Cola the vine-grower, who was filthy rich, everyone said; he had an unmarried daughter. With a good word here and a good deed there Turiddu got Master Cola to give him work on his land, and he began to call at the house and make flattering speeches to the girl.

'Why don't you go and tell Lola all that nonsense of yours?' Santuzza replied.

'Lola's done well for herself! Lola's married wealth!'

'I don't think I'll marry wealth.'

'You're worth a hundred Lolas, and I know someone who

wouldn't look at Lola with you about, or her patron saint either, because Lola's not fit to clean your shoes, she isn't, she isn't.'

'When the fox couldn't reach the grapes . . .'

'He said how pretty you are, you sweet little thing.'

'Hey! Hands off, Turiddu.'

'Are you afraid I'll eat you?'

'I'm not afraid of you, and I'm not afraid of anyone else either.'

'Yes, we know, with a mother from Licodia you've got quarrelsome blood. Oh, but couldn't I eat you up!'

'All right then, eat me up, I won't make any crumbs. But go and lift that bundle up for me first.'

'I'd lift the whole house up for you, I really would!'

To stop herself blushing she took up a piece of wood and threw it at him, just missing him.

'Come on, Turiddu, let's get on with it, talking won't tie these twigs for us.'

'If I were rich I'd look for a wife just like you.'

'I shan't marry a rich man like Lola, but I've got my dowry too, ready for the day the Lord sends me someone.'

'We all know you're rich, we know!'

'All right, hurry up then – father will be back any moment and I don't want him to find me in the yard!'

Master Cola began to turn his nose up over Turiddu, but the girl pretended not to notice, for the tassel of the bersagliero's beret

When Master Cola showed Turiddu the door, his daughter opened her window to him and chatted with him night after night, and soon the whole neighbourhood talked of nothing else.

'I'm crazy about you,' said Turiddu, 'I can't sleep and I can't eat.'

'Fiddlesticks!'

'I wish I were Victor Emanuel's son, then I could marry you!'

'Fiddlesticks!'

'Holy Mary, I could gobble you up like a morsel of bread!'

'Fiddlesticks!'

'I swear it to you!'

'How you carry on!'

Lola, concealed behind the pot of basil, listened to them every night, turning pale and red in turn. One day she greeted Turiddu.

'Old friends don't say hello then, Turiddu?'

'Well,' sighed the young fellow, 'it's a lucky man that has the chance to say hello to you.'

Turiddu went to see her so frequently that Santuzza noticed it, and shut the window in his face. The neighbours grinned to one another whenever the bersagliere passed. Lola's husband was away travelling the fairs with his mules.

'On Sunday I must go to confession,' said Lola. 'Last night I dreamed of black grapes.'*

'Wait,' entreated Turiddu.

'No, it'll soon be Easter and Alfio will want to know why I haven't gone to confession.'

'Ah,' murmured Master Cola's Santuzza, awaiting her turn on her knees in front of the confessional where Lola stood washing her sins, 'I wouldn't send her to Rome for a penance!'

Alfio returned with his mules, his pockets full of money, bringing his wife a lovely new Easter dress as a present.

'Well may you bring your wife a present,' his neighbour Santuzza told him. 'While you're away she cuckolds you in your own house.'

Alfio was a true swaggering carter who wore his cap over one ear, and when he heard his wife spoken of in this way his face changed as if he had been knifed.

'By the Devil!' he shouted. 'If your eyes have been playing you tricks I'll tear them out and you won't have anything left to cry with – and that goes for the whole lot of you!'

'I'm not the crying sort,' said Santuzza. 'I saw Turiddu go into your wife's house at night with my own eyes, and I didn't cry.'

'All right,' said Alfio. 'Thank you very much.'

Since the cat had come home, Turiddu no longer walked up and down the street but whiled away the time at the inn with his friends. Just before Easter they were all sitting over a plate of sausages. When Alfio came in Turiddu knew at once what he had come for by the way he looked at him, and put his fork on his plate.

* Signifying tears and sorrow in Sicilian dreamlore.

'What do you want to tell me, Alfio?' he asked.

'Nothing special, Turiddu. We haven't met for a while and I just wanted to see you – you know all about it.'

When Alfio had come in Turiddu had offered him a glass of wine, but Alfio had raised his hand in refusal. Now Turiddu got up and said:

'I'm ready, Alfio.'

The carter put his arms around Turiddu's neck.

'If you come to the cactus grove by the tannery tomorrow morning we can talk it over, Turiddu.'

'Wait for me on the main road at dawn and we can walk along together.'

They exchanged the kiss of challenge. Turiddu pressed his teeth into Alfio's ear, thus giving his solemn promise to be there.

Turiddu's friends quietly left their sausages and walked home with him. Poor old mother Nunzia was waiting up for him as she did every night.

'Mother,' said Turiddu, 'do you remember how you thought I wouldn't come back any more when I went for service? Give me a big kiss like you did then, I've got a long way to go tomorrow.'

Before daybreak he took his clasp knife out of the hay where he had hidden it when he had been called up, and set off for the prickly pear grove by the tannery.

'Holy Jesus and Mary, where are you going in such a fury?' cried Lola in tears and terror when she saw her husband leaving.

'Not very far,' replied Alfio, 'but it would be better for you if I didn't come back at all.'

Lola began to pray in her nightgown at the foot of her bed, pressing the rosary that Brother Bernard had brought her from the Holy Land against her lips, saying one Ave Maria after another.

'Alfio,' said Turiddu after he had walked a little way with his companion, who was silent and wore his cap over his eyes, 'God's truth I know I was wrong and I should let myself be killed. But before I left home I saw my old mother, she got up early to see me go and pretended she had to feed the chickens, her heart must have told her what's going on, and God's truth I'll kill you like a dog so my poor old mother doesn't have to cry her eyes out.'

'All right,' said Alfio, removing his waistcoat. 'Let's get on with it.'

They were both skilful fighters. Turiddu blocked the first thrust with his arm; when he struck back his aim was good and he stabbed Alfio in the groin.

'Ah Turiddu! So you really mean to kill me!'

'I told you so – since I saw my mother in the chicken-run I've seen her in front of me all the time.'

'Keep your eyes well open then,' yelled Alfio, 'because I'm going to pay you back now!'

He was crouching so that he could hold his left arm over the wound which was hurting him, his left elbow almost trailing the ground; he quickly collected a handful of dust and threw it into his adversary's eyes.

'Ah!' cried Turiddu, blinded, 'I'm dead!'

He tried to save himself by jumping desperately backwards, but Alfio reached him with a second stab in the stomach, and a third in the throat.

'That's three,' he yelled, 'for cuckolding me in my own home! Now your mother can leave the chickens alone.'

Turiddu staggered for a few moments among the cactus plants and then fell like a stone. Blood rushed gurgling from his throat. Not another word did he utter.

The Wolf

GIOVANNI VERGA

She was tall and slim, and though no longer young, had the strong firm breasts of the dark-haired woman. She was pale, as if she suffered permanently from malaria, and out of that pallor her cool red lips and her large eyes devoured you.

In the village they called her 'The Wolf', because she could never be sated. The women would cross themselves when they saw her passing, with the cautiously ambling pace of a hungry wolf, alone like an ill-tempered bitch. She could deprive them of their sons and husbands in the twinkling of an eye, with those red lips of hers, and one look from her devilish eyes could make them run after her skirts, from the altar of Saint Agrippina* herself. It was a good thing the Wolf never came to church, even at Easter or Christmas, either for mass or for confession. Father Angiolino of the Church of Saint Mary of Jesus, a true servant of the Lord, had lost his soul on her account.

Poor Maricchia, a good and decent girl, cried secretly, because she was the Wolf's daughter and no one would marry her, though she had finery enough in her bottom drawer, and as good a piece of sunny land as any girl in the village.

One day the Wolf fell in love with a good-looking lad just back from the army, who was cutting hay with her in the notary's field. She was so much in love that she felt her flesh burning under the cotton of her vest, and when she looked into his eyes her throat felt as parched as on a June day down in the hottest part of the valley. But the young lad went on mowing quietly, his face turned towards the cut grass. 'What's up with you, Mother Pina?' he said to her. In the immense fields where the crackle of

* A virgin martyr whose scourged and beheaded body was buried at Mineo (the ancient Manae) in 262 A.D. – frequently invoked as protection against evil spirits.

81

flying cicadas was the only sound under that sun that beat down from straight overhead, the Wolf bundled up handful after handful, sheaf after sheaf, without tiring, without straightening up for a moment or putting her lips to the flask, just to be able to keep behind Nanni, who mowed and mowed, and kept asking her: 'What do you want, Mother Pina?'

One night she told him. While the men, tired from the long day's work, were drowsing on the threshing ground, and the dogs howled in the vast darkness of the countryside, she said: 'I want *you*. You're as lovely as the sun, and as sweet as honey, and I want you!'

'And *I* want that young daughter of yours!' replied Nanni with a smile.

The Wolf put her hands in her hair and, scratching her head silently, walked away; she didn't come to the threshing ground any more. She saw Nanni again in October, when the olives were being pressed; he was working close to her house, and the screeching of the oil-press kept her awake all night.

She said to her daughter: 'Take the sack of olives and come with me.'

Nanni was busy shovelling the olives under the millstone, shouting 'Ohee!' at the mule to keep him moving.

'Do you want my daughter Maricchia?' asked Mother Pina.

'What are you giving with your daughter Maricchia?' replied Nanni.

'She has everything her father left, and on top of that I'll give her my house. I'll be happy if you leave me a corner of the kitchen where I can spread my mattress.'

'If that's it, we can settle it at Christmas,' said Nanni.

Nanni was all greasy and grimy with oil and half-fermented olives, and Maricchia wouldn't have him on any terms; but her mother seized her by the hair, in front of the fire-place, and said to her through clenched teeth: 'If you don't take him I'll kill you!'

The Wolf looked ill, and people were saying the devil turns hermit in old age. No longer was she seen about, or sitting in front of her door peering out of her mad eyes. When she looked into her son-in-law's face those eyes of hers made him laugh, then fumble for the shred of the Virgin Mary's dress* that he carried as an amulet, and cross himself with it. Maricchia stayed at home feeding the children, and her mother went out to the fields, working with the men like a man, weeding, hoeing, feeding the animals, pruning the vineyards, in the north-east winds of January and in the sirocco of August, when the mules drooped their heads and the men slept face downwards under a north-facing wall. During those hours of 'midday sun and afternoon's heat when no decent woman's on her feet', Mother Pina was the only living soul to be seen in the countryside, walking over the blazing stones of the bridle-paths, across the scorched stubble of the vast fields which faded into the heat-haze far, far away towards cloud-covered Etna, where the sky lay heavy on the horizon.

'Wake up!' said the Wolf to Nanni, who was asleep in the ditch under the dusty hedge, his head between his arms. 'Wake up! I've brought you some wine to freshen your throat.'

Nanni opened his eyes wide in astonishment and stared sleepily at her as she stood facing him, pale, her breasts erect and her eyes black as coal, and he involuntarily raised his hands.

'No! No decent woman's on her feet between midday sun and afternoon's heat!' sobbed Nanni, and with his fingers in his hair he pressed his face against the dry grass at the bottom of the ditch. 'Go away, go away! Don't come to the threshing ground!'

And the Wolf went away, re-fastening her proud tresses, looking straight in front of her feet with her eyes black as coal as she stepped over the hot stubble.

But she came back to the threshing stead, time and again, and Nanni did not object. And if she was late in coming, in those hours between midday sun and afternoon's heat, he would go with sweat on his brow to the top of the deserted white path to await her; and each time afterwards he would bury his hands in his hair and repeat: 'Go away, go away! Don't come to the threshing ground again!'

---

* When the ornate dresses of statues of the Virgin Mary in Sicilian churches are being renewed, shreds from the old dresses are handed to the parishioners and worn as talismans.

Maricchia wept day and night, and every time she saw her mother coming back pale and silent from the fields, she pierced her with eyes that burned with tears and jealousy, herself like a wolf cub.

'Wicked creature!' she spat. 'You wicked mother!'

'Hold your tongue!'

'Thief! Thief!'

'Hold your tongue!'

'I'll go to the police, I will!'

'All right, go!'

And Maricchia did go, carrying her children, dry-eyed and fearless, like a madwoman, because now she loved the husband they had forced on her, greasy and grimy with oil and half-fermented olives.

The police sergeant sent for Nanni; he threatened him with jail and gallows. Nanni sobbed and tore his hair, but he denied nothing and made no excuses.

'It's temptation!' he said. 'It's the temptation of hell!'

He threw himself at the sergeant's feet and begged to be sent to prison.

'For mercy's sake, sergeant, take me away from this hell! Have me hanged or send me to prison, but don't let me see her again, ever again!'

'No,' said the Wolf to the sergeant. 'When I gave him the house as a dowry, I kept a corner of the kitchen for myself. The house is mine, and I won't leave it!'

Not long afterwards Nanni was kicked in the chest by his mule, and looked near death, but the priest refused to come with the Holy Sacrament unless the Wolf left the house. The Wolf went, and Nanni prepared to go too, as a good Christian should; he confessed and took communion with such clear signs of repentance that all the neighbours, and many curious, came to weep at the sick man's bedside. And it would have been better for Nanni had he died that day, before the devil could come back to tempt him and enter his body and soul, after he recovered.

'Leave me alone,' Nanni begged the Wolf. 'For mercy's sake, leave me in peace! I have seen death staring me in the face. Poor Maricchia is in despair. Everyone knows now! It will be better for you and for me if I never see you again.'

He would willingly have torn out his own eyes to avoid seeing those of the Wolf, those eyes that had made him lose body and soul when they stared into his. He no longer knew how to free himself from her spell. He paid for masses to be said for the souls in purgatory, and asked the priest and the sergeant for help. At Easter he went to confession, and publicly crawled over the forecourt of the church and licked six hand's-breadths of cobblestones in penance. When the Wolf came to tempt him again, he said:

'Listen: don't come back to the threshing ground, because if you come after me again, as sure as God exists, I'll kill you.'

'Kill me,' replied the Wolf. 'It doesn't matter to me: I don't want to live without you.'

When he saw her in the distance coming across the field of green corn he stopped hoeing in the vineyard, and went to pull his axe out of the elm tree. The Wolf saw him coming towards her, pale and wild-eyed, with the axe gleaming in the sun, and did not retreat a single step, did not lower her eyes, but continued to walk towards him, with her hands full of red poppies, devouring him with her black eyes.

'Your soul be cursed!' choked Nanni.

Liberty

GIOVANNI VERGA

They hung a tricoloured kerchief from the bell-tower, sounded the tocsin, and began to shout in the square: 'Long live freedom!'

Like the sea in a storm. The mob foamed and surged outside the Club of Gentry, outside the Town Hall, on the church steps: a sea of white caps; the axes and sickles glinting. Then they burst down a side street.

'You first, Baron! You made your field guards flog people!' Leading them all was a hag, her aged hair bristling, her nails her only weapon.

'And you, priest of the devil! You sucked the soul out of us!'

'And you, rich glutton. You can't even run away, you've got so fat on the blood of the poor!'

'And you, copper, you've only brought people to justice when they had nothing!'

'And you, gamekeeper – you sold yourself and your neighbours for two tarì a day!'

The blood flowed and went to their heads. Sickles, hands, rags, stones – everything red with blood!

'The gentry! The Hats! Kill them! Kill them! Get the Hats!'

Don Antonio the priest was trying to steal home by back alleys. The first blow felled him face downwards on the pavement. Blood streamed from his face.

'Why are you killing me?'

'To the devil with you too!' A cripple boy picked up the greasy hat and spat into it.

'Down with the Hats! Long live freedom!'

'Take that! You as well!' they yelled at the priest who had preached fire and brimstone for anyone who stole bread. He was on his way back from saying mass, the consecrated host in his fat belly.

'Don't kill me – I'm in mortal sin!'

Lucia was his mortal sin, Lucia whom her father had sold to him at fourteen in the winter of famine that filled the wheel* and the streets with starving urchins. If that dogflesh had been of any use to them they could have had their fill of it now, but they axed it to shreds on the doorsteps and the cobblestones, just as ravenous wolves, chancing upon a herd, take no thought for their bellies but kill in sheer fury. Next was the Lady's son who had run to see what was happening. Next, the chemist frenziedly trying to close his shop. Next, don Paola returning from his vineyard. His wife, waiting with the five children for what little food he had in his pack-saddle, saw him fall in front of the street door. 'Paolo, Paolo!' The first man in the crowd drove an axe into his shoulder. Another got at him with a reaphook and ripped him open as he clung to the doorknocker with a bleeding arm.

But the worst started after the notary's son, a golden-haired boy of eleven, was knocked down in the crowd. His father had tried to pick himself up two or three times before dragging himself to die in the gutter, calling out to him: 'Neddu! Neddu!' Neddu ran away in terror, eyes and mouth wide open but unable to scream. They knocked him to the ground; he pulled himself up on one knee, just as his father had done; the torrent passed over him; someone trod on his cheek and smashed it in with a hobnailed boot; yet the boy went on begging for mercy with raised hands. He did not want to die, no, not in the way he had seen his father murdered. It was heart-rending. The wood-cutter, out of mercy, dealt him a great two-handed blow with his axe, as if felling a fifty-year-old oak, and he trembled like a leaf. Someone else yelled: 'What does it matter? He would only have become another notary.'

What did it matter! Now that their hands were red with blood, they had to spill the rest.

'Kill them all! All the Hats!'

What kept their rage boiling was not the hunger, the beatings, the oppression. It was the innocent blood. The women, with their

* A device for communication through the outside wall of a convent, often used for handing over unwanted babies to the care of the orphanage that would be attached to the convent.

87

tender bodies clad in rags, were even wilder than the men; they shook their skinny arms and shrieked in fury.

'You came to pray to the Lord in a silk dress!'

'You loathed it when you had to kneel next to the poor!'

'Take that! And that!'

Into the houses, up the staircases, into the bedrooms, tearing up the silk and fine linen. How many earrings on blood-stained faces – how many gold rings on hands struggling to ward off the axe!

The Baroness had had the street door barricaded: beams from carts and full barrels behind it: her field guards firing from the windows, determined to sell their lives dearly. The mob ducked to avoid the shots, as they had no arms to shoot back with: there had been the death penalty for keeping firearms. But 'Long live freedom!' and they tore down the gate. Then into the open courtyard and up the flights of stairs, leaping over the wounded. They didn't bother with the field guards. The field guards could wait till later. First they wanted the Baroness, and that flesh of hers, made plump with partridges and good wine. Her hair dishevelled, her babe at her breast, the Baroness was running from room to room, and there were many rooms. The roar of the mob could be heard approaching through the maze of rooms, like a river in flood. Her eldest son, a sixteen-year-old, with flesh still white like hers, tried to shore up the door with his trembling hands, screaming 'Mama! Mama!' At the first charge they brought the door down on top of him. He clutched at the legs that were trampling him. His screams ceased. His mother had fled out onto the balcony, clasping the baby tight and holding her hand over its mouth to stifle its cries, out of her mind. The other son tried to protect her with his own body by dementedly clutching at the axe-edges as if he had a hundred hands. The mob separated them in a flash. One man grabbed her by the hair, another round her hips, another by her skirts, and they lifted her over the railings. The coalman tore the baby from her arms. The other child saw none of this; all he could see was black and red as they trampled him to death, shattering every bone in his body with their iron-rimmed heels. He dug his teeth into a hand clutching his throat and would not let go. The axes could not strike into the seething mass, and were held glinting in the air.

In that raging carnival of the month of July, above the drunken shouts of the empty-bellied mob, the bell of God continued to sound the tocsin until the evening, with no midday bell or angelus, just as in a heathen country. At last the crowds started to disperse, weary with carnage, abashed, each man wanting to get away from his companions. Before dark all the doors were closed in fear, and the lamps burned all night long. The only sound in the streets in the moonlight, which bathed everything in white and showed the gates and windows of the deserted houses standing wide open, was the rummaging dogs' dry crunching of bones.

Day broke: a Sunday, but with no people in the square, no mass bell. The sacristan was in hiding; as for priests, there were none left. The first few people who gathered outside the church eyed each other suspiciously, everyone calling to mind what his neighbour must have on his conscience. Then, when they had grown into a crowd, they started to grumble: how could they do without mass on Sunday, like dogs? The Club of Gentry was closed and no one knew where to go to get the masters' orders for the week. From the bell-tower the tricoloured kerchief still dangled, limp in the yellow heat of July.

As the shadows on the church-square slowly grew shorter, the crowd huddled together in one corner. Through the gap between two cottages in the square, at the end of an alley that dropped away abruptly, the yellow fields of the plain and the dark woods on the slopes of Etna could be seen. Now they must divide up those woods and fields. Everyone was furtively working out on his fingers how much would fall to him as his share, and casting surly looks at his neighbour.

' "Freedom" means freedom for everybody!'

'That Nino Bestia and that Ramurazzo fellow will try and go on with the arrogant ways of the Hats.'

'If there's no surveyor left to measure the land, and no notary to put it down on paper, who's to stop everybody taking what they want?'

'And if you throw away your share at the tavern, has it all got to be shared out again?'

89

'If you steal, I shall too.'

'Now there's freedom, anyone tries eating a double share and he'll be fêted like the gentry!' The wood-cutter brandished his hands in the air as if still wielding his axe.

Next day word arrived that the General, the one who put the fear of God into everyone, was coming to do justice. The red shirts of his soldiers could be seen slowly winding their way up the ravine towards the little town: all that had to be done to crush them all was to roll stones down from the top. But no one made a move. The women shrieked and tore their hair. The men, dirty and unshaven, just sat on the hillside with their hands thrust between their thighs, watching the arrival of the tired young troops, bowed beneath their rusty rifles, and the tiny general on his big black horse, out in front, all alone.

The General ordered some straw to be brought into the church, and sent his boys to bed, just like a father. If they didn't get up before dawn at the sound of the trumpet he would ride into the church on horseback, cursing like a Turk – that's the sort of man he was. He immediately ordered them to shoot five or six men: Pippo, the dwarf, Pisanello – the first to arrive on the scene. The wood-cutter was crying like a child when they made him kneel down by the churchyard wall: he was thinking of what his mother had once said to him, and her scream when they tore him away from her arms. From afar, from behind closed doors in the further most alleys of the town, the shots that rang out in succession sounded like festival crackers.

The real judges arrived later, bespectacled gentlemen who had climbed the hill by mule and were worn-out by the journey. They went on moaning about the discomfort as they interrogated the accused in the refectory of the convent, sitting on the edge of the high-backed chairs, groaning every time they changed sides. It was a long trial, and it seemed endless. The guilty were marched on foot to the town, chained together in pairs, between two lines of soldiers with muskets at the ready. Their womenfolk ran after them, breathless and limping, along the country roads that wound their lengthy way between ploughed fields, prickly pears, vineyards and golden crops; they called out to them by name every time the road bent back on itself and the prisoners could be seen from in front. Once in the town, the men were locked up in a prison as big as a monastery, with iron grilles at all its windows; and if the women wanted to see them – on Mondays only, from behind an iron gate and in the presence of warders. The poor wretches grew yellower and yellower in that perpetual gloom, deprived of all sunlight. Every Monday they would speak less, reply less and complain less. If their women hung about the prison on any other day, the guards threatened them with their rifles. And then they didn't know what to do with themselves, where to find work in the town, how to get their daily bread. A bed of straw in a stable cost two soldi, and the white bread could be eaten all at once and didn't begin to fill the stomach; if they squatted down for the night on a church doorstep, the police-guards would arrest them. Gradually they went home, wives first, then mothers. One fine young woman disappeared into the city and nothing more was heard of her. All the other folk at home had gone back to doing what they used to do before. The gentry could not work their land with their own hands; the poor could not live without the gentry. They made peace. The chemist's orphaned son stole Neli Pirru's wife, which seemed to him the right thing to do in order to take revenge on his father's murderer. The woman had qualms from time to time, fearing that her husband would slash her face when he came out of prison, but the chemist's son would say: 'Don't worry – he'll never come out.' By that time few people thought about the prisoners any longer – only a few mothers and a few old men if their eyes should wander towards the plain where the city was, or on Sundays when they saw the others, beret in hand, meekly discussing business with the gentry in front of the clubhouse, and they they thought how the devil always took the hindmost.

The trial took not a day less than three years. Three years of prison without seeing the sun. The accused looked like so many disinterred corpses every time they were brought handcuffed into court. All who possibly could came along: witnesses, relatives and many simply curious, as if at a festivity, to see their fellow-villagers again after they had been packed in that capon coop so long – and what capons they had become in there! Neli Pirru came face to face with the chemist's son who had made himself a relation by treachery.

They were made to stand up one by one.

'What is your name?'

Each was heard in turn: name, surname and what he had done. The advocates, between bouts of chattering, would get down to business with their wide sleeves dangling; they would get worked up and foam at the mouth, wiping it at once with a white handkerchief and treating themselves to a pinch of snuff. The judges dozed behind those spectacles that froze the heart. Opposite sat twelve of the gentry in a row, tired, bored, yawning, scratching their beards, or gossiping with each other. They were surely telling each other how lucky they had been not to be the gentry at that little town up there when freedom had been proclaimed. And the wretched accused kept trying to read the expressions on their faces. Then they went out to talk among themselves, and the accused waited, pale-faced, with their eyes fixed on that closed door. When the jurors came back the foreman, the one who always talked with his hands clasped over his paunch, was almost as pale as the accused as he said: 'Upon my honour and my conscience . . .'

The coalman stammered when they put the handcuffs back on him: 'Where are you taking me? To prison? Why? I didn't even get a hand's-breadth of land . . . And they said freedom had come!'

The Sulphur Mine

VIRGILIO TITONE

This is the story of an incident that happened some time ago. It was much talked about at the time, and mentioned in all the newspapers. There was a court case afterwards, or rather two, resulting in two convictions – in the absence of the accused. Then nothing was heard about the whole affair any more.

The young man concerned, named Toto, Toto Russo, in his thirties, lived with his mother on the proceeds of a *senia* which he worked and owned, and which his father had owned and worked before him. The family were respectable middle-class. *Senia* is an Arabic word meaning a smallholding for cultivation of citrus fruit and market garden produce. Russo's was the best cultivated senia in Partanna, and everyone in the district who needed orange or lemon graftings went to him. He was also the only reliable nurseryman for rooted American-type vine cuttings. The sale of these rooted cuttings is a matter of trust, because the peasant is unable to distinguish between good and diseased ones: only the result will tell him.

Russo enjoyed the peasants' confidence. He was in fact entitled to regard himself as belonging to a race apart. A Sicilian people doesn't really exist: the different races which for centuries superimposed themselves upon one another not only failed to fuse, but did not even succeed in getting closer to one another, and never overcame their mutual distrust. It thus happens that next to true negroid types can be found people who recall the old Normans, without of course necessarily being their direct descendants: tall, fair-haired and blue-eyed, differing in character from the more usual types by their strange honesty and sincerity. Russo belonged to this rather rare strain.

On the day in question, 9 August 1913, he had gone to irrigate his senia. Normally it was sufficient to irrigate twice a week, but

93

during the preceding winter he had planted some hundred orange trees in place of an old olive grove which was no longer economical: these young trees had to be watered every second day in order to obtain quicker growth. Together with the adjacent vineyard and the oranges which his father had planted, they would permit him, a few years hence, to build a nursery and storehouse for his rooted cuttings in the curtilage of his home.

He was thinking of all this in the morning as he rode his mule across country to the senia; more precisely, he was thinking of the estimate which the builder Casola had given him the previous day – three thousand lire. He himself could have done it for two thousand five hundred, or perhaps even less. He had a good idea: the municipal council had just begun to demolish the Politi House in order to build a school in its place, and he might buy the large doors that belonged to it. However, as so often happens, events were to take a different course.

When he came to his gate, he could see nothing amiss, nor could he see anything wrong from the stable where he left his mule, or from the enclosure where the harvested fruit was kept. With a hoe in his hand he began to follow the water course, and one after another opened the sluice gates leading to the small water channels dug between the rows of trees. Immediately beside the wall were three rows of medlar trees which prevented him from seeing the rest of the senia. These trees were all right. Beyond, nothing was left: all the trees, old and new, had been cut down. His own work of many years, as well as the work of his father, had been destroyed.

He walked up to the far end of his holding where the land sloped down to a ditch. Even the almond trees that were growing there had been sawn down, with the exception of the two biggest ones; felling these trees would have been a lengthy job and therefore they had been left. Balsamo had done this. There could be no possible doubt. For years Balsamo had insisted that he should be sold the part of the senia that protruded like a wedge into his own vineyard. He had always been refused. That piece of ground, he had been told, was Russo's; it had come to him from his father, and had always been in his family. Not for a moment did he think of selling it, nor indeed did he have any need to do so. On the contrary, he regarded it as his duty to obey the rule that he had been taught, the rule which stated that he must leave behind to his future sons more than he had inherited from his own father.

This had caused his misfortune. Balsamo, a gaol-bird keen to play the mafioso but rejected by the true mafia, was not prepared to accept a refusal, and persisted in his request. Messages had been sent through friends, and several incidents had occurred during the last two years. The theft of a goat, for instance, had been maliciously attributed to Russo, and a mule had broken loose after its halter rope had been cut and had done some damage to the vineyard. There had been other things too which could have caused trouble, but which had been ignored with great patience. His patience, however, had served him no good purpose. Balsamo now had his revenge. One night had been sufficient – the previous night.

He sat down on the stone seat outside his house and lit a cigarette. The lizard came, as it did every day, wanting him to spill a little water over the stone. He rose to fetch a glass. The lizard, which had become a friend, drank, raised its head, gave him a long look, and drank again. He pondered what was to be done. He had to kill Balsamo. This was such a natural and a necessary thing that he didn't give it any thought at all. If he failed to do it, everyone in the town would despise him. It was something else that occupied his thoughts. Why should Balsamo have provoked him like this? He couldn't possibly fail to realise what the response would have to be. Balsamo had no real friends, and all the town would be on his side, including don Carlino, head of the mafia, who was a just and honest man. He would have to go to him and ask for his approval, but he felt quite sure that it would be given. What could possibly have made Balsamo believe that he was *not* going to behave like a man? Everyone knew that he was his father's son.

The lizard was still there . . . He jumped to his feet. He remembered that Balsamo had a brother in America, and was due to join him there. No doubt he had brought his sailing date forward. He might even have left already, to embark in Palermo. No other explanation was possible, unless Balsamo had decided to forestall him altogether by having him shot down before he could make a move.

The countryside around him lay in complete silence. The harvest fair had begun and the peasants had all returned to their homes. The air was as stagnant as a dead cloud, but suddenly it seemed to him that something was moving. He listened intently; no, it must have been a dog or a rabbit. He closed the door, aware that he was closing it for the last time. He took the gun which he normally left in the house, and led the mule by the collar-rope towards home. He did not take the usual road, but followed a narrow lane that led to the Bresciana road, and afterwards took a path. He made up his mind not to mention anything to anyone. Should someone talk to him about what had happened, he would have him believe that he had decided to cut the trees down himself, intending to graft them with tarocco oranges in order to obtain more fruit eventually. No one was to suspect the truth. Balsamo had been to prison several times, but had always been released on account of insufficient evidence. If Balsamo had not yet gone away, the sergeant of the carabinieri would not waste his time with a long search for Balsamo's possible killer. In cases like this it was, of course, not practicable actually to thank the unknown man who had done the killing, but he would be left in peace, and after a while the whole thing would be forgotten.

He saw him next day in San Vito street, and he thought he could detect a mocking smile when the other man looked at him. He turned round to look at him again. Balsamo was now talking to Cosimo, and broke off in his conversation to look at him in turn once more in the same manner. He went quickly home – it was only a few steps away – and took the pistol which had belonged to his father. He had not carried it with him because he hadn't thought matters would come to a head so quickly. He told his mother that he had to go away. The poor old woman knew about his oranges, and understood what 'going away' meant. Men murder, and call down curses upon one another: women must stay at home, and cry quietly. She wanted at least to prepare a few things for him, but he gave her no time to do so, and hastily said good-bye without taking anything. She was always to remember him later, with tears running from her eyes. She looked at the two shirts she had washed a day or two before, which were of no use to him any more. No one went near Balsamo as, riddled with bullets, he lay at practically the same spot where he had been talking to Cosimo. They let him die where he was. The carabinieri were working out of town, and did not return until late that night.

Two days later he was at Casteltermini, a distant town where he was quite unknown, where he hoped to find work in the sulphur mines. He also knew that a woman whom he had known ten years previously was living there. Her name was Filomena; she had gone from town to town as a prostitute. In Michele Sciuto's hostelry there was a room above the straw store which was sometimes let out to a carter or a travelling girl. On the night he had gone to meet her there, a storm had broken. Filomena was frightened of thunder, and he had stayed the whole night with her. Strangely, both of them afterwards had the feeling that they had spent all their lives together. He often thought of her sad eyes and her slender body, and would ask the carriers from neighbouring towns whether they knew anything of her whereabouts. They all knew her, but had lost touch with her. However, only a few months previously a carter from Ribera had said that he had seen her in Casteltermini, and that she had told him she had settled there.

The first thing he did was to find a church to thank Saint Joseph for helping him to murder Balsamo. He was devoted to Saint Joseph, just as his mother and his father had been, and now he prayed especially fervently to the Saint. Only the principal church was open; it was cool and ancient. In the chapel of the patriarch, the first on the right from the main altar, he lit two candles; one for himself and one for his mother.

Next he went to look for a tavern, and found one in a narrow street beyond the square. In a large room with smoky walls a man in his forties, rather fat and red in the face, sat behind an old counter. There were a few tables for the customers; they were obviously all sulphur workers, except for two men talking to one another who looked like itinerant merchants carrying their shop on their shoulders – two bundles wrapped up in a sack lying under their table. He was quite prepared to encounter people here who were very different from those in his own town: in Sicily the towns of the sulphur miners are a world of their own, and their habits and ways of life are quite different from those of agricultural folk. The peasants, for instance, never go to an inn; they drink wine, if they have it, only in their own homes, and always after meals. The peasants used to be given a *quartuccio* – approximately three-quarters of a litre – as part of their hire for a day's work, and this they used to drink in the fields; but it is no longer the practice. The sulphur miners, who had better pay than the peasants, were habitual clients of the inn and spent most of their earnings there.

He sat down at the pedlars' table. One of them was elderly, of strong build, but lean and with a moustache which gave him an air of authority. The other, much younger, who addressed his partner as don Carlo, helped him to visit customers and look out for new ones. Depending on the possibilities, the season and other circumstances, they would remain for one, two or even three days in each place, splitting up its districts between them. One could do more business in a small place – the old pedlar explained to him later – where there were no shops, not even a haberdasher's, than in a large place where everyone had a shop and the poorest peasant had pretensions to dress like the gentry.

'When did he say he was going to let us have that head of cheese?' (The agreed price for a shirt that had been sold to a shepherd the month before).

'At fair time. He says he wants linen for a pair of trousers too. If we agree, he would like to pay later for everything together. That's what he said. What do you say?'

'I say it's best not to have any dealings at all with people of that sort. These shepherds are people who are up to all sorts of tricks. I have no linen for him, but I'll try to get that cheese out of him all the same.' He turned towards Russo and said: 'These are sad times. You can't trust anyone now. Once upon a time you could, as they say, take an ox by its horns and a man by his word. But those were different times.'

'Everyone has his worries,' replied Toto. 'And there are

people about who don't want to be straight.'

'You're quite right; the trouble is, if you're in business you have to deal with so many different people. It isn't like the life of the countryman who looks after his own land – life is easy for him, as long as the crops grow.'

'Enough about that. You can at least travel where you like – but the countryman has to stay put. And when people trample on him and force him to see to his rights, he must get up and go and leave everything behind, he has no bread and no employer, he's like a stray dog . . .'

'I quite understand,' the other interrupted. 'Everyone knows the weak spots in his own pot.'

He understood that Russo was in grave difficulty. Toto would not usually talk of his own affairs, and certainly not to an unknown man, but the old pedlar inspired confidence in him. The place, too, where no one knew him, gave him the feeling that he had left behind some of the tormenting thoughts that had been robbing him of his peace. He felt the need to talk, and he had found the man he could talk to.

The inn-keeper had meanwhile brought three plates of lasagne, home-made and flavoured with oil and garlic.

'The wine is on me,' said don Carlo. Russo thanked him. The younger of the two men, who had gone to look at the kitchen, came back. The old fellow interrupted the conversation and began to ask questions about customers, as if there were an accord between the two older men. In fact, as soon as they had finished their food, don Carlo poured the young man a glass of wine and told him to hurry up and visit a late customer who by now would have returned from the country. When he had gone, his partner began to talk of the good money to be earned in the sulphur mines. Talk among true men in Sicily is full of allusions and veiled phrases, leaving a need to puzzle out and interpret the meaning they are intended to convey. This is particularly so when friendly advice is offered. Advising means assuming responsibility, and respect for oneself as well as for one's friend necessitates the use of such oblique language.

'The mine at Cozzoddisi isn't a bad one,' the old man concluded. 'It's run by serious people who look after their own affairs and don't want to get mixed up in other people's. No policeman has ever been seen there, and it isn't likely one ever will be.'

Toto understood. They continued to talk, about the price of bread which had risen that very week, about the inn and the inn-keeper whom don Carlo had known for some time as a reliable and respectable fellow, about shepherds – the worst payers in the world. They didn't talk of the mine any more. They drank until the bottle was empty, and as Toto didn't want to be under an obligation he offered to order another, but don Carlo refused: he had already drunk more than enough and was now going to bed, because he had to be off early next day. Saying good-bye, they both felt they had become friends even if they didn't know whether they would ever see one another again.

Russo had already decided on his next step, but later he was often to think of the old hawker, and he would look him out at that inn every so often. About a year later an occasion arose to prove that he had not forgotten him: a young mafioso who showed no intention of paying was forced to do so, and to offer his apologies as well. Don Carlo had not requested the intervention, and Russo never mentioned that it was his doing. He just said that the mafioso might never really have intended *not* to pay. The two understood one another.

An old beggar sitting on the steps of a church directed him to the house he was looking for. He had given him a few soldi – rather more than those the beggar called his benefactors normally gave him. Begging is a business like any other. Old beggars have seen many people come and go, and know about things that are discussed, as well as things that must *not* be discussed. The beggar told him that Filomena was a good soul: someone else might recommend a rather younger woman, but to a respectable man a sensible woman means something more, and gives more satisfaction than a four-soldo *tapinella*.

While Russo listened to him, he began to wonder whether it could possibly be true: he noticed that the beggar spoke with a Partanna accent, which was rather different from that of Casteltermini, and the more he looked at him the more he believed that the beggar was Lucio Gangitano, a man he had known when he was a boy; he seemed scarcely changed in appearance. If he was not, then it was a case of extraordinary likeness. It seemed almost incredible. Saint Joseph and his mother's prayers must be continuing to help, just as they had helped him up to that moment. But he still had to be very careful, even though the old man would not readily recognise the erstwhile boy. His own manner of speech would not give him away – he was always told that he did not have the singing Partanna accent. He bade the beggar good-bye and went. If it was not Gangitano but someone else from Partanna, it was all the more important to be on the look-out.

The house was at the far end of the town, where the street became a narrow lane. After the intense heat of the day, it was the hour when one could breathe again. Men and women sat out in front of their tiny one- or two-roomed houses and exchanged a few words every now and again. Most of the time they looked straight in front of them, and it was obvious that they had nothing to say or ask. People can sit for hours like this, without moving and without speaking: in Sicily people speak little, on the whole, and this contributes to general respectability. Some of the women were taking advantage of the moonlight and plaiting ampelodesma cores for ropes and saddle-bags to be sold at the fair. From the street the passer-by could see right into the houses, each with a table, sometimes a large bed and a few straw mattresses on the floor where children of all ages played or slept completely nude – it was the habit of the children of simple folk never to wear anything under their trousers.

At Filomena's house he found a boy. He was in bed, as naked as all the others. He might have been fourteen, and was not asleep. When he asked for Filomena from the doorstep, the boy got up, saying that his mother had gone to a neighbour and would return soon, lit a paraffin lamp, asked the newcomer to sit down and himself sat down on the other side of the table. He remained naked, making no attempt to clothe himself.

Soon Filomena returned. She had no difficulty in recognising him, though she herself had changed greatly, having lost her girlish looks. She had once been like an unbroken colt, yet with such gentle eyes that her business could never have been guessed – a business that she executed with the same simplicity as she would have done any other. In Sicily it used to be so difficult to earn one's living that the way in which it was earned did not matter too much. A thief or a whore who had saved a little money would think himself or herself quite as good as anyone else.

The woman's eyes were unchanged, though she was noticeably tired. She made him feel very welcome, and when he mentioned Sciuto's she too thought of that night of long ago and tears came to her eyes. She told him that the boy was her son. She insisted that he took some refreshment, but did not ask what had brought him to Casteltermini. She knew that he would not have left home without compelling reason, that under such circumstances questions are not asked, and that women are not supposed to know certain things anyway. He told her, in a manner that left no room for doubt, that he had to talk to her. She suggested that they should go to the other room, where there was a large bed as well as another table, and asked her son to bring the flask and three glasses.

'Vanni,' she explained, 'can stay.'

'His name is Vanni?'

'Yes, that's Vanni and he's a man. You can speak freely.'

Russo made it clear that the air at Partanna was no longer healthy for him, and that he had been advised to look for work in the mines. The woman approved of this idea, and there was indeed little else that could be done at Casteltermini: almost everyone lived from the Cozzoddisi mine. There was work enough there, and the only difficulty was that things had to be arranged with a *partitante.**

'I know about this sort of thing because don Lucio told me – now he begs in front of St Peter's, but he was a miner before.'

'I know him.'

'How do you know him?'

* A sub-contractor who employs a number of miners and sees that each is paid according to his output; he supervises the extraction in the oven and is paid by the mine according to the amount of sulphur produced.

'I gave him something on my way here.'

'Do you know he comes from Partanna?'

'Does he? How do you know?'

'He's helped me several times – once they tried to deport me back home. People said I ought to talk to him because he knows everyone and has a lot of friends. This I did, and no one troubled me any more. He lives alone now – his wife is dead and they had no children – so I invite him to a meal every now and again, and that's how he's come to tell me about his life.'

'Mamma,' said the boy, 'I think you ought to talk to don Lucio.'

'Yes, don Lucio might know of a partitante.'

Russo had already made up his mind to go and see don Lucio the next day, and explained that he was going to talk to him himself.

Matters having been thus arranged, he asked Filomena how she liked living at Casteltermini and why she no longer travelled about. She had done it for her boy, she explained, who had been living at Alimena with her sister, who had died four years ago.

'And then,' she added, 'can't you see how I've aged? How could I go on doing what I did before?'

She was now leading a quiet life, she explained. She went in the mornings to do housework for an old notary who lived alone; a few clients had retained their affection for her and came to her home.

'And thank God, I have this house which I bought three years ago, and when my son's working he gives me all he earns – don't you, Vanni?'

'Yes,' said the boy, 'but I haven't had any work for two weeks.'

'Do you want to stay the night?'

'Yes,' he replied, looking into her eyes.

The bottle was almost empty. Filomena had poured only a thimbleful into her own glass, but he and the boy had gone on drinking the strong, almost black local wine that warmed the blood. In the distance a dog barked at someone going home. The last doors could be heard closing and then the street lay empty in the moonlight. The pungent smell of sulphur, penetrating and persistent, made the night air seem even warmer. The scene had a certain familiarity; the little lamp just lit the table, leaving the rest of the room in darkness. He had the feeling of having come home.

'If you wish, I could be your caruso,' said the boy. 'I've been a caruso before, but I quarrelled with my miner.'

'With God's help, this will be your chance to get back to the mine,' said his mother approvingly. 'Don Toto will settle things with your miner.'

'First of all I must talk to don Lucio,' said Toto. 'But if you want to come and work with me, that will be best for both of us.'

Filomena had extinguished the lamp, and only the little oil wick below the picture of the Virgin of Itria now remained aglow. The boy said goodnight, crossed himself and went to bed in the other room.

More than a year had passed since he had begun his new work, and now he was earning as much as if he had always worked in the job. After all, no special ability was necessary, and his arms were well used to the hard work. The money was good: in the whole of Sicily, no worker earned more than a good miner. Vanni had to carry the excavated mineral in a basket on his shoulders, and went nearly thiry times a day from the shaft up the stairway to the kiln where the rock was melted and the sulphur extracted. His wages were paid by Toto, as was the practice with every miner and his caruso. The carusi were boys, sometimes only eight or ten years old, who did all the carrying; the mechanical means of transport that were later introduced did not exist in Cozzoddisi at that time. Toto himself was paid by the partitante, at so much per container consigned to the melting oven. The partitante, in turn, depended for his money on the administration of the mine.

The work in the mine was no harder really than work in the fields. It was much harder for the poor carusi who had to carry almost eighty pounds at a time over stairways of hundreds of steps. As far as living underground was concerned, he got used to that after a few days and even found that the heat was more bearable than the sirocco at home. Reluctant at first, he too became accustomed to being without clothes; everyone worked naked on account of the heat and the sweat that ran down the body. He worked for well over ten hours a day, with a few short rest periods. He ate twice a day and took his meals together with Vanni. The bread and whatever was eaten with it – olives or an onion, sometimes a large sardine or a piece of cheese – was brought by a caruso who went twice a week to the town to do the shopping.

Vanni was pleased with his new boss. In those days the carusi were practically sold to the miners. The miner had to advance a certain sum to the caruso's family as a frozen loan, and no boy could leave him unless that sum of money had been repaid first, a condition that families were often unable or unwilling to fulfil. If a caruso did not make the necessary number of daily journeys, or (with the miner on daily pay instead of piece work) the caruso's load was rejected because the partitante considered it too small, the miner would get his belt out and hit his caruso, naked as he was, as hard as he could. The poor boys knew that the beatings saved them from a far graver punishment – having their money reduced. If their money was reduced they would be punished even more severely on their return home. Before Toto arrived, Vanni had been with a very harsh boss, and he had run away. A caruso who ran away couldn't possibly work for another miner unless the frozen loan was repaid; this would have constituted so grave an offence that no one dared to cause it. It was one of those transgressions for which vengeance in blood was considered to be the duty of every man of honour. Filomena did not have the money for the repayment and her boy would therefore have been unable to work had Toto not given Vanni's ex-boss to understand that he must wait: he gave a pledge that everything would be refunded in full, but requested the other man to give Filomena time to pay.

From that moment onwards people could see that he was not a man to be trifled with, and they began to treat him with respect. Don Lucio had perhaps contributed to this by saying that Toto wasn't the sort of man whose nose you could put a fly on. The notion had also got about that he was a mafioso of the true mafia, the mafia of the big country areas and the towns, people who could do virtually anything they liked. There was another mafia

105

too, in the sulphur mine, but as it consisted of people of little account, miners, partitanti and even carusi, it did not enjoy the same influence. Added to this was the element of mystery which surrounded Toto: no one knew much about him, and what sort of man he really was. Crude jokes, filthy swear-words and the display of aggressive temperament were everyday things among the sulphur miners. Toto was not like the others: he neither joked nor cursed. He talked only when it was necessary, and he never denied a favour to anyone if it was within his capability. For this reason he was approached increasingly frequently when there were quarrels and disagreements which could be peacefully adjusted. Of course, there were also troubles when nothing could be done but to avenge the offence, and Toto was then the first to approve of such action. However, as long as this could be avoided, he nearly always succeeded in making himself heard, and would find the proper words which led the quarrellers back to reason. He thus became the recognised head of the small gangs as well as of the *partiti,* although he was not really connected with either, and deliberately remained completely independent.

In the absence of any legal authority in the mines, groups of mafia adherents known as *cosche* took the place of the law in looking after their common interests, and in the determination of their duties. Among these duties was helping sick or injured comrades. The *partiti,* gangs which formed among the carusi, consisted of from two to ten or sometimes more boys, who often remained linked to one another even when they were grown up and had families. The bond which united them was one of friendship and of homosexual practices, which were common to all, and totally approved of by custom. Though in many instances they continued with their homosexuality long after they were married, those who belonged to a gang had other ties as well: they regarded each other as firm friends who had to help and defend one another. For this reason the gangs formed minor *cosche,* and a particularly important part of their activities was devoted to mutual assistance.

Vanni belonged to a gang of seven boys who were of his own age or a little older. At the end of their day's work they slept together in one of the large rooms at the entrance to the mine which were used as dormitories, and where fifty miners and boys would rest on straw after their strenuous labour. Only on Saturdays did they return to their homes.

Most miners had sexual relations with their carusi, but not Toto. He was fond of Vanni, who had become attached to him, but he treated him rather as he would have treated a son. This did not mean that he spared him beltings if the boy was negligent, or if he lost too much time between his journeys by cuddling with a friend in an out-of-the-way corner of the shaft. After all, one had to earn one's bread – about that fact he understood no jokes.

One day he caught the boy at sex twice in the space of a few hours. The first time he said nothing. The second time, when he was kept waiting even longer and the heap of mineral had accumulated, he hit him harder than usual.

'You'll never become a miner like that. Can't you see how thin you're getting? You'll make me lose my day's earnings!'

He continued to hit him, but without losing his temper or swearing as the others did. The boy neither protested nor cried. When Toto had finished he tried to make the boy understand in a friendly way that he was doing himself harm, and gave him some advice.

'I don't say that you ought to play the saint. We've all been boys, and I was one too, but look, Vanni, you'll lose your health and I'll lose my caruso. Every now and again, of course, I can understand, but if you carry on like this you'll get consumption. We can't afford medicines – we have to work for our living, and you can't work and carry on like that at the same time! You and I are like two wheels on the same cart. Can a cart go forward if one wheel moves and the other doesn't? That's what we're like – just like a cart. I can't go on working if the sulphur stays piled up. And if I don't work, how can I pay you? You know very well that you get more than the others!'

'You're right,' said the boy defensively. 'I know you meant it to be for my own good. But it wasn't my fault, it was Masi's. He wanted me this morning, and as he belongs to my gang I can't say no to him. And if he does it for me, I must do it for him.'

'I shall talk to Masi myself,' replied Russo.

'No, please don't. No one must interfere in our affairs. He

would think I'd made you talk to him, like a baby.'

Meanwhile the time for their first meal of the day had come. The second meal they were going to have at home; they were to go back that night to spend Sunday in the town. When they stopped work, they sat down on a sack and the boy began to ask questions. For him, knowing only the mine, Toto came from a different world, a world full of strange and wonderful things. His punishment seemed quickly forgotten. He asked Toto whether he had ever seen the sea.

'Often,' replied Toto, whose answers were always short. He weighed his words and used them sparingly, as people do who negotiate important matters. However, by and by the ingenuity of the boy induced him to talk of his previous life which now seemed so far away that he almost had to force himself to remember it.

'What's it like?'

'Vast. As large as the sky, and blue.'

'And does it always have water?' asked the boy, who had the rivers of his own district in mind, which dried up after the winter's rains.

'Always.'

'It must be very beautiful.' Vanni became lost in thought, imagining the world so different from his own. 'Is there a road to the sea?'

'There are many, because the sea is not in one place alone. Often there are towns quite close to the sea.'

'What did you have to do to get to the sea?'

'There's a road from Partanna, and from the town you can see the sea.'

'And the fishes?'

'No, you can't see the fishes. Not even when you're very close. They're shy and stay deep down. But you can see the ships.'

'What are the ships like?'

'They're very large and sail from port to port. They go to America too, and America is very far away.'

While the boy was thinking of the sea and they were eating their bread and onion, Nardo walked past. Nardo was an old caruso – there were also old ones about – who had come from the Trabonella mine, where he had seen a ghost, an experience that had left him possessed. There were ghosts in many mines but none at Cozzoddisi. The boy began to ask questions about ghosts.

'Masi has seen ghosts. There's one behind the Church of San Vito. Why are there never any ghosts in some places, and always some in others?'

'After you die, your soul can go to paradise, and then it becomes like a butterfly and flies. Or else it can go to hell or to purgatory – that reminds me, I must have a mass said for the good souls of my father and brother, because I had a brother who died as a child. On the other hand, if you kill someone, his ghost stays on earth and roams about at night.'

'Have you seen any ghosts?'

'Yes, I've seen two at home.'

'What are they like?'

'You can't see their faces. You can only see a shadow.'

The boy tried hard to imagine how a ghost could be a shadow, but he couldn't.

'Can ghosts speak?'

'Of course. They speak and give warnings, so that you can avoid enemies and misfortunes. There are good ghosts and bad ones,' he explained, making the sign of the cross.

'Why did you cross yourself?'

'When you talk about ghosts you should always cross yourself, and better still, say an Ave Maria as well. Otherwise they can do you harm. If a man is pursued by a ghost he can come to a bad end. There was a farm agent at home once who hanged himself.'

'But why do ghosts go against men?'

'For many reasons. Sometimes they're in the right, because they've had no burial or were murdered without good cause. If you kill a man, you must always have right on your side. You must remember that!'

The boy who was on the threshold of the serious part of life, and the man who had seen so much, both lived in the same world, where daily bread had to be earned in sweat, where neighbours had to be guarded against as against so many wolves. However, they were both also familiar with another world, which seemed neither less real, nor less friendly, nor less hostile: the world of mystery, of ghosts, of the devil and the saints, of heroes and generous bandits, and the magnificent paladins of France.

When work had ended, they put their clothes on and began to climb the stairway which led to the surface. Six days on end they had been below ground; now they saw the ground again, bathed in red as the sun was sinking towards the horizon. A long line of miners, every man holding his lantern, was walking along the track which ran across arid ground, and extended on to the first stretch of road which was paved with burnt rubble from the kiln. Here and there pairs of boys could be seen in the dry bed of the stream or behind bushes. It was the same every Saturday; no one took any notice.

They found Filomena in high spirits. She had won a double at lotto. She never failed to play, but had never won a soldo before. This time she had won. She had had a fancy to try a *terno* (guessing three numbers out of five) but had not wanted to play on the 90 (which signifies great fear) and so bet only on the 14 and the 29. The pleasure of her win of fifty lire made her chatter on and on; she had even bought presents for everyone which she had put on the bed to show off. A red handkerchief for Toto, a pair of light-coloured trousers for Vanni, and a turquoise apron for herself. She thought that she had to offer excuses for her apron: she felt she needed it, because with all its patches the one she was wearing was really indecent. Toto accepted his handkerchief, protesting that he didn't want her to waste money on him. Vanni immediately tried his trousers on, and they fitted him very well. Then they went to the small courtyard behind the house, where there was a well under a lemon tree, and undressed. Filomena drew water and threw bucketfuls at her menfolk. Even a piece of soap had been bought. When she rubbed the soap on her son's shoulders, she noticed the bruising caused by the blows with the belt.

'You've hit him good and hard, the poor boy. What did he do to you?'

'Ask him yourself,' replied Toto.

When she was told what had happened, she began to laugh:

'Masi is a good caruso. They've known one another from the

time Vanni first went to the mine, when he was nine years old, and they began it then. If you knew how often I've found them on the bed, one on top of the other! Anyway, it's better he does it with someone two years older and sensible than with the others. They all do it, don't they, Vanni?'

'Of course. What else can you do? But don Toto was right because I did it twice, one after the other.'

Filomena began to laugh again. She really felt jolly that day, and all three of them were truly happy.

'You rascal, you did it twice?' With affection she gave him a resounding smack on the ear, and Vanni began to laugh. 'Well, you were right to let him have it. When he deserves it you mustn't spare him.'

'I won't – you can be sure. I like him, that's why I won't spare him – and he knows it.'

'Don't I know it! When you fetch your belt to me you make my arse burn!'

'My poor boy,' said his mother, caressing his wet hair. 'But I really think it's best if he does it with Masi. After all, he's a man now and he can't let it run out of his shirtsleeves! If he got in the habit of going with some slut, it would be terrible. He wouldn't give me any more money, and he might pick up a disease.'

Meanwhile they had begun to dry themselves, and Vanni put on the new trousers and a white shirt – which suited him, because he was as dark-haired as his mother. He was altogether very much like her – even his hair was as fine and shiny as hers.

Afterwards they sat down to table. Toto had been given half a lamb by a partitante whom he had helped the previous week by getting a long-standing account for two iron girders settled. Filomena had seen to the wine. They all drank more than usual, and even Filomena filled her glass to the brim.

Their happiness was short-lived. Toto had a feeling that it could not last, and every now and again they sensed that he did not follow their conversation. He was thinking of his mother, and it didn't seem right to him that he should be so carefree while heaven alone knew how much she cried for his sake. This thought often occurred in moments of contentment and gave him the foreboding that his happiness could not last. Sometimes he thought that it would have been right to marry this poor woman. She had been a whore until he arrived, but what did it matter? After all, she was simply one of the unfortunates, just as he was. Another thought arose whenever, for a moment, he enjoyed the dream of a quiet life: that of his own fate, which had destined him for misfortune. He would reproach himself for forgetting about it, and sit in silence for a long time. At such moments, mother and son looked at him and became silent too.

When the meal was finished, both men went out. Toto went to the inn to see whether don Carlo had arrived. Vanni went to the puppet theatre where he knew he would meet Masi and the other carusi from his gang, all admirers of Orlando. He never missed the show, neither the Saturday nor the Sunday one, partly because there was another gang who were on the side of Rinaldo.*
When he arrived, the large public storehouse, which was used in the autumn for preserving olives, was already full of boys and adults who had come to see their heroes. On a stage made of beams and planks don Bastiano was ready with his puppets. He had to be careful not to let Orlando appear inferior to Rinaldi, and vice versa, and the number of Moors which either of them managed to kill had to be equal. Similarly, if things went badly, both of them had to have their revenge. Otherwise the spectators might have smashed everything – they were quite capable of wreaking vengeance on the puppets and tearing them to pieces, and those puppets were don Bastiano's whole capital.

Toto was back before Vanni. Don Carlo had not been seen at the inn since Toto had last met him there. On his return he found don Lucio who was looking for him to tell him that two men from Partanna had arrived that morning. One was Balsamo's son, who had just come out of the army – who the other was he didn't know, possibly a relative. He warned Toto not to let himself be taken unawares, and mentioned the possibility of an

* The fame of Orlando and Rinaldi, two of Charlemagne's paladins who figure in many heroic epics, lives on in Sicilian puppet shows. The marionettes are three feet tall or more, and appear to the audience to be life-size figures seen from a distance.

encounter on the lines of the usual countrymen's duels: what did he think of that? Toto replied that he was quite ready to meet the pair from Partanna. But events took a different course.

Next morning he had hardly opened the front door when Balsamo's son – afterwards he learned that his name was Nicola – fired three pistol shots at him from behind a low wall. He didn't hit him – possibly the pistol had jammed. He tried to run away across the fields, but Toto went after him, caught up with him after a short distance and left him lying dead at the foot of a fig tree. He had ripped his throat open with a knife.

Thus his destiny was fulfilled. He would have made the most peace-loving man in the world; instead he had had to slay first father and then son. He looked for a while at the dead youth: a good-looking boy, who had done his duty as a son because a son must kill the man who has murdered his father. He closed the boy's eyes and crossed his arms, a sign by which the murderer shows that he wishes to pay honour to his victim. Then he went back to the house for a short while – and was not seen again.

All this had happened within a few minutes. Vanni was not seen again either – the boy was determined to follow him. After a few months don Lucio received a letter, with another enclosed for Filomena. Toto and Vanni had written from Tunis – no one had known where they were – and there they were working and earning good money. The letter contained two hundred-lire notes, one for don Lucio and the other for Filomena.

A year or so later the poor woman became ill and when she realised she was going to die, she sent for don Lucio and asked him to write to Vanni to make him come back: she did not want to die without seeing him again. Every day she had taken the light-coloured trousers which he had left behind out of the cupboard, together with an old waistcoat of Toto's, kissed them fervently and wept. For a few days she felt a little better and don Lucio, who came every morning to see to her needs, thought that she might be recovering. Then came a relapse. Vanni arrived in time, and was with her when she died; then he left again, for good.

Years went by. The empty little house fell into ruins; the lemon tree by the well, no longer watered, dried up and died too.

In the mine things went from bad to worse, and it was closed down not long afterwards, because sulphur came to be sold at prices much lower than it cost to produce it by mining. Nothing is left now of the life of that time and its strange customs, and hardly a memory remains of the sorrows and the brief joys of those men. But this, after all, will also happen to ourselves and the affairs of our own lives.

Ciàula Discovers the Moon

LUIGI PIRANDELLO

That evening the pickmen wanted to stop work without having extracted enough sulphur to fill the melting oven the following day. The overseer Cacciagallina*, revolver in hand, raged at them by the pithead of the Cace in an attempt to prevent them from getting out.

'By the body of . . . By the blood of . . . Back, the lot of you! Back down the mine the lot of you, get down there and sweat blood till morning or I'll shoot you!'

'Bang!' called someone from deep in the pit. 'Bang!' echoed several others. And with laughter and curses and shouts of derision they began to rush him; all of them elbowed or shouldered their way past except one. Who? Uncle Scarda of course, that poor one-eyed fellow over whom Cacciagallina could play Gradasso† to his heart's content. Jesus, what a terror! He hurled himself at Uncle Scarda as fiercely as a lion, seized him round the chest and, as if he were holding all the others too, shook him violently and yelled in his face: 'Get back the lot of you, I'm telling you, you rabble! Down the mine, the lot of you, or I'll slaughter you!'

Uncle Scarda peaceably let himself be shaken. The overseer, poor man, had to vent his feelings somehow, and it was only natural if he vented them on an old man like himself who was incapable of resistance. And after all, even Uncle Scarda had someone below him, someone weaker than himself, someone he in turn could take it out on later – his caruso Ciàula.

As for the others – there they were, already well down the road

* Literally 'Chase-chicken'.

† A character from Ariosto's *Orlando Furioso*, well-known for his pride and bossiness.

to Comitini, laughing and yelling: 'That's right, hold on to that one, Cacciagallì! He'll fill up the boiler for you tomorrow!'

'These youngsters,' sighed Uncle Scarda to Cacciagallina with a forlorn smile of indulgence.

Still held round the chest, he cocked his head to one side, twisted his lower lip to the other, and remained in this posture for some time, as if in expectation.

Was it a grimace at Cacciagallina, or was he mocking his companions' youth?

Truly this merriment of theirs, this indulgence of youthful high spirits, was completely out of place in that setting. Their hard faces drained of life by the rigours and darkness of those underground quarries, their bodies worn out by daily toil, their rent clothes had the same leaden squalor as that grassless land riddled with sulphur mines like so many huge ant-heaps.

No, Uncle Scarda, frozen in that strange pose, was neither mocking them nor grimacing at Cacciagallina. It was the face he always pulled when, with an effort, he slowly coaxed into his mouth the big tear that every so often ran out of his good eye.

He had taken a liking to the salty taste, and he never let a single tear escape.

Only a little, a drop every now and again; but pitched down there two hundred metres and more below ground from morning till night, wielding a pickaxe that drew a kind of growl of rage from his chest at every blow. Uncle Scarda always had a mouth burnt dry, and that tear did the same for his mouth as a pinch of rappee would have done for his nose.

A treat and a break.

Whenever he felt his eye full, he would put down his pick for a moment and, gazing at the smoky little red flame of the lantern nailed to the rock which, in the darkness of the infernal cave, lit up a chip of sulphur here and there or the steel of shovel or hatchet, he would twist his lower lip and wait for the tear to trickle slowly down the channel hollowed out by its predecessors.

Some of the other miners were addicted to smoking and some to wine; he was addicted to his tear.

The tear was due to a disorder of the tear sac, not weeping; but

Uncle Scarda had drunk wept tears too, four years earlier, when his only son had been killed in an explosive charge, leaving him seven orphans and a daughter-in-law to support. He would still shed an occasional tear that was saltier than the rest, a tear he would recognise at once; and then he would shake his head and murmur a name: 'Calicchio'.

In consideration of Calicchio's death, and also of the eye he had lost in the same explosion, he was still kept working in the mine. He worked, in fact, harder and better than a young man. But every Saturday night when he was given his pay he took it as if it were charity, and putting it in his pocket he would murmur almost in shame: 'May the Lord reward them for it.'

Because as a rule it was to be assumed that a man of his age could no longer be a good worker.

When Cacciagallina at last let him go so that he could run after the others and try to persuade someone to work all night, Uncle Scarda begged him at least to send one of the returning miners to his home with the message that he had stayed behind at the sulphur mine, and so they were not to wait up for him or worry about him. Then he walked round calling his caruso, who was more than thirty but might just as well have been seven or seventy, half-wit that he was; he called him with the mimicking cry used to call a pet crow: *'Te, pa! Te, pa!'*

Ciàula* was busy getting dressed to go back to town.

For Ciàula, getting dressed meant first of all taking off his shirt, or what had perhaps once been a shirt: it was the only garment that covered him, after a fashion, while he worked. After he had taken his shirt off he covered his bare torso – on which all his ribs could be counted – with a long, broad-fitting waistcoat which had been given to him in charity; once it must have been very smart and expensive, but it was now so thickly ingrained with dirt that if placed on the ground it would stand upright. With the utmost care Ciàula would do up the six buttons, three of which hung dangling, and then admire himself with it on, stroking it with his

* The name suggests the crow.

refinement. His scrawny, bandy bare legs would turn goose-pimpled and blue with cold during this act of admiration. If one of his companions gave him a shove or a kick and shouted at him 'Aren't you handsome?' he would open his mouth right up to his jutting ears in a toothless grin of satisfaction. Then he would put on his trousers, which had holes in seat and knee, and wrap himself in a baggy, unbleached cotton overcoat; and at every barefooted step wonderfully imitating the call of the crow, 'Caw! Caw!' – that was why he had been nicknamed Ciàula – he would set out for the town.

This evening too he responded to his boss's call with a 'Caw! Caw!' and presented himself to him stark naked apart from the one refinement of his waistcoat, duly buttoned up.

'Go and get undressed again,' Uncle Scarda said to him. 'Get back into your shirt and sack. The Lord isn't going to give us a night.'

Ciàula did not demur. He stood for a while looking at Uncle Scarda open-mouthed, with the gaze of an idiot. Then he placed his hands in the small of his back and stretched himself, screwing up his nose in pain.

'All right,' he said.

And he went and took his waistcoat off.

But for tiredness and the need to sleep, working by night as well as day would have meant nothing, because down there, after all, it was always night. At least that was how Uncle Scarda saw it.

But not Ciàula. With his oil lamp tucked into the folded mouth of the sack hanging down over his forehead, and his nape bent low under the load, Ciàula would go up and down the steep, slippery underground ladder with its broken rungs, up and up and up he would climb, his croak growing weaker and weaker at every rung with his shortness of breath until it sounded like the groan of a strangled man, and at the end of every climb he would see the light of the sun again. At first he would stand dazzled; and then when he unloaded and took a deep breath, the familiar forms of surrounding objects would rush in upon him; he would stand looking at them for a while, still panting, and without being clearly aware of it, would find them comforting.

It was a strange thing: Ciàula had no fear of the slimy darkness of the deep galleries where around every bend death lay in ambush, nor did he fear the monstrous shadows fitfully raised by the occasional lanterns along the galleries, nor the sudden flash of reddish light reflected here and there in a puddle or a pond of sulphurous water; he always knew where he was; his hand, groping for support, would touch the bowels of the earth; there he was as blind and safe as in his mother's womb.

But he feared the empty darkness of the night outside.

He was used to the darkness of the day down there, interspersed by faint glimmers of light, beyond the bottom of the funnel-shaped ladder-shaft up which he climbed so many times a day with his peculiar throttled crow's croak. But he was not used to the darkness of the night outside.

Every evening after work he went back to the town with Uncle Scarda. As soon as he had swallowed his last morsel of food he would lie down to sleep on a paillasse on the ground, like a dog; the boys, his boss's seven orphaned grandchildren, would pummel him to try to keep him awake so that they could laugh at his stupidity, but to no purpose, for he immediately fell into a heavy sleep from which, every morning at the crack of dawn, he was roused by a familiar foot.

His fear of the darkness of night went back to the time when Uncle Scarda's son, then Ciàula's boss, had his belly and chest torn open by the detonation in the mine and Uncle Scarda himself had been hit in one eye.

Down there at the sulphur faces they had been about to stop work, as it was already evening, when they had heard the tremendous roar of the detonation. All the pickmen and carusi had rushed to the scene of the explosion; Ciàula alone had run off in terror to take cover in a cave known only to him.

In his haste he had smashed his earthenware lamp against the rock; and when, after a lapse of time he could not assess, he had finally left the cave for the silence of the dark and deserted workings, he had had a hard time groping his way back to the tunnel that would lead him to the ladder: but even then he had not been afraid. Fear had seized him only when he emerged from the pit into the black, empty night.

He had begun to tremble with a sense of insecurity, shuddering at every vague, indistinct stirring in the mysterious silence that filled that endless void in which a dense swarm of countless tiny stars failed to diffuse any light.

The darkness where there should have been light, the solitude of familiar objects so altered in appearance as to be almost unrecognisable when no one saw them any longer, had thrown his bewildered soul into such turmoil that Ciàula had suddenly broken into a mad gallop as if someone were chasing him.

Now, after going back below ground with Uncle Scarda, as he waited for a load he felt gradually growing within him the fear of the darkness that he would find on emerging from the mine. And because of that rather than the darkness of the galleries and the shaft he carefully trimmed the terracotta lamp.

Far away in the distance could be heard the rhythmic creaking and thudding of the pump which never stopped day or night. And between the creaks and thuds, in alternate rhythm, came Uncle Scarda's grunts, as if the movements of the old man's arms were aided by the force of that faraway machine.

At last the load was ready, and Uncle Scarda helped Ciàula arrange it and hitch it up on the sack secured behind the nape of his neck.

As Uncle Scarda loaded, Ciàula felt his legs gradually buckling under him, until one leg began to shake so convulsively that, afraid he would be unable to bear the weight, he cried out: 'Enough! Enough!'

'Enough my foot, you carcass!' replied Uncle Scarda, and went on loading.

For a moment Ciàula's fear of the darkness of night was overcome by dismay at the thought that with so heavy a load and the weariness that he felt, he might not be able to climb right to the top. He had worked pitilessly all day. It had never occurred to Ciàula that anyone could pity his body, and nor did it now; he simply felt utterly exhausted.

He set off under the enormous load, which needed balancing as well. Yes, he *could* move, at least as long as he was on the level. But how could he bear such a weight once the climb had begun?

Fortunately, when the climb began Ciàula was once more seized with his fear of the darkness of the night into which he would soon emerge.

Passing through the galleries that evening, he did not utter his usual crow's croak but only a protracted, rasping moan. As he climbed the ladder even the moan ceased, hushed by his fear of the black silence he would find in the impalpable emptiness outside.

The ladder was so steep that, with his head pushed forward and down beneath the load, Ciàula could not see the opening that yawned above, once he was round the last bend in the shaft, however hard he strained his eyes upwards.

Bent double, his forehead almost touching the rung above him, his flickering lamp casting a faint ruddy glimmer on its slippery surface, he climbed, climbed, climbed out of the bowels of the earth, not with eagerness, but with fear of his coming liberation. He could not yet see the hole far above, open like a bright eye, an eye of delicious silvery brightness.

He saw it only when he reached the very last rungs. At first, although the idea struck him as odd, he thought it must be the last gleam of daylight. But the brightness increased, and went on increasing, as if the sun which he had certainly seen set had risen again.

Was it possible?

He emerged into the open and stood in amazement. The load fell from his back. He raised his arms slightly, and opened his black hands in the silvery brightness.

Large, placid, as if floating in a new, luminous ocean of silence, facing him was the Moon.

Oh, he knew, he knew what it was all right, but only in the way many things are known that have never seemed to matter. And what could it have mattered to Ciàula that there was a Moon in the sky?

Only now, emerging from the shaft at night, out of the bowels of the earth, had he discovered her.

In ecstacy, he flopped down on his load facing the shaft. There he was, there she was, the Moon – there was the Moon, the Moon!

And Ciàula began to weep without knowing it, without

wishing it, from the great comfort, the great sweetness he felt at discovering the Moon as she climbed the sky in her ample veil of light, unconscious of the mountains, the plains, the valleys she brightened, unconscious of him, though it was thanks to her that he no longer felt fear or exhaustion in the night now filled with his wonderment.

The Story of Mila

VITALIANO BRANCATI

The trouble was that in May 1895, when he undertook a long voyage around Europe as his first journey abroad, Giovanni Gorgone was still very young. For a Sicilian, to arrive in northern seas with so little experience is an event fraught with great danger: Giovanni came back to Messina a married man. And whom had he married? A Norwegian woman. They all said, 'Well, he's really bought himself a packet of trouble now!' and put their hands to their ears with the index and little finger extended. However, as it turned out, life put horns on many of those who had put their hands to their ears, whilst Giovanni Gorgone stayed a much-respected husband; only a malicious fool could have cast suspicion on his home life.

Within a few days the young Norwegian girl had acquired the oldest and most complex Sicilian habits. Gradually she lost her distinctive colouring, and began to blend with the plainest creatures of my homeland; her pale face slowly disappeared into the darkness of the balcony window where she sat every afternoon, like a leaf that takes twenty years to sink to the bottom of a water tank.

A daughter, Mila, was born to this couple who led so retired a life. When she was about fifteen years old the girl began to go to the beach, and the bathers on the lido rose from the sand where they had buried themselves to sleep, in order to see this 'wonder of a woman'. The sand into which they soon dug themselves back smothered many affectionate if coarse words of admiration.

Between her fifteenth and her twentieth year, Mila continued to grow taller and even more beautiful: her full head of hair now shone above the slow river of hard and soft hats that nightly

123

flowed up and down the corso. Everything that changes the face of a man in love when he sees the woman he desires – the pallor, the trembling lips, the rolling eyes – was hidden and lost beneath those black-ribboned felt hats when her face rapidly crossed the throng, only rarely encountering the face of a man, and even more rarely that of a woman, that rose to her own height. It was not that Mila was a beanpole: on the contrary, she was the best-proportioned woman in the district, and her height would have seemed perfectly normal in the streets of a northern town. But things were different here, and eager young men, passionately longing to dance with her at a municipal ball, often did not even dare to bow and ask her; they would revolve around her in a slow and dismal wheel, like crows circling around something that attracts them but on top of which one of them lies dead. They said that she was arrogant and, to make excuses for their own hapless timidity, claimed that she was hard and cold, a piece of ice. She was, on the contrary, a very sweet girl indeed. She would have loved to befriend those dark and vivacious men with their deep-set eyes whom she found so charming. If she didn't fall in love, it was because she thought herself too ungainly to participate in the game of reciprocated affections.

This perfect woman whose picture hundreds of men carried in their hearts, who caused many of my friends to leave the paternal home and move to pale northern suns under whose feeble light they were never happy again, or else to take almost fatal risks; this woman often found herself envying one of the dark Sicilian girls with her shiny skin, and she would go home murmuring, 'The Lord has helped that girl.' Mila would have given years of her life for those jutting-out cheekbones, that short figure, that full little body rippling with flesh.

Men always behaved well in front of her, because her beauty made them fear that, left on their own, their behaviour would verge on the ridiculous; they behaved, in fact, so well that they appeared cold and bored, or else they assumed sportive and comradely manners that fitted neither their temperament nor their feelings or the mood of the moment – treating the beautiful girl in the mountains and at the seaside to slaps on the back, horseplay and quips from the humorous weeklies: and yet, if only the chance they hoped for to show their true feelings had come, they would have fallen on their knees in front of her and confusedly stammered the words of the five or six love songs they had ever learned.

Of all this, Mila never knew nor even suspected anything, even though one afternoon in July, fate contrived that the whole painful misunderstanding could have been cleared up in a moment. On that afternoon, the mayor's son, whom she thought the most lovable young man in the world, crept towards her along the sand on the beach. As he crawled forward with his face almost buried in the sand, his field of vision was reduced to that of a snail's fumbling antenna. Mila, lying flat on her back, felt herself suddenly touched, and sat up quickly, tossing her head to shake the sand out of her hair. 'Signorina . . . I . . .' the young man began, not quite near enough to use that tone of voice, but the words spilling out of his trembling body, 'Signorina Mila, for some time I have . . . My father knows your father . . . I believe we've already seen one another at the Rowing Club Dance . . . Well, anyway, I . . . I . . .' And a word that might have had the force of a bomb was on the point of exploding when Mila, unable to bear his gaze, turned her eyes towards the sea. What happened to the girl the moment she looked towards the sea? Her face, always strangely serious, appeared now – because of the light that her eyes reflected on her cheeks as she looked seaward – to assume the twilit colour of a statue beside the stained glass window of a church. The mayor's son felt like a thief shown up by the sacristan's lantern as he scrambles towards a statue of the Virgin Mary to steal a bracelet. He became so confused that he trod on the face of a man who lay under a blanket of sand, with only his pipe protruding. Speech failed him, even for an apology, and a violent struggle ensued: blows were exchanged, the pipe flew into a near-by boat, and in the end the mayor's son had his nose flattened. No sooner did he realise his disfigurement than he turned his face away to hide it from Mila and fled, limping like a hare lamed by the first shot. From a distance, peering from behind the trunk of a palm, he saw his adversary – who was a Norwegian, a ship's master – retrieve his pipe and bury himself in the sand again, exchanging a few words with Mila in the process.

'He comes from her part of the world,' thought the mayor's son. 'They'll get on well with one another.'

The Norwegian didn't appeal very much to Mila. Her father, however, said to her, 'My dear girl, you're not a child any longer. Who are you waiting for? Is there anyone among your friends here who wants to marry you? If there is, say so!' Mila had to admit that there was no one, and she hung her head. Some time later, with a bunch of flowers in her arms, Mila left for the north with her Norwegian husband. The Sicilian priest's sermon still rang in her ears; he had bungled his words in a most delightful way – it was the only thing that made her smile in the deep depression that had come over her.

But two years later she was back. They had not managed to get on with one another after all. 'What they say about blood . . . it's all nonsense!' was the comment of the people of Messina. Mila had felt herself dying of despair alongside that cold and courteous man whose head, wreathed in pipe smoke, would appear in the frozen square of the window pane exactly one hour after midday as he said, 'Good-day, Mila. I'm back. Is lunch ready?' However, he too must have had a good deal to put up with in living with that uprooted woman who would look suddenly towards far-away points, now to the right, now to the left, as if she were hearing gates closing on all sides. He was the first to leave the house – with a woman, of course. A week later, Mila left for Sicily.

'What are you going to do now?' asked her father.

'I'm going to find myself a job; I'm going to earn my bread. I don't think the good people here will begrudge me a bit of help.'

Since 1927, Mila has in fact been the secretary of a rich ship-owner, and at six o'clock every evening she can still be seen passing through the crowds on the corso with her leather handbag in her hand. No one can say a word of blame about her, just as nothing could ever be said against her mother. 'When they say Northern women . . . it's all nonsense,' is the comment of the people of Messina. Since 1937, Mila has no longer been an elegant woman; she blends in with the others. She even seems less tall than before. But the men still follow her with their eyes when the light from the shop window enables them to pick her out, even at a distance, as she glides quickly by. How many stories of other people's experience are bound up with this woman who even now thinks she has never roused any feeling among the local men she finds so appealing! The chemist remembers that one evening in 1921 he found himself close to her when she was wearing a white dress, and he was overcome by such happiness that he felt his brain would burst sweetly, like the bud of a flower. The notary recalls that one afternoon in 1917, as he followed her at a distance, he suddenly heard the sound of a piano, and from that moment understood music, which he had previously always hated. And three lawyers remember . . . And a landowner remembers . . . Even a colonel remembers . . . The hem of this woman's dress, which still billows over her firm knees, sparks off memories on all sides.

But now the evening has come. The lamps of the corso no longer light up. The shop windows go dark suddenly.

Mila has faded away.

Story of a Man Who Twice Failed to Laugh

VITALIANO BRANCATI

On New Year's Eve 1900, Giacomo Licalzi was forty years old. Many bottles were opened that night in the houses of Catania: some say the mayor got so drunk that he took off his trousers and hung them on the window-sill; some say it snowed between two and three in the morning; others say it didn't snow, but that a very strong wind hurled itself for an hour against the window shutters and then ceased all at once, like a tree felled by lightning; according to others still, there was neither storm nor snow, but is was a quiet, fragrant and splendid night.

They toasted the new century: they said all sorts of things about happiness, progress, brotherhood, love, and so on; they talked a lot, and laughed even more. Only Giacomo Licalzi did not laugh; he passed the night with a melancholy face, smoking his pipe, poking at the ash in the bowl, and every now and again getting up and asking his children, 'Are you asleep?'

The children would wake up, rub their eyes and answer, 'Yes, Daddy, we're asleep.'

'Well,' their father would say, 'go on sleeping.'

Until a short time before, he had been a light-hearted man; then all at once a strange shadow descended on his face. He ceased to go out at night, to play cards, to visit the theatre. He gave up his shotgun, his dogs, his horse, his pet monkey; cut down his conversation, his needs, his pleasures. He prepared to enter the new century like a good captain who lightens his ship before entering dangerous waters.

'What a horrid century,' he sniffed. 'Horrid things, horrid events, horrid deeds, horrid tricks. Tedium, nausea, and on top of everything else such very, very horrid people!'

When the bombardment of Sicily began in 1943, neither the face nor the heart of this old man, now eighty-three, held any more room for fear or surprise. He looked at people in deepest silence, with he same cold, unfathomable stare as that cast by the half-closed eyes of a dead man on a thief stealing his shoes.

He lived on a top floor, under a thin flat roof that the smallest splinter could easily have pierced; but neither his children nor his granchildren could make him go down to the shelter. When the war came nearer and the people of Catania fled from the town, the whole of the quarter around him – including the cathedral and the public library – had only one inhabitant: that taciturn old man who, during the first night of the twentieth century, had been the only one who failed to laugh.

The retreating Germans occupied the house, and a general came to visit Giacomo Licalzi – more to survey the position from the window, of course, than for the pleasure of making his acquaintance.

'You're an inhuman lot,' said the octogenarian in German, although he had not spoken for three years, even in his own dialect.

The general extracted seven photographs from his wallet – two old people, a woman, three children and a girl – spreading them on the table like a pack of cards as a player does when he wants someone to choose one, and he said, 'They're all dead.' Then he took out his revolver and shot recklessly towards the balconies opposite. 'As far as I'm concerned,' he shouted, 'the whole world can go to blazes! Let them all die! Heil Hitler!'

The old man got up and led him towards the door. The other man, giving way to that half-alive look, jumped to attention, saluted, and went out.

When the Germans disappeared towards the horizon, and while their guns still rumbled from the woods of Etna, the town fell into the hands of the looters. Dressed up as Germans, British, Fascists, police, the thieves broke down the doors of the houses, went up to the balconies and appeared on the roofs. Every conceivable item was stolen, and carried off by robbers who hid themselves beneath it; wardrobes, mirrors, beds, statues, chests of drawers began to walk about the deserted, rubble-choked streets.

From his high window, Giacomo Licalzi looked down at the sorry spectacle and smoked his pipe. Nothing surprised him; all these things he had already seen in his mind's eye during the first night of the twentieth century, and he congratulated himself that he had not taken part, in the slightest degree, in the stupid laughter of those who greeted 'the dawn of the new century'. Those people who had uncorked bottles, laughing and guffawing, appeared in his memory like a crowd of drunken, tripping apes. To the devil with them! How horrid they were!

Eventually the British arrived. Carefully they looked even under the church pews to see that no German foot was there. They climbed up to the attic where the old man was smoking his pipe. A sergeant and a private asked his permission to fly the Union Jack from his little window. An imperceptible spark lit Licalzi's eye at the sight of that ragged piece of cloth dangling over a flattened town, symbol of an armed multitude advancing in fear behind another retreating in fear.

'You're an inhuman lot,' said the old man in bad English.

'No!' said the sergeant. 'Not at all! We're very kind!'

He could speak Italian, and he wore a string of rosary beads. 'I'm a Catholic,' he said, and as the old man remained unresponsive, the sergeant, thinking that he hadn't understood him, raised his voice. 'Catholic!' he repeated. He made the sign of the cross – 'Father, Son and Holy Ghost' – and seeing a statuette of the Holy Rita above the shabby bedstead, knelt down on the hair mattress and kissed the feet of the image. Then he got up again, and jumped off the bed. With a courteous gesture he removed the pipe from the old man's mouth, filled it with tobacco for him, and put it back between his teeth.

'Let's drink!' he exclaimed. 'Grandad, let's drink!'

He produced a bottle, filled a glass he saw on the table, and handed it to the old man. Impetuously he himself drank straight from the bottle.

'Long live peace!' he shouted. 'Peace! Peace! Let's have peace forever! Grandad, you will live to be a-hundred-and-eighty, three hundred years old!'

The old man was about to smile when the other man, in his ardour, went on: 'Peace! Peace forever! A new age is beginning!' The old man's face clouded over, and once more, beside a person contorted with fits of laughter, he failed to laugh.

Joy and the Law

GIUSEPPE DI LAMPEDUSA

When he got onto the bus he irritated everyone.

The briefcase crammed with other people's business, the enormous parcel which made his left arm stick out, the grey velvet scarf, the umbrella on the point of opening, all made it difficult for him to produce his return ticket. He was forced to put his parcel on the ticket collector's bench, setting off an avalanche of small coins; as he tried to bend down to pick them up, he provoked protests from those who stood behind him, who feared that because of his dallying their coats would be caught in the automatic doors. At last he managed to squeeze into the row of people clinging to the handles in the gangway. He was slight of build, but his bundles gave him the cubic capacity of a nun in seven habits. As the bus slid through the chaos of the traffic, his inconvenient bulk spread resentment from front to rear of the coach. He stepped on people's feet, they trod on his; he invited rebuke, and when he heard the word *cornuto* from the rear of the bus alluding to his presumed marital disgrace, his sense of honour compelled him to turn his head in that direction and make his exhausted eyes assume what he imagined to be a threatening expression.

The bus, meanwhile, was passing through streets where rustic baroque fronts hid a wretched hinterland which emerged at each street corner in the yellow light of eighty-year-old shops.

At his stop he rang the bell, descended, tripped over the umbrella, and found himself alone at last on his square metre of disconnected footpath. He hastened to make sure that he still had his plastic wallet. And then he was free to relish his bliss.

Enclosed in that wallet were 37,245 lire – the 'thirteenth monthly salary' received as a Christmas bonus an hour before. This sum meant the removal of several thorns from his flesh: the obligations to his landlord, all the more pressing because his was a controlled rent and he owed two quarters; and to the ever-punctual instalment collector for the short lapin coat ('It suits you better than a long coat, my dear – it makes you look slimmer'); the dirty looks from the fishmonger and the greengrocer. Those four bank notes of high denomination also eased the fear of the next electricity bill, the pained glances at the children's shoes, and the anxious watching of the gas cylinder's flickering flame; they did not represent opulence, certainly, but did give that breathing space in distress which is the true joy of the poor; a couple of thousand lire might survive for a while, before being eaten up in the resplendence of a Christmas dinner.

However, he had known too many 'thirteenths' to attribute the euphoria which now enveloped him to the ephemeral exhilaration they could produce. He was filled with a rosy feeling, as rosy as the wrapping on the sweet burden that was making his left arm numb. The feeling sprang from the seven-kilo Christmas cake, the panettone that he had brought home from the office. He had no passion for the mixture – as highly guaranteed as it was questionable – of flour, sugar, dried eggs and raisins. At heart he did not care for it at all. But seven kilos of luxury food all at once! A limited but vast abundance in a household where provisions came in hectograms and half-litres! A famous product in a larder devoted to third-rate items! What a joy for Maria! What a riot for the children who for two weeks would explore the unknown Wild West of an afternoon snack!

These, however, were the joys of others, the material joys of vanilla essence and coloured cardboard; of panettone, in sum. His personal joy was different – a spiritual bliss based on pride and loving affection; yes, spritual!

When, a few hours before, the baronet who was managing director of his firm had distributed pay envelopes and Christmas wishes with the overbearing affability of the pompous old man that he was, he also announced that the seven-kilo panettone, which had come with the compliments of the big firm that produced it, would be awarded to the most deserving employee; and he asked his dear colleagues democratically (that was the word he had actually used) to choose the lucky man then and there.

The panettone had stood on the middle of the desk, heavy, hermetically sealed, 'laden with good omens' as the same baronet, dressed in Fascist uniform, would have said in Mussolini's phrase twenty years before. There was laughing and whispering among the employees; and then everyone, the managing director first, shouted his name. A great satisfaction; a guarantee that he would keep his job – in short, a triumph. Nothing that followed could lessen the tonic effect; neither the three hundred lire that he had to pay in the coffee bar below, treating his friends in the two-fold dusk of a squally sunset and dim neon lights, nor the weight of his trophy, nor the unpleasant comments in the bus – nothing; not even the lightning flash from the depths of his consciousness that it had all been an act of rather condescending pity from his fellow-employees: he was really too poor to permit the weed of pride to sprout where it had no business to appear.

He turned towards home across a decrepit street to which the bombardments of fifteen years previously had given the finishing touches, and finally reached the grim little square in the depths of which the ghostly edifice in which he lived stood tucked away.

He heartily greeted Cosimo, the porter, who despised him because he knew that his salary was lower than his own. Nine steps, three steps, nine steps: the floor where Cavaliere Tizio lived. Pooh! He did have a Fiat 1100, true enough, but he also had an old, ugly and dissolute wife. Nine steps, three steps – a slip almost made him fall – nine steps: young Sempronio's apartment; worse still! – a bone-idle lad, mad on Lambrettas and Vespas, whose hall was still unfurnished. Nine steps, three steps, nine steps: his own apartment, the little abode of a beloved, honest and honoured man, a prize-winner, a book-keeper beyond compare.

He opened the door and entered the narrow hall, already filled with the heavy smell of onion soup. He placed the weighty parcel, the briefcase loaded with other people's affairs, and his muffler on a little locker the size of a hamper. His voice rang out: 'Maria! Come quickly! Come and see – what a beauty!'

His wife came out of the kitchen in a blue housecoat spotted with grime from saucepans; her little hands, still red from washing up, rested on a belly deformed by pregnancies. The children with their slimy noses crowded around the rose-coloured sight and squealed without daring to touch it.

'Oh good! Did you bring your pay back? I haven't a single lira left.'

'Here it is, dear. I'll only keep the small change – 245 lire. But look at this grace of God here!'

Maria had been pretty; until a few years previously she had had a cheeky little face and whimsical eyes. But the wrangles with the shopkeepers had made her voice grow harsh, the poor food had ruined her complexion, the incessant peering into a future clouded with problems had spent the lustre of her eyes. Only the soul of a saint survived within her, inflexible and bereft of tenderness; deep-seated virtue expressing itself in rebukes and restrictions; and in addition a repressed but persistent pride of class because she was the granddaughter of a big hatter in one of the main streets, and despised the origins of her Girolamo – whom she adored as a silly but beloved child – because they were inferior to her own.

Indifferently her eyes ran over the gilded cardboard box. 'That's fine. Tomorrow we'll send it to Signor Risma, the solicitor; we're under such an obligation to him!'

Two years previously this solicitor had given him a complicated book-keeping job to do, and over and above paying for it, had invited both of them to lunch in his abstract-and-metal apartment. The clerk had suffered acutely from the shoes bought specially for the occasion. And he and his Maria, his Andrea, his Saverio, his little Josephine were now to give up the only seam of abundance they had hit in many, many years, for that lawyer who had everything.

He ran to the kitchen, grabbed a knife, and rushed to cut the gold string that a deft working girl in Milan had beautifully tied around the wrapping paper; but a reddened hand wearily touched his shoulder. 'Girolamo, don't behave like a child – you know we have to repay Risma's kindness.'

The law had spoken: the law laid down by unblemished hat-shop owners.

'But dear, this is a prize, an award of merit, a token of esteem!'

'Don't say that. Nice people, those colleagues of yours, with their tender feelings! It was alms-giving, Giro, nothing but alms-giving.' She called him by his old pet name, and smiled at him with eyes that only for him still held traces of the old spell. 'Tomorrow I'll buy a little panettone, just big enough for us, and four of those twisted red candles from Standa's* – that'll make it a fine feast!'

The next day he bought an undistinguished miniature panettone, and not four but two of the astonishing candles; through a delivery agency, at a cost of another two hundred lire, he forwarded the mammoth cake to the solicitor Risma.

After Christmas he had to buy a third panettone which, disguised by slicing, he took to his colleagues who were teasing him because they hadn't been offered a morsel of the sumptuous trophy.

A smoke screen enveloped the fate of the original cake. He went to the Lightning Delivery Agency to make enquiries. With disdain he was shown the receipts book which the solicitor's manservant had signed upside down. However, just after Twelfth Night a visiting card arived 'with sincerest thanks and best wishes'.

Honour was saved.

* A multiple chain store of household goods, comparable to Woolworth's.

Remote Past

CARMELO CICCIA

When the solicitor Venanzi returned home after an absence of many years, everyone who knew of his engagement expected to see him married, and perhaps with children as well; but when he came back he was still alone. People only gradually learned the true reasons for his return and his remaining a bachelor, because he was by nature shy and reticent; he told very few that his fiancée had been killed in a car accident. To a close friend he also confided that he was still very shaken, that he felt himself to be a wreck and scarcely capable of starting his life again.

Among the things of his fiancée that he had kept and not returned to her family were her letters. He had not kept them to show to others; in fact the only person who knew about them was his closest friend, to whom he occasionally mentioned matters connected with the accident. The letters were for himself alone. In moments of nostalgia and depression he would shut himself up in his office and read passages from them, looking again at every stroke of the pen, trying to experience once more the effect these letters had had on him when he received them, abandoning himself to dreams and fantasies about a reality which now lay buried. But it should be said that he was one of the most sought-after lawyers in the area, and even had too much work. When he read the words of those letters again, he turned back the years, experienced old scenes and gestures once more, heard familiar voices of former times; especially that voice . . . her voice, the voice that he still heard so often in his mind, causing turmoil in his thoughts, with its different shades and tones expressing her state of mind in varying circumstances.

The style of the letters was lively and rather hurried; they were not without mistakes, and in places muddled and repetitive. He had once scolded her, and shamed her by saying that schoolchildren wrote better than she did. This had led to a quarrel but, like all the others, it was soon forgotten. Her mistakes were mostly due to her highly emotional nature, the tumultuous feelings that overwhelmed her in her impetuousness and high spirits, but partly also to her anxiety to get the letters to their destination as quickly as possible. Thus, just as they had been conceived, without ever having been re-read or corrected, so they still were, her scribbled thoughts and opinions on those pages. It must have been a great love, indeed an extraordinary love, if it was this love that kept the lawyer Venanzi alive – alive, that is, as long as he could read the letters again and again, or at least those parts of them that he had underlined and knew almost by heart.

'You know how happy I am that you find me so lovable, and that you are so much in love with me! I want this to last forever, for our love to go on growing and growing, just as it says on that medallion which you gave me: *today more than yesterday but much less than tomorrow.* I hope you didn't think too badly of me when I opened up and asked you about your true feelings for me . . . '

'God, wasn't it funny that day at Forni when your feet kept slipping in the mud! I saw straight away that you were embarrassed and shy. But that little spot you made on my flowery dress still won't go away, not with the best detergents. And don't be cross, darling, if I've dirtied your new shirt, at least you're left with the imprint of my lips . . . '

'You don't know how happy I was that day in the wood! I was happy because I could see you were happy, and I could read your happiness in your eyes. You gave me a little handkerchief, soaked in Eau-de-Cologne, and it burnt my skin: I can still feel the burning, but it doesn't hurt at all – quite the contrary! . . . '

'I wish you would come more often to Sabbiadoro. I like swimming with you so much, and not only because it's good for our figures. And it's so beautiful down there, especially in the pine woods . . . '

'Don't tell me again that I don't understand anything. I'm not a child. If you tell me again that I don't understand anything, you're not going to see me again. Understand? . . . '

'I only want our happiness. We've been so happy together. And if marriage is based on love, we won't feel alone again for the rest of our lives. You can't imagine how lonely I've felt these last few days when you've been angry with me, and I think you must have felt lonely too . . . '

'For me, life without you is no longer life, and you ought to know that. Everything here speaks of you and how happy we have been in this place or that place. Why must our love finish like that? I could never be happy with another man. You are my love and you know that I can't be happy without you. Haven't I always tried my best so that I could see you happy beside me? I am your dream, and you can't live without me . . . '

'Happy Christmas and Happy New Year from someone who thinks of you. Think of me at midnight, because at that moment my thoughts will be flying towards you . . . '

'The lines of poetry you dedicated to me are quite beautiful and they express such fine thoughts! I knew that you wouldn't be able to be without me for long. You said so many times that I am your "destiny" and that you "feel me in your blood". I thank you with all my heart and I'm longing to see you soon . . . '

'The ring you have given me is so beautiful! It's thrilled all my friends. I love it all the more because it's not the usual type of engagement ring, but different and original. This ring is a token of our love and strengthens it at the same time, and for me it is also the chain which binds me to you forever. I must tell you of a strange sensation I have every now and again when I feel as if we were already married: yours forever! . . . '

'I'd like to have a bungalow. You know I'd really love to have a little piece of garden where we could keep a few animals and breed chickens. But perhaps you're right: it's better to be in a block of flats as it's cheaper and does offer some comforts, even if it brings a few troubles as well . . . '

'I've been thinking that if we saved some money we could buy a bit of land in the country, so that we could have somewhere to escape to and amuse ourselves, we could even have our own fruit . . . '

'I am your dream' was the phrase that had impressed itself most strongly on the lawyer Venanzi's mind, because it was the truest. In second place was 'You can't live without me', but this was only partly true since he continued to live without her, although it was more an existence than a life. Finally, the words 'I could never be happy with another man' were the ones that bound him to his solitary life, because he could not be happy with another woman, and although it was over twelve years since that tragic day, he still felt her in his blood, felt her as a part of himself, and was as convinced as ever that she was his destiny. This was why he remained single, and lived in the past.

Sometimes he would lose himself so completely in his meditations that he seemed to leave the present world in pursuit of his fantasies – living memories, dreams, wanderings towards an imaginary world glimpsed beyond thousands of images of a different past, seen again and again as if on a cinema screen; a communing with himself as well as with the object of his imagination; a feeling of elevation at having been so loved, although that happiness had lasted for only one year – such was now the life of the lawyer Venanzi, eternal bachelor, convinced misogynist and professed atheist. A life in the past, while living in the present, a life in the remote past.

And if someone seeing his greying hair – he was now over forty – asked, just to tease him or tempt him: 'Don't you ever think of getting married?' he would reply by shrugging his shoulders as if to say 'Why should I?' with an absent, wandering gaze that seemed to go beyond visible boundaries and fix itself on a non-existent image.

A few people who chanced to have seen his bedroom said that they had glimpsed a large, framed colour photograph on the wall portraying a beautiful young girl in a green crocheted dress, with a lock of blond hair falling over her cheek; she sat in a field, her head and shoulders stretching towards the photographer. She appeared to be grace itself; the picture was so vivid that she seemed to smile out of the rectangle of the frame, as if just about to speak. He maintained that it was an artistic photograph he had bought in Jugoslavia; but those who knew him well said that it was his fiancée of twelve years previously, and that he spoke to her every night.

How Filippa Died

GINO RAYA

Newspapers of 11 December merely reported that Filippa took poison and died three days later – that's all. What really happened is known, however, to Father, Son and Holy Ghost.

Filippa was not plain like Maria, her married sister, but a beautiful blonde, and so well-grown that she appeared older than her eighteen years. She was keen to get married.

First on the scene was a carabiniere; for six months they went out together. He was going to take up a new post, and was already preparing his move. The girl's mother said: 'If Filippa goes away, how can I see her? How will I ever find this treasure of a daughter of mine again?' As the marriage date approached, the bride's mother began to have screaming fits; the carabiniere went away alone.

Then there was an electrician. He was going to stay at home, so the mother had no worry on that account, but Filippa herself was undecided: after a police officer, an electrician seemed a come-down. She went to her sister for advice.

Sister Maria had the family's flat at the back of her mind. If Filippa marries here, she thought, I won't be able to have the flat for myself when our parents die: she's bound to want at least half of it. Maria's advice was therefore that Filippa should not marry anyone from her home town – exactly the opposite tune to her mother's. That courtship, too, fizzled out.

The same thing happened with a solicitor's son, and a customs officer, with whom they even reached the stage of ordering the wedding dress. Again, the mother made them break it off, as she could not bear the thought of Filippa leaving home.

Then Pippo appeared, a glass-maker, working only a few yards from Filippa's home. Pippo had a wife and a three-year-old child in Messina – but no one knew about that here. And on whom should his eye settle if not the best-looking girl in the street?

Filippa thought: If I talk too much about him, mother is only going to spoil everything again: perhaps it would be best to elope, and get things straightened out afterwards.

Many marriages in small towns take place through elopement. But Filippa's fate was otherwise.

On Tuesday 6 December, at about ten o'clock at night, Filippa eloped with Pippo. Only Maria knew of the plan, but she feigned ignorance and asked the neighbours: 'Is Filippa with you?' She wasn't. Everyone had a good idea of what was in the air, and went to bed happily.

At four o'clock in the morning, while it was still dark, knocks were heard at the door of the house. Pippo had brought the girl back! They had been to a hotel, and it was all over.

Filippa's father, who had not yet gone to work, called to Pippo from the second floor landing: 'You really have brought her back early!'

They began to talk on the staircase, and some of the neighbours listened. Pippo said: 'I've brought her back because I must leave for Messina to see to the marriage documents. I'm a bachelor, and here's my identity card – do you want to see it?' But he held it tightly in his hand, because it was all lies.

His voice sounded strained and apprehensive. Suddenly the card fell out of his hand, and Filippa picked it up. He knew she would instantly realise the truth, and changed his tune: 'Let's conceal the whole thing. I took her away at night, and I've brought her back at night – no one need know anything about it. I'm a married man – I have a three-year-old child.'

But how to conceal it? Filippa's mother, as usual, began to scream 'Mamma mia!' and 'My daughter!' While the neighbours came, Pippo made off in a hurry. Thus began the fateful Wednesday.

The father left early in order to talk the matter over with his step-brother's son, a solicitor, who maintained that the police must trace the dishonest fellow.

Filippa stayed at home. Her mother's words were like a dagger in her flesh: 'What are you going to do, you wicked daughter? There's fire in our house! I am a mirror of chastity. Your sister

– a mirror of chastity. Your grandmother – a mirror of chastity. You have dishonoured us all. What a fire – in our house! What are you going to do, you wicked daughter?'

At last Filippa burst out: 'Have you finished yet? If you go on like this, I'll take poison.'

And her mother: 'What are you waiting for? You either take poison or jump from the quay. Mamma mia, what a fire in our house! What are you going to do? Either you take poison or you jump in the sea.'

Maria intervened: 'That's enough, mother. On the other hand, Filippa, mother is right. You were thoughtless; you should never have run away.'

When the father came back he said to Filippa: 'What's done is done. You should leave here, and stay for a while with your brother and sister-in-law in town. Best try to take a job; I'll see you have enough money.'

But mother and sister disagreed with this plan, which would be to dishonour Filippa's brother and her sister-in-law too – another mirror of chastity – so what was the wicked girl going to do?

At about eleven o'clock that morning the wicked girl, by now half-demented, rushed out to a neighbour who kept a salt and wine shop, and asked her to lend her a bottle to buy a quarter of marsala for her splitting headache.

When she had the bottle she left the shop, called a little girl and said to her: 'Go and buy me half a quarter of spirit of salt, will you?' But the girl replied: 'They won't sell it to me. You have to go and get it yourself.' Filippa returned home and found Maria standing inside the front door.

'Shall I go and get it?' Maria asked. And so she did.

Filippa waited upstairs, outside the door to their flat. Maria soon returned and gave her the bottle: 'You must never tell anybody I bought it!'

The poor girl gulped down three mouthfuls of the acid, and immediately collapsed and rolled down to the first floor landing, in front of the door of the nurse who was working at the hospital. The bottle broke and the acid bubbled onto the stairs.

Three neighbours hurried from below. On the stairs above, the mother appeared and immediately cried: 'What's happened?

Filippa has poisoned herself!' There were shouts, and other people came as well, and they all wanted to carry Filippa to the hospital.

But instead the mother made them carry her into the flat, and place her on the bed. 'No, not the hospital just yet – first we must call my husband. He must decide – he's doing some tiling near the beach.' Two men went to get him, but it took them the best part of an hour.

At last the husband returned; they took a car and were driven to the hospital. The doctors said the whole throat was burnt, and there was nothing to be done; but they kept her there for the whole day, and for the night as well.

On Thursday morning, when the parents saw there was no hope, they took her home again and waited for her to die. Again and again the mother said: 'What a fire, what a fire!' but the real fire was in Filippa's throat; she was a pitiful sight.

Every now and again Maria and her mother said: 'You won't tell them, will you?' and she would reassure them with her eyes. Later in the day she added: 'Bury me in my white wedding dress', the dress that had been made for the wedding with the customs officer. So Thursday and Friday passed, and then came Saturday, the day that was to end with her death.

On Saturday afternoon the magistrate and the doctor came to the house together, and spoke to Filippa in the presence of her father, her mother, and her sister Maria. All five stood in Filippa's room. She was asked: 'No one suggested you should take poison?' And she answered: 'No, no one.' This was the point that concerned them most. Then she added: 'Send me a priest,' and her mother asked the doctor to do so.

When the priest came, the neighbours who had entered Filippa's room went out again, and the priest remained alone with her; he left after a very short time.

Then Filippa said: 'Dress me – I am going to die very soon.'

'What are you saying? Keep quiet,' said her mother.

Filippa answered: 'Give me the light blue sheets with the embroidery, and the pink coverlet.' But foam was dribbling from her mouth, and her mother did not want the good sheets to be soiled, so she took her time.

The girl had been right. A dark ring rose around her eyes; she

144

gave a profound sigh, and gave up her soul to God. Margherita, a neighbour, closed her eyes for her. It was about seven o'clock in the evening.

Another neighbour, Nella, brought a kerchief to keep the mouth firm, and Margherita tied it over the head of the dead girl. A third neighbour stood at the door and prevented the men from coming in.

Maria was howling. She and her father went into another room while her mother, Margherita and Nella stayed to dress Filippa up. Nella took the linen out of the box; the mother changed the shoes; Margherita did most of the work.

When Filippa was laid out, she looked almost happy, wearing her white wedding gown and veil at last. Her hair was loose, down to her shoulders, her feet pointed towards the balcony instead of towards the door, and around her were the candles. It must have been about ten at night, and once more the room was as full as an egg.

The mother wailed: 'Who is to have this treasure of a daughter now? I kept her like a jewel. Wherever we went I always kept her close to me. Who is to have her now, this treasure of a daughter?' She tried to tear her hair, but was restrained by the other women. 'Who was to know that my daughter was going to be dead tonight? Breath of my soul, when your grandmother died, you said in the graveyard: "How many young people this earth has eaten up!" Who could have told that it would eat you too?'

In the room was the woman who had provided Filippa with the bottle. 'And you gave her that bottle!' the mother accused. But the woman replied: 'How was I possibly to know?'

The night advanced amid tears and talk. Several people left to go to sleep, but so many were waiting to come in that one of the relatives had to stop them from all coming in together. Towards midnight the married brother arrived.

The other two brothers, who were in the army, came on Sunday morning. Maria's eyes were so shiny that Nella said: 'I think you've got a temperature.'

The funeral took place about midday. There was a beautiful mass for the dead, and several people wept. The mother did not go to the funeral, and Nella, Margherita and the nurse from the first floor kept her company.

Afterwards the three friends brought clear soup and macaroni, six cutlets, and two bottles of wine. During the mourning period there were seven to feed – the father and mother of the dead girl, the sister Maria and her husband, and the three brothers.

For breakfast they had only milk and coffee, but they all greatly enjoyed their midday meal, the 'consolation lunch' that was brought to them for the next three days in succession.

E.A.

DANILO DOLCI

In Partinico, in summer, some people earn a bit of money by selling ice-cream and fruit drinks from carts, and as soon as a cart stops at the top of a road you see all the children pestering their mothers to buy them an ice-cream, it's a sight which tears your heart to pieces, because those mothers who can afford it satisfy their children's wishes while the others, who can't, tell them it's muck that they mustn't eat, made out of donkey's pee; but their children don't believe them because they can see other children buying it.

And those mothers have to lie to their children, fondling them and coaxing them with fibs, and they cry silently to themselves. But how can they afford ice-cream when they can't even buy bread for their children? Families like that live on carob beans.*

I'll tell you one case of misery that's stayed in my mind for years. In 1944 I got engaged to my present wife. In April of 1946 we eloped – in Partinico many young couples elope because they haven't any money for a wedding, I'm speaking of the working people of course, therefore first they run away, and then they marry as best they can. When we ran away, a friend of mine let us have some rooms in the Via Madonna quarter. Almost opposite us lived a family consisting of husband, wife and four children, the youngest was a baby of about four months and the others were about five, seven and nine years old. The day after we arrived, the biggest child, a girl, came to help my wife with some housework hoping to get a piece of bread, my wife and I had no idea of the wretched conditions in which that family lived, though I'd seen the children going barefoot and poorly dressed, but in Partinico being without shoes was a common thing and so we'd taken no notice of it.

* Essentially animal fodder.

147

The third evening after we arrived, my wife was preparing some pasta for the two of us when the eldest girl came in and said: 'Donna Titidda, my mother says when you have cooked the pasta will you let us have a bit of boiled water from it?' My wife didn't think anything about this and said, 'Yes, wait a moment. As soon as I take the pasta out I'll give you the water.' But when I heard the girl ask this I thought it was odd, and out of sheer curiosity I asked her what her mother was going to do with the boiled pasta water, and that child replied, completely open and innocent, that for the last three days no one in that home had eaten a single piece of bread or pasta, and since the mother had no more milk to feed the baby she'd asked for the boiled pasta water to drink to see whether this would bring a little milk to her breasts.

The moment I heard of such a pitiful thing, I cursed God who caused us to be born, I cursed the government which governs us, I cursed the father of the child for a monster and a coward, for in his place I would have stolen anything from anyone to satisfy my children's hunger – only a worthless degenerate could tolerate such misery and torment and do nothing about it. I would like to put the most honest of our Ministers in that family's place and see if he wouldn't become a robber and a thief, and a dangerous one – unless, of course, he could behave as despicably towards his children as the father of that girl did to his.

Instead of the boiled pasta water I told my wife to give the girl a kilo of pasta which we had in store, as well as some oil and a piece of bread, and I told the girl to tell her mother to have that instead of the water.

As soon as the girl had gone we both felt tears in our eyes and my wife got our own meal ready, though it now only consisted of pasta since we'd given the bread away. But as soon as we began to eat my wife started telling me she wasn't hungry, and she made up all kinds of excuses and when she thought she'd convinced me she said, listen, as I'm not hungry can I give my food to those children?, and I understood why my wife wasn't hungry, and I said I wasn't hungry either and told her to give them my share as well, and so we spent the third night of our married life with empty stomachs, but at least me and my wife would have the memory of being able to satisfy the hunger of those poor for one evening.

A few days later the owner of the house had the family evicted, probably because they hadn't been able to pay the rent, and he sent the bailiffs and they threw out the few things that were left in the house, an old bed and a few chairs, threw them out.

Santuzza

DANILO DOLCI

I can't go gleaning any more because I haven't got spectacles, I can't work any more, I can't see anything far away, only near-by. I used to go gleaning in all the fields every year, I would leave at three in the morning, or two, the earlier I went the more I could collect. My back used to ache with bending over all day long, but at least I got something to eat. How else could I have lasted in winter? I've been a widow for twenty-four years, and some years there was very little wheat, some years there was more. If the corn was heavy we'd pick up eight kilos in a day, if it was thinner, five or seven kilos. When we got it home we'd thresh it with a wooden stick to separate the grain, then take the straw away. When there was any wind we tossed it in the air with our hands. We winnowed it with a sieve to get rid of the chaff, and at last there was the wheat, nice and clean.

This year I've tried but I can't pick up a thing. For four days I've gone to the fields, but I wasn't able to see anything and so I've brought nothing back. I can only see straw and stubble, a while ago when I bent down low to see if there were any ears of wheat left in the stubble a piece of straw went in my eye. That was about six months ago but it still feels as if I'd been hit, as if I'd been punched in the eye. From a distance I can't recognise people any more. I keep wanting to rub my eyes, and I try to clean them with my handkerchief to clear them but they always stay cloudy. Here, when you have no money, you're set apart, and you stay at home. If only I could gather wheat I could sell it and buy myself some spectacles, then I'd be able to work again. I used to go gleaning for a whole month. I'd gather tomatoes, those dry ones, and do other jobs as well. When I can work I'll have money, and then I can buy myself a pair of spectacles and work, I'm still fit to work. But when I haven't got work all I can do is stay put. They told me that with spectacles your sight has a rest and comes back.

Here we're all poor. Who can I ask for help? My daughter's married, her husband couldn't find any work here and had to go away to France – if my daughter had any money she'd give me some. But how can I ask her to give it to me? If she was still single I could . . . But now that she's married, would it be right? She hasn't been able to help me anyway. Shall I ask the priest? But I don't know whether he has anything to do with this. The Eca?* I don't know what that is really, or what it's supposed to do. Shall I ask the mayor? But when I needed medicine once he told me there was no money. For my sight I must get spectacles, so I'll have to go to Palermo. If I go by coach it'll cost eight hundred lire for me alone, and sixteen hundred lire if my daughter comes with me. And on top of that comes the price for the spectacles, I don't know how much they cost, I've never bought any. I've heard that they cost ten thousand lire – I know someone who once had a cataract and got spectacles for it and he said that they cost eight thousand lire, or was it ten thousand? I don't know, I get confused. When I have something to eat my sight seems to clear a little, and that cheers me up.

* *Ente communale di assistenze* – Communal Assistance Board.

Antimony

LEONARDO SCIASCIA

*The Italian edition of this story is prefaced by the following lines in
English from Archibald MacLeish's 'Conquistador':*

> 'And the Cardinal dying and Sicily over the ears –
> Trouble enough without new lands to be conquered . . .
> We signed on and we sailed by the first tide . . .'

*In a note the author explains: 'The sulphur miners of my district call
antimony* grisou, *and the story is current among them that the name
derives from* anti-monaco: *that in the old times the monks worked it
and that they died from handling it carelessly.* To this one must add
that antimony is also used in the composition of gunpowder and
typographical characters, and, in former times, the composition of
cosmetic preparations as well. These reasons were suggestive enough to
lead me to entitle this story* Antimony.'

I

They were firing from the campanile: in response to our own
movements came short bursts of machine gun fire or accurate rifle
shots. The entire village consisted of one single road with a blind
ending; low, white houses; and at the far end a church with a
rough sandstone façade, two ramps of stairs and a simple brick
bell-tower with three arched openings. They were firing from this

---

* The notion that the word *antimony* is derived from *anti-monk* is certainly not restricted
to the sulphur miners of Agrigento: the *Shorter Oxford English Dictionary* states that 'in
popular etymology, antimony = antimoine, monks-bane'. *Brewer's Dictionary* explains that
the word probably comes from the Arabic, since it was introduced through alchemy, and
that *Johnson's Dictionary* derives it erroneously from the Greek *antimonachos* (bad for
monks).

campanile. We had entered the village believing that they had given it up completely, but the machine gun bursts and the rifle shots made us stop by the first houses. Our company was ordered to go behind the church to the other side of the village: but behind the church was a protruding rock which looked as if it had been sawn off, it was so smooth and sheer, and the captain decided to make us lie in wait in the graveyard which was on high ground near-by, about level with the roofs of the church and the campanile. When they caught sight of us, they began to direct bursts of machine gun fire at the graveyard.

For more than an hour I had been on my knees behind the pillar of a grave, and I rubbed my face against the marble to get cool. My head felt as if it were frying inside that burning hot helmet, and the blaze of the sun made the air vibrate, like air coming out of an oven. On my right, under the arch of an ancestral vault, the captain and a journalist I knew stood rigid, as if they'd been nailed to the door: the slightest movement would have made them a target. If I turned my eyes to the left and slightly to the rear I could see half of Ventura's face behind a thick slab of marble – in every action we seemed to find ourselves close together. There was a long inscription on the marble and the words SUBIÓ AL CIELO in big letters which at a certain point began to dance before my eyes and in my head as if the letters had come, one by one, white hot out of a blacksmith's forge. For me, I was certain, the hour of ascending to heaven had not yet come; and if it had, it would have been better to go down into the earth where moisture clung to the finest roots. The soldier who had moved from the grave in front of me towards the shade of the chapel had certainly not gone up to heaven: his head was split wide open and his body, which had been quite thin before, had swelled up like a leather bottle; forty in the shade, the captain had said – in the shade of the vault where he was standing.

'Here come the Moors,' Ventura said to me.

They came towards us, running in a crouched position, looking as if they were curled up into balls. The firing from the campanile switched to their direction, and the captain and the journalist stretched their necks like giraffes while their bodies stayed glued to the door of the chapel. A bullet whistled by, close to their heads; the journalist's monacle fell onto the step and shattered with a silvery sound. 'Red bastards,' he said – but he had another monocle in his pocket, and took it out of its tissue paper and put it into his eye. I knew him – he came from my home town and he couldn't live without a monocle. I remembered what he had been like as a young man, in 1922, in his black shirt and boater, an ox whip hanging from his wrist, and always with his monocle. His friends called him The Count to tease him, he was the son of an old money-lender. In the summer of 1922 he had set the doors of the Trade Union Council on fire, and almost burnt the whole town down. Afterwards he had left – I didn't know he'd become a journalist; the last time he had been to our town was ten years before when he'd come to give a lecture on D'Annunzio in the municipal theatre. I like things to do with books, but from his lecture I didn't take to D'Annunzio. I'd met this journalist again in Spain and introduced myself to him, because when you're abroad it does you good meeting someone from home, even though at home I never went near him because I disliked him. He said he was pleased to meet a fellow-townsman who was serving the Fatherland in Spain – 'Bravo,' he said, 'Let's make them feel proud of us.' He didn't understand a thing.

The Moors had lost a few feathers. From where I stood I could see two of them dead, their arms spread out and their faces to the sun: the Falangist hymn began with the words *Face to the sun,* the faces of the dead eaten up by the sun. The hymn referred to the living marching with their faces towards the sun – for me the sun was part of death's coat of arms. Our own machine guns were firing furiously; the arrival of the Moroccans was always encouraging – they seemed to relish risky actions.

There could not be more than four men and two machine guns in the campanile. The machine gun suddenly became silent and only the *ta-pum* of the rifles continued. This *ta-pum* reminded me of a summer day of long ago, when some bandits had fired from the rocks down onto the road to frighten the peasants into leaving their mules behind: my father had explained that it was Austrian muskets which made that noise; it had been in the years after the war, and the countryside around home swarmed with bandits. Behind the tombs the Moroccans began to move, and then they broke cover – more bursts came from the campanile, but the Moroccans took no notice, and the last burst died down: we knew that it was the last, just as a peasant says on the threshing ground 'The wind's going to change, the wind's died down.' Their machine guns no longer served the men in the campanile.

One of our patrols was left in the graveyard, the others ran towards the first houses. Shooting from both sides of the road, and creeping along the house-fronts, the Moors advanced towards the church. From the campanile came rifle shots, and one of the Moors fell headlong onto the cobbled road.

'Good men,' said the journalist.

'They're tarred with the pitch of hell,' said Ventura.

The Moors reached the bottom of the stairway, and only now did I realise that the church looked exactly like our church of Saint Mary at home. There were no more shots from the campanile; then came a piercing shriek like a boy's when he is terrified and on the point of crying.

'They're surrendering,' said the journalist.

The Moors squatted on the stairway, their rifles trained on the church door. I could feel the silence increasing. Whenever there was a surrender I felt a cold shivering inside me, I felt icy blades in the small of my back, a painful lump in my stomach, and dream-things and fantastic pictures came into my head.

The church doors opened with a creaking sound and two people in overalls came out; one was wounded, his face a deadly colour. They were FAI, I knew that from the moment I realised they had no hope of escape and knew it. We all gathered round. The wounded man collapsed onto a step; the other took off the helmet – and straw-coloured hair falling all over the face and the movement of the hand adjusting it revealed a girl. She had large grey eyes. The Spanish colonel began to ask her questions; she answered rapidly, and we could tell that between one answer and the next she pleaded with the colonel for her wounded companion. The journalist explained to us that there had been four, two were dead; she was German.

With a smile on his lips the colonel spoke to the Moors; the girl screamed, and shouting with joy the Moors dragged her away.

The journalist said: 'He's given her to them as a present, they're going to make her give them some fun! She'll get more than she bargained for!' and behind his monocle his eye gleamed with malice.

They also carried away the injured man, who could only groan. Ventura and I sat down on the steps of the church. We took out our tobacco and cigarette papers – my hands were shaking so badly that the tobacco fell on the ground. One or two house-doors were opened, two or three windows displayed red-yellow-and-red flags.

'If he comes into my range at the right moment,' said Ventura, 'I'll bang that journalist from your home town right in his glass eye.'

'And the colonel too,' I said.

'Yes, the colonel too,' he said, 'I'll put them right at the top of my list. I've been making that list for six months now, it's getting too long — I ought to get a move on and start . . .'

Ventura, who had a bit of the mafia in him, would tell me how during the 1915 war his father, his uncle, his uncle's child's godfather and a cousin of his father – in fact all the people from his home town who were at the front together, didn't think twice about getting rid of officers and NCOs who 'stank', whenever an attack gave them the chance to do so. According to him the Italian army must have lost more officers and NCOs through his relatives' bullets than through the Austrians'. But I accepted his story because I found a sort of escape in it, and it helped me to get rid of that lump of terror I felt inside. Ventura was a good companion, and perhaps he told me those things to cheer me up; we had been together since Malaga, and always found ourselves close to one another in moments of danger. We had become friends one day when he had come to blows with a Calabrian who enjoyed watching executions, who said 'I'm going to watch the executions' whenever he had a free moment, as gaily as he'd go to see the fireworks on Saint Rosalie's day. Ventura told him not to talk about executions any more, and if he really had a taste for such bastard's joys he should go and have a look without pestering people who felt sick at the mere mention of such things. The Calabrian reacted by trying to hit him with his

156

bayonet, and Ventura socked him one which made his face swell up. After that scuffle I asked Ventura to have a glass of wine with me: we spent an hour together munching crabs and drinking the good-smelling wine that was like Pantelleria wine, and only then did I begin to understand what the war in Spain was about – I had thought that the Reds were rebels who wanted to overthrow the regular Government, but Ventura explained to me that the rebellion was made by the Spanish Fascists who were quite unable to do the Government in on their own, so they asked Mussolini for help, and Mussolini says: 'What am I to do with all my unemployed? I'll send them to Spain and everything's fine.' Also, it was quite untrue that Spain had a Government of Communists.

'And then,' said Ventura, 'what do the Communists do to you? What are they doing to us, I mean you and me? Communists and Fascists, they don't matter to me – I spit on them both: I want to go to America.'

'How are you going to get there?'

'That's what I've come to Spain for,' he said. 'I'm going to go across the lines: the Americans are helping the Republic, there are Americans fighting in the brigades, and there's one completely American: if they kill me, I mean if you fellows killed me . . .' – the thought that I or one of us might kill him took him by surprise – 'but I'm not going to get killed in this tangle here, I'll get to the States, even if there's a piece or two of me missing, I'll get there . . . My mother's in America, my brother, two married sisters and their children . . . I went there when I was two with my father and mother; then my father died and I got myself mixed up with every hooligan in the Bronx; one night a policeman was killed, and I found myself involved in the affair, I don't really know how, it wasn't me who did the shooting – a fortnight later I was on the boat to Italy . . . My mother wanted to come with me, I was still a boy really, but they persuaded her to stay, some big lawyer was going to see that I could go back, a Senator as well . . . My mother's been chasing that lawyer and that Senator for ten years, and there I was in Italy, desperate, out of work – though they kept me going with their dollars . . . just waiting . . . I tried to get into France several times, but they always fished me out . . . As soon as I heard of the war in Spain, and that they wanted volunteers, I became the most fanatical Fascist at home, and they let me leave with the first lot. But I really spit on Fascism – and on Communism too.'

I thought it had been the wine that had made him want to talk, and open his heart for relief; he shouldn't have spoken like that to me, he hardly knew me! And about such intimate things, such dangerous stuff – it really scared me. But a few days later he told me it hadn't been the wine that had made him talk to me, he had known that he could rely on me, he could judge men. I still believed that it had been the wine and always told him to be careful and not to drink more than half a bottle.

'You know,' Ventura had said to me that day, and the wine was already making him feel great friendship for me, 'You're one of those that Mussolini managed to get shot of – you're one of the unemployed: let's make that poor unemployed chap fight a war, there's no bread for him in Italy – in Spain he'll become a hero, he'll do great things for the glory of the Duce...'

Now, sitting on the steps of that church which was so much like the one at home, rolling lumpy cigarettes between my fingers, I myself felt the need to talk and talk, like a drunken man – about home, my wife, the sulphur mine in which I had worked, and my flight from the sulphur mine into the fire of Spain.

We heard rifle shots. 'They've shot the wounded man,' said Ventura.

'I'll come with you,' I said, 'I'll come over to the other side – so that I won't hear these executions any more, or see the wounded slaughtered, see what I've just seen happening to the German girl – I don't want to see the Moors any longer, the colonels of the Tercio, the crucifixes and the Hearts of Jesus...'

'You won't see the tassels of the Tercio* any more, or the Moors, the crucifixes and the Hearts of Jesus: but no one can take the executions and all the rest away from you.'

I knew it was true. Yet it seemed a great deal to me just not to see any more of those crucifixes that the Falangists, out of piety, had fitted to all the things that spread death – cannons, armoured cars; to stop hearing the great Mother of God invoked

* The Italian unit who wore tassels on their caps in the Fascist style.

by soldiers from Navarra who were shooting prisoners for fun, to stop seeing the blessing chaplains or that monk who had passed through out lines exhorting us with outstretched hand in the name of God and the Virgin . . .

'At home,' I said, 'just now they'll be celebrating the Feast of the Assumption – the Mid–August Madonna as the peasants say. Here they're shooting peasants to the glory of the Mid-August Madonna . . . The peasants walk in procession with their mules all decked out. The mules have bells, and every mule carries a brand-new saddle-bag full of wheat. They arrive at the church and unload the wheat, hundreds of little heaps of wheat, as a thanksgiving for rain which has come just at the right time, for the fact that a baby got over the worms, that a kick from a mule only grazed a peasant's head . . . True, many children die, the wheat may have had the rain it needed but the almonds had a bad frost, it won't be a good year for the olives, and a peasant was kicked on the head or in the belly. But only the good things count when it comes to faith. God has nothing to do with afflictions, it's fate that brings us those. We have a good Sunday meal, with real soup and meat, and my mother says that we ought to thank God for it – they bring my father back burned from antimony and my mother says that a horrible fate has burned him. I would like to show my mother that here in Spain God and fate have the same face.'

'I don't want to know anything about God or fate,' said Ventura. 'Only fools believe in fate. Say you go up to an ant heap and think: Am I going to put my heel into it or not? Is it fate that I'm going to kick it in or leave it alone? If you start to think about fate you'll drive yourself mad standing and looking at the ant heap. As for God, it's more complicated. In the ten years I was out of work I had enough time to think about God too, and I'm convinced that death is God, every man carries within him the God of his death, like a woodworm; but it's not a simple matter, there are moments you wish that death were like sleep, and that something of you could stay in a dream, in a mirror still reflecting your shape while you yourself are far away . . . That's why men make themselves a God. But I tell you — I don't want to know anything about it, I'd feel like a child beginning to walk, and suddenly becoming aware that his mother's hand has stopped holding him, and falling over: then I'd have to walk alone without God – all the better never to have had one. If I had to make myself a God, it would have to be a good God: and in Spain he would certainly have left me by myself. The God of the Tercio and Navarrans is not a good God.'

'I shall tell my mother,' I said, 'that her God's on the side of the Tercio.'

'She'd tell you it's right that way. Perhaps at this moment she's doing her nine days devotion for the Tercio and the Navarrese – the priest will have preached: "And when you do your nine days devotion for the Mid-August Madonna, invoke God's protection and strength for the armies which fight for His name and for His Glory." '

'I hate those Spaniards,' I said.

'Because they've pulled God over onto their side like a blanket, and left you out in the cold. Your God is your mother's God. In the Republic there is no God: there are some who've always known it, like me, and others who are scared of the cold because the Falange has pulled the blanket of God right over onto the other side.'

'It's not only that,' I said, 'they're inhuman.'

'Listen,' said Ventura, 'it's only because of my burning desire to get back to America that I've come here to risk my life in Spain; America is rich and civilised and full of the good things of life; there's freedom there, and from nobody you can become as rich as Ford, or President, or what not. But two innocents are sent to the electric chair, and the whole of America knows they're innocent, the judges, the President, the people who write the newspapers and the people who sell them. To me that seems worse than the executions here. And these two were condemned in a free, rich, well-run country, with all kinds of laws, for the same reasons that the Falangists here slaughter the FAI. Haven't you heard of Sacco and Vanzetti?'*

'No,' I said, 'I've never heard of them.' He told me the story of Sacco and Vanzetti, and there was nothing to be surprised at

* Two young left extremists executed in the United States in 1930 amid great public outcry.

of Sacco and Vanzetti, and there was nothing to be surprised at in Spain any more.

'And think of Sicily,' said Ventura, 'think of the Sicily of the sulphur workers and the land workers who hire themselves out by the day. In winter when there's no work, think of the house full of children who go hungry, the women going about the house with swollen legs because of their sick kidneys, and the donkey and the goat next to the bed. I'd go mad myself. And if the land workers and the sulphur workers one fine day kill the mayor, and the secretary of the Fascio, and Don Giuseppe Catalanotto, the owner of the sulphur mine, and the Duke of Castro, the owner of all the cultivated land – if that happens in my district, and if yours gets stirring too, and if that sort of wind starts to blow over the whole of the island, do you know what would happen? All the gentry, who are Fascists, would get together with the priests, the carabinieri and the civil police, and they would begin to shoot the land workers and the sulphur miners; and the land workers and the sulphur miners would kill the priests and the carabinieri and the gentry; the killing would go on and on, and then the Germans would come and arrange a little bombardment so as to make the Sicilians lose their desire for revolt for ever – and the gentry would win.'

'That's how it's going to end in Spain,' I said.

'Thanks to us,' said Ventura, 'because without Italians and Germans the gentry here would have died like mice. We're really worse than the Moors.'

I should like to remember the name of that village, I only remember that the church was Saint Isidoro's – he is a peasant-saint, but in that church the peasants had used him as a shooting target; the journalist took photographs of Saint Isodoro with his head off so that he looked like a flower pot, and without arms, just like the soldier who lost his at Guadalajara. Sitting on the steps by that church I began to understand many things about Spain, about Italy and about the whole world and the men in it.

At Malaga the Calabrian who went to see executions said: 'It's just like a theatre – the ladies are going too: they stand a little way away and watch, there was one old lady who looked through mother-of-pearl opera glasses.' That old lady became a sort of vision to me, a symbol of savage and fanatical Spain. Now donna Maria Grazia came to my mind, she had let us live in a box-room without windows at her mansion and my mother paid the rent by washing the floors and staircases of the house twice a week; donna Maria Grazia would look at the work with her lorgnette and say: 'You've left these stairs dirty – get into that corner with the floor cloth and go over the drawing room once more' – twice a week my mother would come back completely worn out and so tired she could hardly eat. Donna Maria Grazia didn't have a good opinion of me, and she'd say to my mother: 'Your son is growing up badly, he isn't polite, he hardly greets me, and he dresses as if he were a gentleman. Who knows what wrong ideas he has in his head? You must teach him that everyone should stay where Providence has put him. The poor who are presumptuous always come to a bad end.' And my mother would say to me: 'Greet her, just for me, greet her,' though I had always greeted her, doffed my cap and said good evening – but she would have liked me to say: 'I kiss your hand, madam' – that was why she looked at me through her lorgnette and didn't reply. She would have come to watch my execution through opera glasses.

Until I arrived in Spain I knew nothing about Fascism, for me it didn't really exist, my father had worked in the sulphur mine just as my grandfather had done, and like both of them I worked in the sulphur mine too. I read the papers; Italy was great and respected, she had won an empire, and Mussolini made speeches which were a pleasure to hear. I disliked priests because of what I had read about them in stories, and because of confession – it annoyed me that my mother and my wife should go and tell the priest what went on at home, their sins and mine and the neighbours' too: the women in our parts confess by talking more about the sins of others than about their own. And the gentry annoyed me, living on the income from their lands and the income from their mines; and when I saw them on Sundays, in uniform, it seemed to me that Fascism was dealing them some sort of justice by forcing them to dress up and march about the Castle square in such a foolish way. I believed in God, I went to mass and I respected Fascism. I was fond of my wife and had

162

married her for love and without a soldo in dowry. And I worked in the sulphur mine, one week on night shift and the next on day shift, without ever complaining. But I had a great fear of antimony because my father had been burnt, and in the same mine. It was a mine that the owners had exploited for as long as anyone could remember without any care for the safety of their workers; 'unfortunate accidents' happened quite frequently, either through collapsing walls or explosions of antimony, and the families of miners who were crushed or burnt would deplore their fate. There had been a time, in 1919 and 1920, when miners who escaped from 'unfortunate accidents' blamed not fate but the owners, and went on strike and issued threats. But the time for strikes had passed, and quite truthfully I did not myself believe that a strike was a good thing in so orderly a nation as Italy had become.

On the eighth of September 1936, the day of Maria the Child, when bonfires were lit in her glory all over the countryside around my home town (my mother said later that it was a 'special' day and on special days no one should work), I was on day shift. Day shift meant getting up at three, leaving the house at half past three, walking along the road for an hour and going down the shaft at five. My uncle Pietro Griffeo, my mother's brother, an old hand in the sulphur mines, had been saying for several days: 'Keep the lamps low, boys, there's something about that I don't like' and on that morning he gave his usual warning. Our section was the worst ventilated one; there was no timbering, and the paddings were still incomplete. We undressed, and the air on our naked bodies felt like a wet sheet. Our lanterns were acetylene ones, the administration kept the safety lanterns just as we keep our Sunday best, for appearances, when the inspection engineers came; but quite apart from that the old sulphur workers didn't really like them – when it's your fate, they would say, you die with safety lamps as well – who knows why they disliked them, but they were very fond of their old acetylene lamps.

After our midday meal – bread with salted sardines and a raw onion for most of us – we started work again. Once more my uncle warned 'Low with your acetylenes' and a minute later came a roar of fire from the far end of the gallery – just as I had seen

163

water rushing out of opened lock gates on the cinema screen, so the fire came roaring towards us – I'm not sure it was really like that, but that's how I remember it now. I saw fire all around me, I was utterly bewildered; my uncle yelled 'Antimony!' and dragged me away; I had already begun to run as if in a dream. I was still running when I got out of the mine gates, and I raced barefoot and naked across the fields until I felt my heart was bursting, and threw myself on the ground crying aloud like a child and shaking with terror.

That night I was delirious. I wasn't feverish but I couldn't sleep, every word that was said, every noise I heard, every thought that came to my mind seemed to explode like a photographer's flashbulb; then the flashes went out and I was left with a violet light, the sort of light, I thought, that the blind carry inside them – I had always been frightened of antimony because I knew that it burnt your guts out (that's how my father had died) or your eyes; I knew a lot of people who had been blinded by antimony.

The next morning I felt a hundred years old, and decided I would never go back to the sulphur mine. I knew that there was a war in Spain, and many people had been to the war in Africa and made quite a bit of money and only one fellow from our town had died there. But the thought of dying in broad daylight didn't frighten me and throughout the war in Spain I had no fear of death, only the thought of the flame-thrower made me sweat with terror. I put on my Sunday best and went to the Fascist Party Headquarters. The political secretary was there, I had been to school with him and afterwards he had become a schoolteacher, he didn't dislike me but he feared I might treat him with familiarity as an old school friend and address him by his Christian name – but I spoke to him very respectfully.

I said: 'I want to go to the war in Spain.'

'Well,' he said, 'actually there's something just come in, a request for volunteers – though it doesn't say it's for Spain.'

'Even if it's to hell,' I said.

'Yes, quite so, but what they're after is soldiers, soldiers have preference: you're not in the Fascist Militia.'

'Please enrol me,' I said.

'That's not such an easy thing to do.'

'I belong to the Fascist Trade Union,' I said, 'I've been in the Young Fascists, I've done my pre-military service, and I've been in the Army, and I don't know why they didn't take me in the Militia when I came out.'

'You should have put in for it.'

'Well, I put in for it now. I haven't been in the African war, but I want to be in this one, I think that someone like me has a right to go to war – or else I'll write to the Duce and offer myself as a volunteer.'

That was a good argument – once a workman had written to the Duce about a bonus they didn't want to give him, and had caused trouble which the secretary still remembered; but they'd certainly made that workman pay for the trouble afterwards.

'Let's see what can be done,' said the political secretary. 'I'll speak to the Militia Colonel and we'll see. Come back on Monday.'

They enrolled me. My mother and my wife cried, but I left with peace in my heart. I was terrified of the sulphur mine, and compared to it the war in Spain seemed a picnic.

Cadiz was beautiful – rather like Trapani but even more dazzling on account of the whiteness of its houses. And Malaga was beautiful too during those February days full of sunshine, and that good sun-ripened wine and cognac. From November to February the war was good too, it was good to be in the Tercio with those officers who went into attack without drawing their revolvers, and only a whip in their gloved hands. I saw the whole essence of our war in one man with a goatee whom the Spaniards cheered. He wasn't an officer, but certainly a big shot among the Fascists: on his black shirt he wore the emblem of the Fascio, the cross, and the bow and arrow of the Falange; he was good-looking, and looked very well on his horse. The Spaniards said that he had done great things, and later I was told that a Frenchman had written a book about the tremendous things he had done – I'd like to read it.

In Malaga I first heard about the executions, and later Ventura opened my eyes. But the Spaniards at Malaga cheered us, everyone wanted to speak to us and give us something, and the women smiled at us. The men said 'I'm of the Right' and invited us for a drink. I never knew what they meant, and thought that to say you were 'of the Right' was a sort of Spanish greeting. Ventura explained to me that Fascism was the political party of the Right, and Communism and Socialism were of the Left. All the Spaniards of Malaga were of the Right. Six years later I saw all the Fascists at home calling themselves men of the Left. The town was intact, the promenades joyful with women. But there were interminable shootings.

Up to Malaga I couldn't say I had risked my life. I had only taken part in small actions around villages and little towns, and I had entered Malaga in parade march. The war proper began for me a month later, with the battle for Madrid which was later named after the town of Guadalajara. It is a memory of hell, more because of the wind that blew sharp as a razor, the snow, the mud and the loudspeakers, than the artillery and rifle fire that came from all sides. The loudspeakers drove us mad, the voices seemed to come from the forest, the branches above our heads, on the wind as if they belonged to it, from the snow. The trees, wind and snow would say:

'Comrades, workers and peasants of Italy – why do you fight against us? Do you want to die in order to prevent the workers and the peasants of Spain from living in freedom? They have cheated you! Go back to your homes and families. Or come over to us: your comrades who have become our prisoners will tell you that we have welcomed them with open arms...'

Then there'd be another voice:

'Listen comrades, we have been cheated and betrayed. It's not true that the Reds shoot prisoners. They're better armed than we are, and better fed than we are. It's not true that they have no generals. I have seen them myself and they've questioned me. It is Pinto speaking to you, Calogero Pinto – '

At every name that came over the loudspeakers our officers would say: 'It's a lie. I've seen Pinto' – or whatever he was called – 'fall with my own eyes – he's dead. They're using his identity disc' – and perhaps it was true that they used dead men's identity discs, but I found it suspicious that so many officers should have seen the same soldier fall.

Ventura said to me: 'I'm going to go, I'm only waiting to find out where the American Brigade is, I want to be with the Americans at once.' But he didn't go – I think he felt he couldn't leave us while things were going so badly.

On the fifteenth of March we went out on patrol and stopped at one point, stopped dead in absolute silence as if every one of us had had some mysterious warning. But I think we must actually have heard something, I don't belive in mysterious warnings. We moved on, and then a voice said: 'Throw away your arms.' We moved our heads like puppets to see where the voice was coming from, a volley of shots went high over our heads and the voice said again: 'Throw away your arms and give yourselves up.' The voice and the words were Italian – as calmly spoken as if giving us a friendly invitation. Our lieutenant was taken in and he said: 'Stop joking, it's us.' And the voice answered in amusement: 'Of course it's you, we recognise you very clearly – throw away your arms.' Ventura made a rapid movement and his grenade exploded among the trees. There came a hail of shots, we threw ourselves onto the ground behind the tree trunks and left behind the lieutenant and one man dead. When we got back to our own lines and were drying ourselves by our fire, Ventura said to me: 'When I want to go I'll go – but the man who can catch Luigi Ventura like a fool hasn't been born yet.'

We were in a miserable little house, half of it blown up. The corner that was left would have made a good setting for a Nativity scene – the last piece of roof was mantled in snow, and round about there was snow too, softening the scene of destruction. We were mulling some wine over the fire.

I said: 'They were Italians – your grenade could have killed one of them.'

'I'm sorry,' said Ventura, 'but even if it had been the Americans I'm looking for, I still would have thrown that grenade. Under certain circumstances there's no Italy and no America and no Fascism and no Communism. That's how it was today – there was Luigi Ventura, and there was a chap who wanted to take him prisoner. Once in New York I was in a brawl in a bar, and the police came and made us stand against the wall with our hands up. For ten minutes I stayed glued to that wall and to stand with your face against a wall with your hands stretched up isn't at all nice for a man. And I thought: from today, anyone that tells me to put my hands up – either his skin or mine. Dignity is over when you have to stand with your hands up while someone points a rifle at you. Executions make me sick as well – there's no dignity in putting a man against a wall and shooting him with twelve rifles. People who order executions make an utter disgrace of themselves and so do those who carry them out – disgraced people, that's what they are, people with no honour.'

'There's no honour in killing,' I said.

'There's honour even in killing', said Ventura, 'when you kill in anger – when it's your skin or mine, or when you kill a swine who informs out of cowardice or for gain, or when you kill officers who stink – those you can kill in cold blood too, and still act with honour.'

He regarded it as an honourable deed to kill a policeman in the Bronx, or a policeman in the fields at Naro, or to shoot an officer dead from behind. This attitude wasn't really new to me. It was the same as the foreman's in the sulphur mines who took money from us and from the owners, guaranteed us our work and the owners efficient manpower, and those who didn't pay up 'violated' their honour. Ventura was rather like those people, and in the sulphur mine I should probably have hated him, but in this war his arguments about honour seemed more sensible and somehow closer to true human dignity than the arguments on Fascist banners. For me, for Ventura and for many of us, there were no flags in a war we had gone into without understanding it, and that gradually pushed us towards the arguments and opinions of the enemy. But every one of us felt the need for a pledge of honour towards himself; not to be frightened, not to give way and not to abandon his post. Perhaps all wars are waged like this, with men who are just men, without flags; perhaps for men who fight against one another there is no Italy or Spain or Russia, no Communism, Fascism or Church, only dignity in staking your life honestly and accepting the gamble of death. I say perhaps, because as far as I'm concerned I would have liked to see a true and human flag under which to fight. When the voices inviting us to desert stopped, we heard the tune of the Workers' Hymn over the loudspeakers. The invitations and declarations of fraternity worried me a lot: even true things appear false when shouted over loudspeakers – but the Workers' Hymn made me feel differently. My father had died in 1926, when I was sixteen, and the thought of his death and the way he died never left me; but I had forgotten he had been a Socialist. The sound of that Hymn made me see my father holding me by the hand, I saw the brass band playing the tune and a man with a bow tie coming onto a balcony and making a speech, and my father saying 'Very good' and clapping his hands. But who could remember that hymn? It was fine music and at one point it seemed to disperse dark clouds – the words 'The sun of the future shines upon the flag of the free' truly opened up hope.

But what was Socialism really about? It certainly had a good banner, as my father said, with justice and equality. But there can be no equality if there is no God – you won't found the Kingdom of Equality in front of a notary; only in front of God. Or in front of death, if it's true that we always see ourselves reflected in death. A world of equality would be so unjust that only in the name of God or by reflecting ourselves in death could we live in it. Justice, however, can exist without God, I never believed that God was justice, He is far removed from any hope of justice. My father was not satisfied with justice, he wanted equality. He thought that important lawyers with their large hats and bow ties took the place of God, lawyers like Ferri and Cigna* took the place of God.

But Socialism too must be rather like a religion, a cauldron with many things boiling in it, so that everyone can put a bone in to give the broth the taste he likes. For me it was simply the memory of my father, his beliefs and the way he had died, and the thought that I had risked my life in the same way; and donna Maria Grazia's remark about me 'He has his father's twisted ideas' – whereas I had neither straight not twisted ideas but only a sweet memory of my father and great sorrow at how he had died, a terror of antimony, and a little hope for justice.

After Guadalajara they said we had let ourselves be beaten because on the Madrid front Communism had begun to spread amongst us like a disease. Perhaps they really thought the morale

* Early Italian Socialists.

of our troops had been undermined by all the shouting from the loudspeakers and the leaflets that the planes rained down on us – but it rained bombs as well, and you can't accept truth and bombs at the same time. There were some enquiries afterwards and a few of us were sent home. I remember one day we were made to stand in line and Teruzzi, who commanded the whole of the militia, reviewed us. At one point he stopped in front of a legionnaire and asked: 'Well, what did you come to Spain for?' and the legionnaire began to babble: 'A friend came to see me and said "There's a war in Spain, go and apply." I'd just got married, I had a piece of land for crop-sharing together with my father and brother. When I got married they threw me out, and my father said: "You go and look for a piece of land for crop-sharing on your own" and I said: "You think it's easy to find land for crop-sharing? Where am I going to find it?" and then luckily that friend of mine comes and says there's a war on in Spain.' Teruzzi looked at him as if the soldier had told him a great secret, and his face was thoughtful and serious. They said that before Fascism he had been a sergeant, and I believe that at that moment he understood the soldier as a sergeant, as the poor fellow he had once been, and not as the commander of the militia. But the colonel who was accompanying him said to the legionnaire 'You idiot!' and without saying a word Teruzzi walked on, looking absent-mindedly at the soldiers' faces. Then he stopped again and said: 'You there – let's hear what you've come to Spain for!' By that time we all understood what you had to say not to be called an idiot by the colonel, and the legionnaire spoke up in a firm voice: 'For the greatness of Italy and the salvation of Spain.' Teruzzi gave a sigh of relief, said 'Bravo!' and to the colonel: 'We'll give that man a prize' – and later they gave him twenty-five pesetas. On the other hand the fellow who replied with the story of the friend and the crop-sharing was repatriated. Carried out in this way, of course, the whole investigation was utterly stupid. Later the colonel came on his own to interrogate us, and Ventura, who had the gift of the gab, cut a splendid figure and spoke of the Duce and Fascist Italy and religion like a party secretary and a preaching padre rolled into one – and no one hated Fascism and priests more than he did. As always, the Fascists asked for the lie. Every one of us, except for a few dyed-in-the-wool Fascists, had enrolled for the sake of the money, and been forced into it either by unemployment or by our working conditions. And yet we fought with responsibility, and died. Certainly we were greatly worried by the fact that there were Spanish land workers and miners on the other side and that the Falangists shot them. And though I knew nothing about Socialism, that music and that banner were enough to stir up dangerous memories in me, like the memory of my father.

Guadalajara, the battle for Madrid, was an inferno. After the mild spring in Malaga I wouldn't have believed that such a violent winter was possible in Spain. My lips were cracked and my hands chapped by the snowstorms, and we stood in mud, soaked to the skin. We saw our aeroplanes only occasionally, but Republican ones passed over us as if they wanted to cut off our heads – you really did almost feel your head being torn off. And their armoured cars were like houses compared to our sardine tins. On all the walls they had written: *Madrid is the bastion of Anti-Fascism,* and they fought with great valour and discipline to keep it that way. Up to Malaga we had fought against bands of peasants and workers who came forward without order or caution to be mowed down by our machine guns, or lay in ambush behind low walls in fields, or on roofs or campaniles, and put up a desperate resistance – often they were armed only with double-barrelled shotguns. At Malaga there was a large force of militia men – there were ten thousand prisoners – and they might have been able to put up much more resistance and perhaps even beat us, but they had no idea of order. I knew nothing of war, but their way of moving like a herd in attack as well as in retreat made me feel that they lacked any proper command. Perhaps they threw themselves into war with the same dream of equality that my father had had, and thought that the war might give birth to a world of equality. No officers, everyone an officer – what pleasure my father would have found in throwing himself into that war. But in war someone is needed to give orders, even if he has a head like a watermelon. By now they had learned this lesson and for the defence of Madrid they had disciplined soldiers and good officers. Our officers said that theirs came from Russia and were always ordering executions in order to impose discipline, but I don't think this could have been true, I never saw a Russian prisoner – I saw Germans, Americans, French, and even an Italian prisoner, but never a Russian. The truth is simply that they had realised their error – they had made a bad beginning, but now they knew how to wage war.

If I said that I understood how the battle went and that I had the feeling of defeat I would be saying things I only realised ten years later; in those days I had great admiration for the generals who, out of all that disorder of men and motor cars in mud, in between trees, under snow, wind and fire, mangaged to disentangle something like a front line and could see where we stood, and where the Republicans were. But perhaps they didn't see things so clearly after all, as we were beaten. Or was it General Franco who got us defeated, as the rumour went among us? On the part of the front that his own troops held, he left the Republicans in peace – as if it had been agreed that the battle of Madrid was to be won by Mussolini's men. What is certain is that the Spaniards greatly enjoyed our defeat. Whenever a quarrel broke out in a café between Spaniards and Italians, 'Guadalajara' was mockingly said in order to offend us, and even though I never took part in quarrels that name upset me.

However, we got our own back when the Republican army at Santander would only discuss their surrender terms with Italians – trusting our generals but not Franco's: and I must say I would never have trusted Franco's word either. There were pictures of the young Franco in which he looked like a San Luigi Gonzaga* with his little moustache, and he always had the air of a man who has just finished saying his prayers: he reminded me of don Carmelo Ferraro in the Corpus Domini procession at home, holding the gilded canopy of the Eucharist – every afternoon he used to go to church to lead the recitation of the rosary, and the murmur of the old men and the women followed his fine deep voice; he always walked looking towards heaven, his eyes as if pulled by a magnet towards the sky; he was a money-lender, charging high rates of interest – for fifty thousand lire he got

* A young saint, often depicted with a beaming, rubicund face.

172

an olive grove belonging to Baron Fiandaca which was worth more than a million, he had choked him with interest – and he fleeced the poor with his interest too. Just like don Carmelo, Franco had a full, smooth face with his eyes turned to heaven. I was convinced that he was one of those men who look as if they have stepped out of an altar-piece, and yet do all the evil things a man can do – steal and get people murdered, and then leave legacies to churches and hospitals in their wills. Even the general who spoke every night on the radio was better – Queipo de Llano his name was – he amused the Spaniards vastly, as if they were at a farce in the theatre: everyone knows what he did at Malaga, which was only to be expected from that dog's face of his and the vile things he said on the radio. Franco was serene and elegant, a man who had just got up from his velvet-covered praying stool – no good can ever be expected from a man who prays on a velvet-covered stool. Anyway, the Santander army wanted to surrender to the Italians; the Italians guaranteed the lives of their prisoners, and it gave us some satisfaction that the Republicans regarded us as human. But it was a bitter satisfaction because Franco got up from his praying stool and said that General Bastico was beginning to get on his wick – not that he would have said it like that, I'm sure he would have expressed his anger in a more polite expression. He informed Mussolini that it was insane that an Italian general should defy his orders and prevent him from achieving *limpieza* at Santander – making a clean sweep of that Red town – and would he therefore whistle Bastico back home. Mussolini understood – can anyone imagine he would not have understood the need for *limpieza,* for he too believed in cleanliness. So Bastico went, and the Falange had their fun in Santander as well.

However, while I was sitting on the steps of the church of Santo Isidoro in that village whose name I can't remember, the battle for Santander had hardly begun. It was the fifteenth of August 1937, and we were swarming around Madrid like moths around a light – like moths coming nearer until they feel themselves singeing and swoop away and approach again, and in a sudden gust the flame catches them. That's how it was at Madrid, and the gust of wind was Brunete, where the Republicans took

173

us by surprise, and my admiration for the generals vanished at a single stroke. They took us, as one says, while we were asleep, and perhaps they didn't make a really sweeping advance because they were so surprised at finding an empty space that they thought a trap must have been set for them – and instead there was nothing. They went beyond the Brunete crossroads and halted. Their general, Lister, gave our generals far too much credit on this occasion; like the labourer he had once been he thought, just as I did, that the generals could see everything, and that leaving an empty space like that on the Madrid front must have been secretly arranged beforehand. When he realised that he could have pushed on much further, it was too late. His forces closed in on Brunete where many of our soldiers were, but we were already beginning to counter-attack to prevent a further advance and to break the pincer movement that had closed around our men. We didn't succeed in breaking it, but we forced Lister's army into defence. His initial success, which he didn't know how to exploit, was nullified in ten days, and we began to clean up the small villages again. The one we had taken on the day of the Mid-August Madonna was in the region of Brunete and I seem to remember that there was a small river nearby. We had passed through a place called Maqueda – I was told that a duke from there had been Viceroy of Sicily many years ago, and that's why the finest street in Palermo is called Maqueda – but perhaps my memory is faulty and we went through Maqueda a few days earlier or later. I don't know why, but I have no clear memory of the towns of Spain, whether big or small, not even Seville which is the most beautiful town I have ever seen. My memory for places has never been good, and even less so for places in Spain, perhaps because I found them so similar to places I've known since childhood, my own and neighbouring towns, and I would say: This town is like Grotte, here it feels like Milloca, and this square is just like the one at home – and even in Seville I felt sometimes I was walking through the streets of Palermo near the Piazza Marina. The countryside too was like Sicily: Castile was as bleak and lonely as the country between Caltanissetta and Enna, with the bleakness and loneliness on an even vaster scale; as if the heavenly father, jotting down Sicily, had amused himself with a game of enlarging with one of those apparatuses they sell at fairs, engineers use them – pantographs they're called. What an idea to put a capital city right in the middle of the plain of Castile! It seemed incredible that there was a big, beautiful town in the middle of that desert, rising up like a mirage. But it existed – Madrid, and at night the sky glowed red from the fires our aeroplanes had started. Only occasionally did I think that there were children and old people in that town, women who were crying in distress, and houses where thousands and thousands of people lived. I thought of antimony and fire, but the glow was so far away, and this city of hallucination cost us so much blood and sorrow, that I would usually look at the red aureole of death in the same way as I had looked as a child, from the countryside, at the faraway Catherine wheels on Saint Calogero's day – it was a faraway luminous game of the night.

Evening was beginning to fall upon that little town in Castile or Estremadura, that countryside of clay, thorns and burnt stubble, a countryside that made you think of feudal domains, violent land supervisors, thieving estate managers and the duke who lived in Palermo and Madrid, burning up his rents with women and motor cars, and the peasants who tilled the clay soil under the hostile eye of the land supervisors – a countryside that breathed sadness over me, and gave me the feeling I had had coming out of the sulphur mine, with the smell of the soil and the sun wafting towards me and filling me with a desire to work on the land. We pushed forward beyond the last houses. A man in a dark suit greeted us, his hand held high – 'Viva l'Italia,' he said. Ventura replied quickly: 'Arriba España!'

I usually enjoyed this sort of exchange, with the names of Italy and Spain crossing in salute.

The man stopped and said 'Es magnífico.'

'Yes,' said Ventura.

'Mussolini,' said the man, 'nos ha prestado un gran servicio ... Es magnífico.'

'Cómo no!' said Ventura.

'Una pandilla de asesinos, los rojos' (A gang of murderers, the

Reds), said the man.

'This fellow's beginning to get on my wick,' said Ventura, and he asked *'Por qué?'*

'Qué opinion tiene usted?' asked the man in sudden anxiety.

'Arriba España,' said Ventura.

The man breathed again. *'Falange ama España sobre todas las cosas...'* - and then *'Es terrible estar entre cuatro paredes cuando fuera... Los dias son largos entre cuatro paredes... Pues, ahora empieza nuestro triunfo...'* (Terrible to stay inside four walls when outside... The days are long inside four walls... But now our triumph is beginning...)

'Cómo no!' said Ventura. *'Ahora limpieza: y hombre profético partido único sindicato vertical...'* He read the Spanish newspapers and knew so much.

'Claro', said the man, *'España no se aparta de Dios.'*

'Spain does not leave God,' translated Ventura and to the man he said: *'Naturalmente: así es ... Manos a la obra, ahora: limpieza.'*

'Es magnífico,' said the man again, looking for a moment as if spellbound by a vision, and then moving his hands like a mowing machine-gun: *'Falange fusilará, a todos, a todos... Es terrible estar entre cuatro paredes...'*

'Arriba Falange' said Ventura, turning away from him.

'Viva Mussolini,' the man saluted.

'That bastard,' said Ventura, 'wants to shoot down half Spain to avenge himself for the days he had to stay at home. He's probably the chemist or the medical officer of health or the brother of the archpriest - they're the forces of Fascism at home - altogether a gentleman.'

On the square in front of the church a loudspeaker had been put on a chair; it began to make sounds like the breaking of guitar strings and then, as every evening, a voice announced: *'El excelentisimo señor general don Gonzalo Queipo de Llano, gobernador de la Andalucia y jefe del glorioso ejercito del sur...'* and the slander began.

'That bastard taught me every Spanish swearword I know,' said Ventura.

II

Zaragoza was full of prostitutes – never have I seen a town with so many whores. They swarmed about the bars like flies; every soldier found one for himself, and there were thousands of soldiers in Zaragoza. During the Republican bombardments, bars and restaurants suddenly looked like the refectories of monasteries with all the women invoking the Virgin of Pilar and rattling off their prayers, some producing their rosary beads and kneeling. The rapid change from a group of gay, half-drunken women to a doleful congregation of the daughters of Mary had its own mixed savour, like a delicacy made up of different ingredients you wouldn't eat separately, but put together you no longer recognise the flavour of them.

The Virgin of Pilar was protecting Zaragoza. She had already performed miracles at the time of Napoleon, and she continued to give protection with the rank of captain-general of the troops of Aragona (the Falangist ones) and the appropriate stipend. My mother made the sign of the cross when I told her later about the Virgin of Pilar who held rank and pay in the army; she thought that I had invented this obvious piece of devilment just to infuriate her, for the Virgin does not take part and hold rank in a war in which the sons of mothers kill one another, and draw a salary on top of it . . . Only after I swore by the souls of the dead of our family did she believe that such a thing could be true: but as the Virgin of Pilar didn't really receive her pay, which no doubt was drawn by some priest, she had no special obligation to the troops of Aragona, or rather she was thinking of the Aragonans as well as me, a Sicilian, and all those who fought in Spain, and she directed her prayer to God that he might end the slaughter.

Zaragoza was only a short distance from the front line but the war seemed a thousand miles away. Only the occasional bombardment which caused no great damage reminded you that the war was still close by. It had become a war of position, with the lines changing sides, trenches and points taken and given up and re-taken. At Belchite we were in serious trouble, but by mid-September the front line had, as they say, returned to normal. That means we lost a few men and killed a few. The weather was good and cloudless again, the countryside was fresh, the Ebro was like a living vein in the soil. Opposite us was Lister, by a *coup de guerre* we had almost taken him – he had to leave his belongings behind for us, as well as a monkey which was said to be his and which he took around with him as a lucky charm, or perhaps just for amusement. I even have a photograph of Lister's monkey being held by a legionnaire who looks exactly like it – the lieutenant selected him specially – and us in horseshoe formation around him with laughing faces. Lister was a devil – he always escaped us. He was a good commander. I have never seen a picture of him, and I don't know what his background was, whether he was a manual worker or a philosopher – I'd like to know where he ended up and whether he's still alive. I'd like to know so many things about this war, not only about Lister.

When I got back from the front to Zaragoza I always looked for the same woman – her name was Maria Dolores. Her husband had gone to the militia but she had different feelings – her father had belonged to the Catholic party and the Reds had shot him. She hoped that her husband might be dead already, but in any case she felt sure he would not come back.

Maria Dolores was full of hatred – she wanted all those who fought for the Republic to be slaughtered to avenge her father, and to ensure that her husband would not survive her. For her, Mussolini had entered the war in Spain so as to liberate her from a husband whom wine and politics had pushed towards the rabble, and to avenge the death of her father, and she went to bed with the Italians as if she were giving pleasure to Mussolini as well. Never would I have been able to be friends with a Spaniard so full of hatred as she was: but with a woman it was different and for me her hatred played its part in love, not because her hatred of others could have produced love for me, but because of the magic she made out of the hatred, because she was a bit of a witch. The pleasure you find in love is very complicated: it is greater if there is some dark curse in a woman, if there is a core of evil mystery in her; I say the pleasure, because love itself is a much simpler and clearer matter. This woman attracted me more than any other, not only because her body, her eyes, her hair and her voice 'made my blood come alive' as they say at home when a woman attracts you irresistibly; but also because she violently loved all that my own conscience rejected. In those days the thought that my wife could be unfaithful to me, or perhaps was being unfaithful, didn't worry me as much as when I first began to leave home; I had found a strange equilibrium between the crude and confused lust of making love and the painful clarity which this war was beginning to take on in my eyes, and my previous life had become so unimportant, and seemed so far away, that it seemed not to belong to me any longer, apart from the things that had brought me to Spain – poverty, the sulphur mine and Fascism. The memory of my father and his death and the picture of my mother who at the age of sixty, plagued by painful arthritis, had to work half-days in the houses of the rich never left me, though only because I had had the grim revelation that I had come to Spain to fight against their hopes, against the hopes of people like them and myself. My wife, on the other hand, represented a love which became more and more distant, dim and insignificant with every day that passed, and with every letter of hers I received. Her letters were heedless and stupid – she wrote about her domestic troubles as if I had gone on holiday to the country, not to war: that it was a nuisance she had to queue for the money I was earning for her in the war, that some days she was driven almost insane with loneliness, that my mother reproached her for expenses which she thought unnecessary or excessive; she would tell me about the dresses she was sewing and the people she met; she wrote a whole letter about Mussolini who had passed through the railway-station at home, and how she had gone to see him: he was really a good-looking man, better-looking than in photographs, with a pleasant, sun-burned face, and there were so many people at the station that Mussolini at one point was worried that the mass of people might push the boy Balillas and the Little Girls of Italy under the wheels of the train. My mother on the other hand wrote that she was praying on my behalf and also for all other mothers' sons that this war might end soon, and she would say: 'I don't know what your wife is writing about me, but you mustn't think that I play the mother-in-law with her – I only ask her to save, and to realise that the money she's getting is earned by you so bitterly' – my mother couldn't possibly imagine the bitterness of going through a war full of regrets and shame in one's heart, she thought only of the harsh work of war, of shootings and bombs and the death always lying in wait. My mother couldn't write, and she dictated her letters to a neighbour who sometimes amused herself by giving me news on her own initiative; I knew my mother very well – never would she have written to her son at war about what happened at the Festival of San Calogero, or about the bishop who came to our parish for the confirmations.

I had married for love – the love that in our parts springs from furtive looks and encounters without words: every day you walk along a street and suddenly you become aware that there is a lovely girl on a balcony – yesterday she was perhaps still a child; and from that day onwards you look towards that balcony every time you pass, and she looks every day at you; you go to midday mass every Sunday to see her; and in your eyes she becomes more and more beautiful, and you are in love with her and she with you, just from looking. And apart from the fact that she wants you, you know nothing about her thoughts, her life, the things she likes and the things she fears, nothing of her heart, her way of feeling joy or pity at the things that go on in the world. But instead of this, love should spring from the calm discovery that a man and a woman fit well together to face the suffering, beyond everything else the suffering, of life; together for life, and in the knowledge of its pains, in order to help one another in this knowledge; and together in pleasure, which is only a moment, leaving our feelings naked, so that in our hearts we understand each other better. In this way the meaning of love revealed itself to me and I discovered that I did not love my wife. I was therefore contented with pleasure, and a soldier's wench satisfied me, a woman who had the evil of that war within her. I searched for her like a thirsty man, but when I had to return to the lines a few days later, I left her with relief. The thought that other soldiers would take my place in her room and feel that hatred in her, that dark pleasure of her hatred, gave me grim delight.

Ventura went from one woman to the next – once he went with Maria Dolores, they left me at the bar and went away together. I suffered a little because Ventura was my friend, not because she went with someone else. Come to think of it, it was rather stupid. He enjoyed himself at Zaragoza, wanting to make himself forget the war. Each time he had to return to the front he seemed more depressed and angry; he picked quarrels and became increasingly careless in what he said. His desire to get away had apparently left him.

Life at the front in Aragona that autumn was not nearly as hard as it had been in Guadalajara and Brunete – the really dark days were to come in the winter. We were only engaged in small actions, and sometimes I had the impression that they were making us run like a dog chasing its tail, or like a spinning top. There was a certain amount of confusion in our orders, and perhaps Lister knew it. One night we were asleep in a farmhouse near Zaragoza when we were woken up by an alarm call: intelligence reports were spreading that enemy cavalry had infiltrated our lines and occupied a small town that lay within our own defences. In darkness so thick you could cut it with a knife, that seemed to enclose each of us separately, we marched for an hour, and felt the dampness of the night soaking right into our bones. We reached a village full of dogs, so many of them that it seemed as if we were moving in the middle of huge packs. We each tried to coax them – 'Good dog, good dog!' – for fear of being bitten, and threw the pieces of bread we carried with us into the night. In the darkness we could hear the clicking of their jaws as they seized the bread in their teeth, and the violent gnawing of bread hard as bone. We were told to stop – the town in front of us, two and a half or three miles away, was the one that the enemy cavalry had occupied. It was three in the morning and the officers told us to rest as best we could till dawn. In my memory, even now, that movement of men and dogs in the darkness, the calling to the dogs and the swearing, and the gnawing of the dogs, all seems like a dream.

The day broke leaden grey; the dogs yawned as much as we did. Motorcyclists were sent off. Half an hour went by, an hour, they didn't return. The officers conferred together, and a lieutenant, a young Sicilian who was always with the major and whom I rather liked, came and said: 'Twenty men to come with me, to see what's going on.' Ventura was the first to go, and I followed him. When we came within sight of our objective, the sun was already shining down on us, that autumn sun which in Spain just as in Sicily is sometimes worse than the summer's. There was dead silence. It would not have been the first time that militiamen had captured a town and gone off to sleep – that sleep of exhaustion and wine – without posting sentries, and let themselves be taken by surprise in their sleep.

But what about the two motorcyclists who had not returned? With extreme caution we moved in among the first houses. Nothing. On tip-toe we came to a little square: there was a priest with three or four old women, the priest with the old people for the first mass, just as at home. When they saw us appear at the corner of the square, with our rifles at the ready, they almost died of fright. It has never given me so much joy to see a priest as on that occasion – it meant that there were no Reds in the place, or else the priest would not have been there. He was so scared that he looked as stiff and yellow as a slice of frozen cod – it took him some time to reply to the lieutenant's salute. The lieutenant asked about the Reds; the town, he said, had already been reported as being in the hands of the Reds. The priest began to tremble, and instinctively pulled up his robe as women and priests do when they get ready to run. It needed all the lieutenant's tact to soothe him, and to find out that the Reds were not even talked about in this town, nor in the neighbouring ones. And the motor-cyclists? The priest couldn't tell us anything about them either. We went back to the road and marched on. After a few miles we came to another town, rather bigger. A sentry stood beside two motorcycles in front of a villa. Above the gate hung a wooden sign: *Comando*. Irritated, the lieutenant slipped in through the gate, and after five minutes he came out again with a major. The major said plaintively: 'Well, my dear fellow, I just don't understand what's going on. They all take it as easy as they can, officers and men alike. Yesterday a lieutenant said to me "Sir, I'm off" and I say "Where are you off to?" He says "I don't feel well, I'm off to the hospital." I say "But what the hell do you want to go to the hospital for? You're fitter than I am. I'm the one who should be taken there – on a stretcher!" He says "I'm going, I'm not well." Now what am I to do? Break him, that's what I should do. But that's only one story – I can't tell you what I go through. I have the worst skrimshankers in the world here, they must have been hand-picked for me – we'll give this shower to Major D'Assunta because he has such patience and such strong nerves – but my nerves are like guitar strings, I'll take one of that lot and sort him out for good – I'll break him.'

'What about the enemy cavalry?' asked the lieutenant.

'That, my dear boy, is another kettle of fish. Or rather, the same kettle of fish. I have to do everything here myself, every day I go onto the bastions and look around with field-glasses – but that's nothing, I do many other things as well that aren't my job at all. Anyway, yesterday when I looked over there' – and he pointed in the direction of the place where we had met the priest – 'in the valley there, where the stream is, I saw some men on horseback and some men on foot, carrying planks from that ridge up there right down to the bank of the stream. Ah, I said to myself, they want to make me look a fool! So I call everyone to report, and one man says to me: "What's happening with those planks? I've been watching those goings-on for a couple of days." Do you understand, my boy? For a couple of days! And he keeps it to himself, as if he'd seen a pretty girl in Via Toledo!* They take it easy, I can tell you! What sort of war is this? They make it into a holiday in Capri. Anyway, so I send a coded message: "Infiltration by enemy cavalry." Now you've come we'll sort it all out presently.' He passed a hand over his face, which was hard with stubble. 'You haven't a barber by any chance among your men? Mine hasn't turned up for two days, the son of a bitch.'

We sent the two motorcyclists back, and the rest of the battalion joined us. Our major looked through his field-glasses, and patrols were sent out. They came back gay as could be – down in the valley they had found a unit of Requetés† cavalry and workmen putting up a bridge. Major D'Assunta, now freshly shaved, said happily: 'Oh, that's all right then, I was worried they wanted to make me look a fool' – and he began to tell our major about all the troubles he had been having with his men, but more

* This remark reveals the major as a Neapolitan, with his resigned and easy-going sense of humour.
† A clandestine local paramilitary citizen's force which supported the Falangists.

to amuse him than to complain seriously of them, just as a father talks of his sons' misdeeds but deep down would feel sorry if they didn't commit them any more.

'They've been here for a month now, these poor boys; they've settled down well though, they have their girl-friends, their warm beds and fresh eggs; they've made themselves well-liked here, and they're really fond of me, you know – although they sometimes make me wild with rage, in their hearts they like me ... "Sir, I milked that with my own hands" – a nice jug of milk – "Sir, it's still warm" – an egg – "Sir, the chorizo you like, sir" – a sausage as thick as your arm.'

Major B who commanded our battalion (I remember his name but I don't want to write it – I have other things still to tell about him), looked at him with a face like a mastiff about to tear him to pieces at any moment. Major D'Assunta interrupted the story of the attentions of which he was the fond object to ask: 'Do you like chorizo too?'

This was the last straw; Major B's rage boiled over. 'I have not come to Spain to eat chorizo,' he said. 'I've come to fight a war, and to fight it properly.'

'Of course,' said Major D'Assunta, 'we're fighting a war, of course we are, we're fighting a war. What else have we come to Spain for? The Piedigrotta church fête? Perhaps I'm not doing it as well as you are, if by fighting a war you mean ... but we'd better drop that. Anyway, I like chorizo.'

Major B gave the Fascist salute and turned his back on Major D'Assunta.

'Tomorrow,' said Ventura, 'Major D'Assunta won't have fresh eggs or fresh milk – who knows what part of the front he'll be thrown at.'

The motor transport arrived to pick us up, and we went back to Zaragoza.

When I went to Palermo for the first time I was ten years old. I went with my father and a brother of his who was leaving for America. It was the first time I had travelled in a train, and the train, the railwaymen, the stations, the countryside, everything was a delightful novelty to me. I spent the whole of the journey there and back on my feet, looking out of the window. I thought how I would love to be a railwayman when I grew up – and jump off the train a moment before it stopped, blow my horn, shout out the name of the station and leap expertly back onto the train when it moved off. At one stage of the journey the guard shouted: 'Aragona – change here!' and those who didn't want to go in the direction of Girgenti got off and carried their suitcases and bundles to another train which was waiting for them. Later when I used to play with other boys at home I repeated that call, which was indeed the voice of fate itself, fate which caused some people to be born or brought to live east of Aragona and others west, but I cannot now describe exactly the sort of attraction this call had for me then. I remember the little town of Aragona as you see it from the train, a few minutes before it reaches the station. You seem to turn round on a hinge, making a half turn around a palazzo which dominates the little town and the barren countryside below. Although it was only a few miles away, I never went to Aragona itself – I only remember the view of it from the train.

In Spain's Aragona, a region which has so many places similar to Aragona in the province of Girgenti, I thought of that journey of long ago and the game I played afterwards with the other boys, and that call was always in my head: 'Aragona – change here!' just as a snatch of a tune sometimes comes into your brain, or the words of a song, and goes round in your head for days on end with variations. I thought: you change – my life changes trains – or am I getting on the train of death – I must change: Aragona – change here – you change ... and the thought became a musical obsession. I believe in the mystery of words, that words can become life and fate, just as they can turn into beauty.

Many people study, go to university, become good doctors, engineers, lawyers, officials, deputies, ministers – I would like to ask all these people: Do you know what the war in Spain was like, what it was really like? If you don't know, then you'll never understand what is happening today under your very eyes, you will never understand anything about Fascism, Communism, religion – you will never understand anything because all the errors of the world and all the hopes of the world were concentrated in that war; like a lens gathering the rays of the sun and kindling a fire, so Spain came alight with all the hopes and errors of the world, and this fire still goes on crackling all over the world. When I went to Spain I could hardly read and write, just enough to read the newspapers and *The Story of the Kings of France** and write a letter home – but when I came home I felt I could read the hardest things anyone could think and write. And I know why Fascism does not die, and if it ever did die I am certain that I know all the things that would have to die with it, everything that would have to die in me and in all other men for Fascism to die forever.

'Today Spain, tomorrow the world' said Hitler on the propaganda postcards that the Republicans dropped on us: he was shown with his arm extended over Spain, and his hand seemed to create squadrons of bombers, and the land of Spain was shown with a wreath made of the faces of crying children. 'Today Spain, tomorrow the world' said Hitler and I knew that these were not words invented by propagandists, the whole world was going to become a Spain, breaking the bank of Spain didn't mean that the game was going to come to an end. Apart from Mussolini, no one was prepared to risk all his cards on Spain. The Germans tested their new intruments of war. We, on the other hand, threw in everything we had, our latest fighters as well as old Austrian guns, the best regimental armoured cars as well as 1914 machine-guns, and our poor soldiers with their grey-green puttees that became soggy in the rain like bread boiled in soup, the poor unemployed of the Two Sicilies.† And on top of that, not even the Franco Spaniards were grateful to us for all our commitment – out of the initials of the Corpo Truppe Volontarie they made up the phrase *Cuando te vas?* – 'When are you going away?' – as if we had come to Spain to annoy them. How I would have loved to see them manage on their own, those priests, gentlefolk, daughters of Mary, boys of the parish club, career officers and a few thousand *carabineros* and Civil Guards, I would have liked to see *them* pitted

* A story book read by every child in Italy.
† Another way of saying 'Sicily and South Italy': Sicily and Naples formerly comprised the Kingdom of the Two Sicilies.

against the peasants and the miners, against the red hatred of Spain's poor. Perhaps, though, they felt the humiliation and shame in having us witness all that misery and bloodshed, like people who are forced to let their friends see the poverty of their homes and the foolishness of their relatives. All that irrational Spanish pride went into their desire to get rid of us. On Franco's side too there were some who were uneasy about what they saw, there were quite a few who said that if only José Antonio* were there everything would be different – without José Antonio the generals' rebellion didn't convince them – 'It isn't right that Count Romanones should own all the land at Guadalajara,' they said – and they were sad to feel that Franco certainly wouldn't rob Romanones of a single acre of ground, and they were ashamed at the way Spain was being torn to pieces by foreign arms – the Germans who flattened whole towns with their bombs as a man on a walk flattens ant-heaps, and the Moors, led by Spanish officers, who were now taking their revenge on the sons of Christian Spain which had rejected them for hundreds of years. When prostitutes and gentlefolk in a conquered town shouted 'Long live the Moors!' as the Moors marched past, I could read shame and hatred in the faces of some of the Spanish soldiers. As far as we Italians were concerned, the fact that we accused them of executing too many people – and it seems that our commanders were always protesting – made the ones who wanted the executions impatient and the ones who didn't want them ashamed. There was therefore no Spaniard who didn't feel irritated by our presence.

At Zaragoza all these feelings and resentments came to a head, perhaps on account of the prostitutes, because when close to a woman, whore or not, every man wants to prove himself. And then there was the wine, with that moment of truth wine brings just before the glass that makes you drunk. At Zaragoza there were also Moors and Germans, Requetés and Falangists, Spaniards from Aragona and Spaniards from Andalusia and even among us there were Fascists who had been Party members from the beginning, and North Italians who had enrolled to fight anti-Fascism

* José Antonio Primo de Rivera, founder of the Falange.

187

in Spain and looked at unemployed Sicilians in the same way as Castilians looked at Moors. And with wine within and a woman beside him, everyone became even worse or better than his normal self.

I say that if I had brought the dullest peasant from my home town to the front line in Aragona – the 'darkest' as we say, the most ignorant, the least aware of what goes on in the world – and if I had said to him: 'Now guess which side has the likes of you, and go and join them', he would have gone without hesitation to the Republican trenches. He would have done so because on our side the ground was almost all left uncultivated, whereas on the Republican side the peasants worked even under artillery fire. It seemed the Republicans had distributed the land among the peasants, and the old peasants – the young ones were all fighting – applied themselves to their piece of ground with such passion that nothing could keep them away from it, not shell-fire, not the thought that from one moment to the next the land they tilled could be turned upside-down into trenches. On a clear morning, from a hilltop and with field-glasses, I could see the peasants behind the Republican lines in their black trousers, blue shirts and straw hats with their ploughs pulled by mules, a pair or just one – those cross-shaped ploughs with a ploughshare no bigger than a hatchet, that the peasants where I come from still use, and that leave only a scratch of a furrow and hardly take the dry crust off the ground. Ventura had a pair of field-glasses and it gave me pleasure to watch that ploughing: I forgot the war and thought I was at home. The countryside was lovely in the autumn, with the patridges rising suddenly and the light mist letting the earth shine through in browns and blues. Aragona is a hilly country, and the mist gets trapped and makes the hills even lovelier: it isn't a beauty that strikes you at once, it's beautiful in its own special way and I think you have to have been born in a country like this to see its beauty and to love it.

The front line was a broken line like the Greek key pattern on a general's uniform. There had been no large-scale movements since the beginning of the war, and Belchite hadn't produced much change. There were actions where there was such an infernal din that you'd have thought the front would have been carried forward by God knows how much, or back to the houses of Zaragoza, but everything came to nothing – we ended up occupying the trenches which had been held by the Reds up to the day before, or the Reds ended up occupying ours – and then we'd go back again to our old trenches. Ventura enjoyed this type of exchange because he found American newspapers and books in the Republican trenches, and he loved everything American.

This situation went on till the beginning of December. Apart from the town being so near, and the relaxation and the women that Zaragoza had to offer, the Aragona front didn't really have any advantage. When a war stagnates for months on end in the same places, even if the risks are only stray bullets and patrol skirmishes, you feel the nausea of war, the real nausea, in your throat, like a doctor making you sick by thrusting an instrument down your throat. The earth smells of bad eggs and urine and seems to be rotting, it's as if you're cutting trenches and communication lines into sick flesh, into a putrescent tumour of the soil. In fact this deathly smell doesn't belong to the earth but to man, going back to the wild state and making his den in it, digging his den and spreading his smell like any other wild animal. I believe that nothing is more degrading for man than trench warfare: to be compelled to live in his own stench, to eat his food while the ground breathes out vomit and faeces, greedily drink water that seems to have been collected drop by drop from the slimy discharge of a horse-pond.

The snow that brings happiness when it falls and covers the roads and the countryside and preserves a clear outline of every object, a token of brightness that sends joy into all hearts at home when it falls and makes you discover your own house as if for the first time, as if it were some wonderful boon to live in it – this same snow brings despair to the trenches. The man of the trenches looks at it with the same eyes as a fox standing at the entrance of his earth.

The offensive launched by the Republicans against Teruel, in spite of all it cost me, saved me from a terrible winter in the trenches. I should have gone mad if I had been in a hole of a trench for the two months of December and January, with nothing but the wind howling over a world of white death.

189

Teruel is a town situated as high up as Enna, and about the same size. Since the beginning of the war it had been in the hands of the Falangists, and the Civil Guards had simply slaughtered the Reds – not only the ones in the town. The militiamen who hurried along to occupy the town were deceived by the Civil Guards, who pretended to have remained loyal to the government, and were killed like mice. Teruel was well situated to keep Valencia under the threat of attack, and the Republicans decided to seize the town from Franco. From the Republican side this was a strange war – I should have very much liked to be in the thick of it. It was as if facts could be made by words – as in religion or poetry where words make things holy or beautiful, bread becomes the body, blood and soul of Jesus Christ, and a piece of country or a town that you hardly looked at before now expresses beauty because poetry has come to it. I don't know whether I am explaining this clearly enough: I mean to say that from certain slogans they had written on walls or on posters, and from their leaflets, I had the feeling that the outcome of an event was already decided even before the action that was meant to decide the outcome had begun; I imagined that for every soldier of the Republic the words of those slogans took on the truth and the beauty of destiny, and became decision and power. *Madrid es el baluarte del antifascismo* (Madrid is the bulwark of Anti-Fascism) . . . *Teruel sera hoy nuestro* (Teruel will be ours today) . . . Phrases like these gave me a sense of destiny. The words flowed quickly, but a few words or a phrase would emerge as if carried on the crest of a wave, and engrave themselves with the strength of truth or faith. The Commissar of the Nineteenth Army Corps said beautiful things in one proclamation – the offensive was already launched and the Commissar said: '*Que en estas tierras ásperas de Aragón, sea donde florezcan las primimicias de nuestra victoria definitiva*' ('Here in these arid lands of Aragon will flower the first of our decisive victories') – but these were only flowing words, the certainty was in words that were plain but essential – *Teruel sera hoy nuestro.*

On the fifteenth of December 1937 the Republicans launched their attack on Teruel: not that it was a surprise to us; it was a war in which there were no surprises, on one side or the other.

There were as many spies in Spain as maggots in a mouldy cheese. In fact, they got us moving before the fifteenth. During the last few days we had Anarchist militia in the trenches opposite us, men who amused themselves by shooting hundreds of shots over our heads every morning, and afterwards hurling first brotherly invitations and then furious contempt at us through their megaphones: in short, they were men who would have come over for a game of cards if we had invited them; and if they constantly put bullets a hair's-breadth over our heads, it wasn't so much that they wanted to kill us, but that the Spaniard can't resist the temptation to pull the trigger once he has a rifle in his hand. The Anarchists had a definite preference for hand grenades: only the distance persuaded them to use their rifles. Their yielding to the temptation to shoot or throw grenades even at the most unsuitable moments led to countless actions that ended in bloody failure, especially at night, when a rifle-shot or the bang of a grenade would alert us just in time to receive them with deadly fire. However, one cannot deny the possibility that some of them warned us intentionally; Franco fifth-columnists infiltrated the Anarchist battalions by taking advantage of the fact that the true Anarchists were so insane and so absurdly courageous that they hardly noticed it when someone gave us a warning, whether it was through impatience or treachery.

I liked the Anarchists – I mean the true ones. But you couldn't possibly ever win a war with such men – on the contrary, you would be bound to lose. Events convinced me that if the Republic had had more Communists and fewer Anarchists, Franco would never have won. Just as you can't live with others if you tell them everything you think of them, so you can't fight a war like the Spanish war by throwing bombs under everything you hate. The Anarchists hated too many things: bishops and Stalinists, statues of saints and kings, convents and brothels; they died more for the things they hated than for the things they loved, and for that reason they were insanely courageous and only too ready to sacrifice themselves; each one of them felt like Christ, ready to redeem the world with his blood. And of course you can understand that someone who wants to be crucified, and regards himself as a symbol of sacrifice, doesn't need officers to tell him when to move and when to stand still. It's possible that I am wrong as I'm judging entirely from their actions and I don't know anything about their doctrine, but it seems to me the Anarchist regards himself as a bomb which is made to be hurled and to explode; and just as in action you're impatient to hurl the grenade in your hand at the enemy at the first sign of movement, so the Anarchist is impatient to hurl himself and explode against the objects of his hatred. You could ask an Anarchist in the trench opposite for his ration if you were hungry, and he'd come over and bring it to you cheerfully – even give you his rifle if yours had jammed, but a minute later he'd come over even without a rifle and attack your trench with all his hatred.

Insincerity is necessary, even in such a war as that one, and the Communists knew it. If they had been in control from the beginning, there would have been Te Deums and not target shootings in the churches of the Republic, and they would have found priests by the wagonful who would have sung mass for the Republic without hesitation, instead of ending up in front of a platoon of militiamen. The Spanish middle classes, the good middle class people who go to mass, killed peasants by the thousand simply because they were peasants. The world closed its eyes so as not to see. But when the first priest fell before the Anarchists, when the first church went up in smoke, the world jumped up in horror – and sealed the fate of the Republic. But when all is said and done, killing a priest because he's a priest is more justifiable than killing a peasant because he's a peasant: the priest is a soldier of his faith, while the peasant is only a peasant, but the world doesn't want to know it.

Teruel was the seat of a bishop who was in the town when the Republicans tightened their pincers of fire. There were also women and children, soldiers and Civil Guards who couldn't escape, but the whole of Franco's Spain mourned only the bishop. They said that the Reds had shot him, but I read a year later of the death of the Bishop of Teruel: the Anarchists had killed him before passing into France, and as not even a bishop can die twice, it's obvious that the Republicans didn't murder him when they took Teruel.

When we occupied a town the gentlefolk came pale and flabby

out of their hiding-places, the priests so thin with anxiety that their cassocks seemed to hang from a clothes-peg, and wealthy women with their large eyes and faces haggard with fear, and those gentlefolk came out as if to watch a gala bullfight, and the priests were ready to grant ultimate absolution to any Republican who wished to receive it. One day at Zaragoza I saw people swarming in front of the Grand Hotel and I thought it was some sort of elegant function, but instead they had come to see the prisoners walk past on their way to execution – a hundred men or so, in threes tied together with ropes, the Moors with rifles at the ready around them, and in front of the procession an officer with a long-barrelled pistol in his hand and a priest with his surplice on his back; among the prisoners there were mere boys who stumbled along in a trance, and only the firm step of the older condemned men pulled them along in fits and starts on that terrible march. When I saw that sort of thing I gave myself bitter comfort with the thought that the Republicans would come back, even if only for a few hours. Of course, if I had been on the Republican side, and seen a string of priests and gentlefolk roped together walking towards their execution, I would have felt horror too. And yet it was a different matter to see people go to their death who were just like myself, people who had left their pick or their plough to fight their own war. And that was why I found a certain justice in the fact that the Republicans should take Teruel, take by surprise people who believed themselves victorious and safe, middle class people and Civil Guards who had committed the most outrageous savageries against the lower classes. A civil war is not as stupid as a war between nations, Italians against British, or Germans against Russians, and I, a Sicilian sulphur miner, murder an English miner, and a Russian peasant shoots a German peasant. A civil war is far more logical, every man is prepared to shoot for the people and the things he loves and for what he wants, and against the people he hates. And no one makes a mistake in choosing which side to be on, only those who shout for peace make a mistake. I believe that of all Mussolini's sins, bringing thousands of Italian poor to fight against the Spanish poor will never be forgiven. In spite of its cruelty, a civil war is a kind of moment of truth, as Spaniards call the critical moment of the bullfight. People for instance say 'police' contemptuously and despise the arm of the law which safeguards the public's peace, but this contempt seems unjust and uncivil, all the more so if you consider that a policeman is a man of the people. But civil war soon makes you understand what a policeman is, and why people despise him. I have asked myself frequently what reasons the Civil Guards had to be on Franco's side. They betrayed their oath of loyalty to the Republic, as well as betraying the very people whose sons they were. It wasn't that they were forced by circumstances to stick to Franco, or for fear of their officers, or for the sake of obedience; they risked their lives deserting from the Republic, a few at a time or in small groups. The only reason could have been this: they were policemen with all the malice and wickedness that people attribute to policemen, and they knew that in Franco's Spain they would be able to go on being policemen, spreading fear and raising themselves from the scum they were to a position of powerful authority over others. The Spaniards say 'with respect' whenever they mention the Civil Guards, just as our peasants do when they name certain parts of the body or unclean things – not all Spaniards, of course.

At Teruel the hour of death struck for many Civil Guardsmen ('with respect') but to their sole honour it has to be admitted that they were not cowardly in war, they too knew how to fight and how to die. For that matter I never saw a Spaniard who was afraid of death in the whole of the war; from the moment they became prisoners they would be indifferent to their fate, and even look at us with ironic sympathy; you could see that the youngest ones – and there were many boys in this war – would have wept if they had been on their own, but they learned stubbornness from the cool bearing of the older ones. Ventura said that of all people the Spaniards show the greatest dignity in the face of death.

When an army is launched in a major offensive, as the Republican army was against Teruel, an army on its flanks can't do much to stop it, unless the resistance of the forces against which the offensive is directed is prolonged. I don't know anything about the art of war and this statement is based on the single experience of Teruel: we stood, as you might say, on the flanks of Lister's divisions, like a dog running alongside a motor car – the car accelerates and the dog realises that he can't keep pace and stops, panting, by the roadside. In a little less than a week the Republicans took Teruel, and it took another week before we could even counter-attack Lister in earnest.

I had thought that Spain couldn't give us more snow or wind than at Guadalajara, but at Tereul it was even worse. I felt as if I were made of glass, and the wind cut me like a diamond; the images my pupils gathered seemed to break up like spiders' webs, as if they were on a pane of glass which a bullet had hit in the centre. Perhaps these impressions come to me from the sound that the continuous wind made, which was like the sound of glass-cutting, and from the glassy creak of the snow under our feet, and from the prickling of the tears in our eyes.

Below Concud which Lister held like a bulldog, I spent the most terrible Christmas of my life. All the ideas of peace and home, midnight mass, the Christmas game of seven-and-a-half around the fire, the smell of the capon boiling in the kitchen, the colour of the oranges on the white tablecloth came to my mind in contrast to the reality of the war. Our feast in a stable half-demolished by gunfire consisted of an acid-tasting wine which still savoured of must, and a couple of packets of American cigarettes. Each of us saw himself reflected in the others, with a beard, shiny eyes and a blanket around his shoulders: we looked like prisoners, not combat troops, and in fact we felt like prisoners too, not only because the Reds were winning and we might fall into their hands at any moment; we felt like prisoners on account of the war we had been made to fight, those of us who understood it because they understood it, and those who didn't understand it because they didn't understand it. Altogether it was not our war, either for those who thought that fighting *against* Franco would make it a good war, or for those who felt that it was the sort of mange the Spaniards should be left to scratch on their own. It occurred to me, that Christmas night, that in every soldier the war produced thoughts which in one way or another revealed the face of Fascism: for most it was a face of madness, the madness of a man who led the destiny of millions of Italians on the advice of bullies and fools and had brought them to the brink of God knew how big a precipice.

Christmas and wine produced logical reasoning in Ventura. There was a thread, he said, between Mussolini's folly and that of millions of people who at this moment were walking to church to celebrate the birth of Jesus, and that thread was in the hands of the clever; they had pulled that thread – and the war in Spain exploded. Jesus Christ, he said, was born in a stable like this one; then came the clever ones, and they erected golden pillars, put a golden roof on top, and built a church; and then they built their fine big houses beside the church and built a town, the town of the clever. Comes the peasant from the country, and sees how lovely the place is, and says 'I would like to stay here'; and the clever ones take him to the church, show him the stable and say: 'You have a stable, and you want to come into our houses? Just look where Jesus wished to be born, so that he could be like you: don't offend him by leaving your stable!' The peasant returns to his stable, but afterwards he thinks: 'But if Jesus Christ wanted to be born in a stable, perhaps he wanted to show that it's not right to keep people in a stable.' And he goes to the big house and says: 'Let's put things to rights, because they don't seem to me to be going the way God wants them to.' The clever ones get angry but they say: 'If you want to sort things out, you can rely on us.' Then they call Mussolini.

'And Mussolini begins to sort things out with a big stick,' a man from Palermo chipped in, 'just like that: I remember my father came home one day – I wasn't ten at the time – he had a slash in his face and he kept on being sick the whole day long and nearly died from the castor oil they poured down his throat. He told us he'd been arguing with a man who said the railwaymen on strike ought to be hanged, and the man called his friends and they knocked my father about. That's what it's like – as soon as you begin to argue, it's the big stick.'

'Let's stop all this talk,' said a Neapolitan sergeant who had a lot of children and his wife and in-laws to keep as well, the whole battalion knew of his troubles by now. 'Let's leave it at that, it's Christmas, it's a family feast – at Christmas and Easter everyone should be with his own people, so let's be with our families in thought.'

196

'What are you thinking about them?' someone asked jokingly. 'Just now your in-laws are feasting, and perhaps they're saying "Let's drink to that fool who went to war to keep us going."'

'You don't know my in-laws,' said the sergeant. 'You think you're making a joke to annoy me. But they really do think like that, and if I got killed tomorrow they'd feel they'd hit the jackpot! For heaven's sake don't make me think of them.'

'You shouldn't think of them either,' said Ventura. 'Think of Mussolini instead. What would you say to Mussolini if he suddenly appeared right here in the stable?'

'I would say to him: Duce, thou standest for all of us.'*

'And Mussolini would say to you: Bravo, go on fighting in this little war. Meanwhile I'll get another one ready for you – a bigger one with any luck!'

'Mussolini thinks of nothing but war,' said a soldier from Catania.

'Long live our Duce,' said the sergeant from Naples, 'Salute to Mussolini, the founder of the Empire.'

On the twenty-eighth of December we attacked Lister in strength – the offensive broke against Lister's positions like a jug breaking against a wall; however, news reached us that the Republicans were yielding on the opposite side. The journalists who went around with us looked through their field-glasses at Teruel and began to write in their papers that Franco had retaken the town. The war in Spain had taught me not to believe them. Theirs is a salesman's trade: out of a heap of stones they make a garden, and a horse fit for slaughter becomes Astolfo's wonder-charger. Teruel was not retaken until the end of January 1938 – I don't know the exact date but it's definite that the Republicans resisted until the eighteenth of January, because after the eighteenth I left the Teruel front – and the war in Spain – for good.

Early in January Ventura found out that the American brigade had gone to the front. He didn't say anything about going – he only told me that the Americans were there and I didn't ask any

* Mussolini was frequently greeted with this solemn phrase.

questions. I saw him for the last time on the fifteenth. We were crawling up a steep slope in the gathering dark and machine-gun bullets were exploding in the air above our heads like sparks flying off a grindstone; they were special bullets – Ventura said to me 'They don't kill, but mind your eyes', he was just by my side, but a moment later he had gone and I never saw him again. The day before, something had happened that had shaken me very much, and made my admiration for him increase enormously. We were engaged in a small-scale encounter, standing among some trees that were stripped of every branch by shell-fire, and thick snow was coming down from the skies as if through a sieve, when a Republican soldier appeared like a ghost – he had his rifle on his shoulder and was holding his hands up, and he said 'Fascista, Fascista,' his face open wide in an anxious smile. Major B fired, the smile on the soldier's face closed like a zip-fastener, his eyes looked like the eyes of a man feeling his foot slip while standing on top of a ladder; he fell to his knees. Major B was a great marksman and fired two shots holding his left hand sideways over the pistol in Tom Mix style – fortunately for him the Red soldier was only a couple of steps away. It all happened as quickly as the flash of a photographer's bulb, for ten seconds or so we saw it without taking it in, just as a camera is only an eye that collects pictures. When we took our eyes off the body which was lying face downwards on the snow, and looked one another in the face, the Sicilian lieutenant, the one I liked, was beginning to sag at the knees just as the Red soldier had done a moment before under the major's fire; horror and disgust were written on his face. Major B noticed this and gave him a furious look, the lieutenant pulled himself together and looked upwards so as to let the snow fall on his face. 'We cannot afford the luxury of keeping prisoners,' said the major; the lieutenant's reaction had obviously got on his nerves.

A couple of hours later one of our patrols came back bringing two prisoners with them. I thought the major would shoot them, but instead he asked whether they had been taken armed, as Franco had promised since Gaudalajara that he would spare the lives of Reds who let themselves be taken prisoner without their arms; but the two had been taken with their rifles in their hands.

The major looked at the lieutenant in a way that suggested that what he was going to do was for his own good, that it was necessary he should get used to certain things; he gave him the order to take the prisoners away and liquidate them, and get them buried as best he could. For a moment the lieutenant seemed on the verge of showing his fury, but he said 'Yes sir', called the four of us who were nearest to him, and with the prisoners in front we marched off. Ventura hadn't been among those he had called, but he came with us all the same. We were all full of terror, us six Italians just as much as the prisoners themselves, two boys who knew they were about to die and were crying silently as children do when they're tired of crying aloud. The lieutenant held his pistol in his hand, shaking all over, and drops of sweat ran down his face like tears; he looked at us and then at the prisoners with an utterly bewildered expression. After about a hundred metres he stopped and said 'Here', we stopped too with the prisoners, and one of them asked the time, and Ventura looked at his watch and said five past eleven, then he told them to move forward: *'Más adelante'*, and said to the lieutenant: 'Further on', the lieutenant obeyed and we set off again.

Ventura said to the prisoners: *'Calma: nada que temer'* and they looked at him without understanding, with the eyes of animals suffering unspeakable anguish.

A bit further on Ventura halted them. We were behind a hillock, with bushes thickly covered with drift snow all around, the lieutenant and Ventura looked each other in the eye, then Ventura turned towards the prisoners and said: *'Con cuidado: a la izquierda'* – 'Be careful, turn to the left' – and motioned with his left hand that they should turn to the left.

The prisoners stared in disbelief and hope at the same time, but they didn't move. *'A vuestras casa – adiós,'* said Ventura.

The boys looked at one another, beginning to understand, and ran off to the left, turning round again and again to look at us; we stood as still as statues while they disappeared behind a hedge. Ventura took the pistol out of the lieutenant's hand and fired four shots into the snow, then he handed the pistol back and the lieutenant mechanically put it back into its holster.

'Let's have a smoke,' said Ventura.

The next evening he had disappeared. He was reported killed – there was always someone who would say 'I saw him fall with my own eyes', but I searched for him and looked at the dead one by one, and didn't find him. Perhaps he really is dead or ended up a prisoner, or perhaps he managed to find the Fifteenth Brigade, the American one – but I've asked all the Sicilians from America I've ever met afterwards, and no one has ever been able to tell me anything about Ventura. I only hope he is alive, and with his relatives in the Bronx; I hope he's a gangster now, or selling beer or ice cream as he always said he would; I hope he is alive and happy.

On the eighteenth of January another big offensive was launched. After the first thrust forward, our unit was brought to a halt by a machine gun that fired accurately at us in between some trees with those explosive bullets. I was behind a tree, and just as they say about the ostrich which believes it has found cover by burying its head in the sand, I thought that with my head under cover the machine gun wouldn't be able to get me; I was lying face downwards and stretched my left hand, which had fallen asleep, outside the cover of the tree. Suddenly my hand felt as if the air around it had turned into boiling water. Unexpectedly seeing yourself with a bleeding hand, a hand that isn't a hand any longer, you feel as if you're being hurled out of yourself: like the film trick when a person looks at himself in a mirror and the image in the mirror walks away while he's standing still.

I dragged myself behind the lines. The fingers I had lost burned painfully, I had the curious sensation that the fingers were still there and burning. In the field hospital the doctor began to work on us, and I felt nothing any more, perhaps I fainted for a moment.

Four days later I was in hospital in Valladolid. The Spanish war was over for me.

III

The Spanish war was over for me: the snow, wind and sun of

Spain, the days in the trenches, the assaults on trenches, farms and houses, the battles for the roads to France and to the Ebro, the pitiful sight of prisoners, the women of the executed in their black dresses with their dried up eyes, the women of the grand hotels and the prostitutes – all these things were over for me. I would see no more of Major B, the officers of the Tercio, the Civil Guards, the Moors, the Navarrese with their Hearts of Jesus, and all the banners of this war, the hope, the hate and the death that invented flags and raised them in the skies of Spain like a ship decked out with festive flags. But inside myself, in my thoughts and in my blood, the war of Spain went on: every moment of my life was connected still with this experience, the experience that had become the roots of my life, silently moving in their obscure nourishment; my left arm had become a dead branch, but the roots of my life were still growing.

This idea of the tree comes from a dream I had in hospital in Valladolid. I was naked, just as at an army medical, and a man without a face touched me with icy hands and murmured to himself, and from his words I understood that he took me for a tree; I wanted to tell him that I was a man, but my voice failed and I felt my words bursting noiselessly in my throat like soap bubbles; the man touched my left hand, which in my dream had become whole once more, and said: 'This one must be cut – it's a dead branch, the tree will grow new branches, the roots . . .' I yelled, voiceless, that my hand was all right, that it was a hand and not a branch, but then everything became dark and in the dark I could hear the click of the pruning shears. During my days in hospital I had many dreams in which my hand was whole again, but they always ended with something falling on top of it and crushing it, or someone wrenching it or cutting it, and then the pain woke me up.

I didn't suffer much from the loss of my hand. I suffered a little when they removed the dressings – under the bandages it felt, I don't know why, as if the hand were still there; the uncovered stump reminded me in both shape and colour of the closed part of a hanging sausage, and it filled me with despair at first; dressing and undressing, doing up buttons, shoelaces and bandages, lighting a cigarette – all these things made me sweat in despair.

After a few months it didn't bother me any more, it was as if I had been born with only one hand – except for lighting a cigarette, there I still have no hope.

The war had marked my body with a sentence of guilt. But once a man understands himself as an image of dignity, you can chop him until nothing is left but a trunk and wound him all over his body – and he still remains God's greatest creation. When fresh troops arrive at the front and are thrown into battle, the generals and the journalists say that they are having their 'baptism of fire' – one of those solemn and stupid phrases that are used to cover up the bestiality of war, but I did seem to have had a baptism in the war in Spain, from the fire of that war: a mark of freedom in my heart, of awareness and justice.

I spent my hours outside the hospital in Valladolid walking alone up and down Calle Santiago trying to sort out my thoughts, or else I would sit in the café Cantabrico and hours seemed to fly past while I was thinking; at times my thoughts got all tangled up like skeins of wool, God and religion confused everything, and I didn't manage to find my way back to the beginning and unravel it all. I went to the College of San Gregorio and when I entered the courtyard my thoughts became free, they rose above the words of man, the harmony of stone and light created by the hand of man; and the stone was no longer the stone of the *sierre,* and the light was not the light that beat so harshly over the countryside of Castile; I came from a world in which the heart of man was like the stones of the mountainside, and the light devoured the face of the dead; I realised that man with his living heart, for his heart's peace, can bind stone and light in harmony, and raise everything up, and place it in order above himself.

The façade of San Gregorio, full of symbols of the history of Spain, enchanted me, though I knew very little about Spanish history – the story and the beauty of Spain seemed to be reflected in that façade. Valladolid is a beautiful old town – I would have liked to stay there, I hope to end my days in a place like Valladolid or Siena, a town in which man's past is in every stone. But for me the war was over, and the rubber stamps of military headquarters and the embarcation authorities fell on the 'loyalty and honour' with which I had served and the hand I had lost and Spain was a last glimpse of land and houses in the night, as if she had become a land at peace again in that ice-cold February night. As the ship drew away, a soldier was ironically singing a popular song of a few years before, 'When Spain's asleep in clear and tranquil nights', one of those songs that cast an evil spell (I say this but I don't believe in that sort of thing – though it seems odd that during those years trouble arose in the countries that the songs so fondly described – perhaps it was the songs that put ideas into Mussolini's head). In the darkness an angry voice shouted: 'Shut your mouth!'

IV

Relatives and friends came to visit me, showed some sympathy about the hand I had lost, pondered about my future as a man with a pension, and concluded that after all one ought to thank God that nothing worse had happened. Then they would ask 'What's Spain like?' as if I had been on a pleasure trip and only incidentally had a hand missing.

'Terrible,' I replied.

This left them astounded. The bullfights, the songs, the guitars, the women behind the arabesque grilles, the jasmine, the processions – wasn't that Spain?

I had left a bullfight after the first bull, I had not heard the sound of a single guitar string, the women I had seen were drunk in bars and not mysterious behind grilles; and I had seen other women too, packed together in a black tearful mass behind the doors of the military command; I had not smelled the scent of jasmine at night, nor seen processions with gold and incense.

'But isn't Spain beautiful?' they persisted.

'Just like Sicily,' I would say. 'Very very beautiful by the sea, where there are a lot of trees and vines, but arid in the interior – the 'breadland' we called it, and scanty bread too.'

'Are the Spanish poor?'

'The poor are even worse off than we are, and the rich are frighteningly rich – it takes a whole night in the train to cross a duke's lands, the feudal domains are simply endless.'

'Good for him!' said my friends. 'Here Mussolini has set himself against the feudal properties, he says he's going to divide the feudal lands among the peasants, there are big placards in the square saying AWAY WITH THE LARGE ESTATES in huge letters.'

'But in Spain we're fighting against those who want to divide the big estates among the peasants.'

'Are we fighting for the rich, then, in Spain?'

'For the rich, the priests and the police,' I said.

'But how can that be? For the priests and the police, that's understandable. But Mussolini treats the rich like pigs.'

'With words you can do anything,' I explained, 'but no one will ever see anything being taken away from the rich while Mussolini is about.'

When my mother heard me talk like this she made signs to me with her eyes and lips to keep quiet; when we were alone she begged me to be careful, and told me that I made her heart stand still when I talked in that way with other people about. My uncle Pietro said he simply didn't recognise me any more: when I left home I could hardly manage to say four words in a row, and now I spoke like an advocate of lost causes – it was silly to make myself liable to banishment after losing a hand in the war. My wife said nothing, the bank-book with the ten thousand lire she had been able to save seemed to her to make up for everything – for the war, the lost hand, the revulsion she felt when she looked at the stump or was touched by it; I felt her tremble as if she had a fever when I touched her. There had never been love between us, but during the few months we had been together we had at least had satisfaction; that maimed wrist, always cold as a dog's muzzle, was enough to dry up her desire just as some flowers wilt as soon as they are touched by hand. She was good-looking and my desire for her would blaze up in me, but as soon as I was satisfied she would go out of my mind like writing on a blackboard disappearing as you rub it with a duster. She had become more beautiful, her body had filled out, and in making love she feigned her climax dutifully; the further she was away from me the more she simulated her desire – she was a good wife. Perhaps I had become embittered towards her, I felt myself different in body and in mind, and imagined cunning and sham in her; and her excitement when she spoke of the bank book and what could be done with the saved money I condemned as greed, the shabby joy of the woman who loves only money – yet perhaps it was simply the poverty we came from that made money glitter in her eyes, for my mother too saw the future as rosy because of the savings and the pension that was coming to me. I suffered for that money, I saw myself as a murderer who had done his horrible job and had his reward, a Judas with his thirty pieces of silver; I remembered the moment, the only moment of the war when I had felt the cold pleasure of killing: the Republicans were running away and I shot with cool calculation, my aim slightly in advance of the running man I wanted to hit – the savage joy of seeing a man collapse to the ground after he had been shot. I fail to understand why the pleasure of killing should have come out in me at that moment with such violence and clarity. War is terrible for this reason more than anything else: it reveals us to ourselves as murderers at certain moments, with a pleasure in killing which is as intense as the desire to possess a woman. And it was for that moment when I had committed murder that I felt I had earned the money that stood in my red bank-book. Perhaps my mother might have understood if I had explained to her that in my eyes, in my conscience that money represented shame – shame for a war that was not mine, a war against people like myself, and shame for the moment in which I had been a murderer; she might have understood, but she would have thought that everything would resolve itself, for my present peace of mind as well as for eternity, if I only told a priest my thoughts on my knees, and gave a small part of the money as an offering to the Virgin Mary. That's what troubles me about religion: people take their conscience with them as they take a dirty blanket to the wash-house, and stretch it out clean again over their sleep. But my wife didn't even understand that washing of the conscience – she had a healthy appetite, she enjoyed herself and went to church in the same way as some people make a warding-off gesture when they see a black cat; copying a crochet design was the highest point of her mental effort and her sense of beauty. The idea of having a child from her body appalled me.

In those days I was like a child with a new, complicated toy which he can't leave alone for a single moment. I had discovered that to think about myself and others and everything on earth was a game as inexhaustible as the endless chain of numbers: it wasn't that I was conscious of my discovery and deliberately threw myself into the terrible game – it came naturally, as a plant stunted in a pot sprouts foliage and roots when it is transplanted to open soil. As children at elementary school we used to play at numbers: we'd put a nought behind a one and read ten – another nought, one hundred – and more noughts, one after the other, until we reached figures that even the teacher couldn't read, and we added still more noughts – that's what thoughts are like. I felt like an acrobat balancing on a high wire and looking at the world in airborne delight, and then turning upside down and seeing death below him, as the wire suspends him over a whirlpool of human heads and lights and the drum beats out death. I had a rage to see everything from the inside, as if every person, every thing, every face were a book you could open and read; a book is a thing too – you can put it on a table and look at it, use it to put under a wobbly chair leg to keep it steady, or hit someone on the head with it – but if you open it and read it, it becomes a world; and why shouldn't everything be opened and read and become a world?

What hurt me most of all and made me feel most isolated was everyone's indifference towards the tremendous things that I had seen and that Spain had lived through. I felt like a man walking in a funeral procession on the day of the Festival of Saint Calogero or the Assumption, when everyone is mad with joy and the big square is decked out in the gayest colours; you'd walk behind the black and yellow hearse containing the dead man, have to cross an amusement arcade with your heart full of sorrow, and a deep grudge would well up in you against the festival and the people enjoying themselves. Perhaps it's only natural for veterans to be stung by the indifference of others and lock themselves up inside themselves until everyday life, work, friends and family absorb them again: but if someone comes back from a war like the war in Spain with the certain feeling that his own house is going to burn down in the same fire, he can't just push his new experiences and thoughts into memories and dreams – he wants others to be awakened too, and to know.

But the others wanted to sleep. The people of my town are so poor, and so mean-spirited in their abject poverty, that everyone said to me enviously: 'Now you've made your money you can live safely' – and the rich said it to me too. If I hadn't lost my hand I would have gone back to the sulphur mine; Spain was a sulphur mine too, with men exploited like beasts of burden, deadly fire waiting to burst through a hole like a flood, man with his cursing and his hatred, and noble hope like the white sprouting wheat on Good Friday inside his cursing and his hatred. But with my lost hand I was condemned to idleness spent in conversation with old people, at the miners' social club, or long walks alone; with the old people I could talk endlessly – they listened to me as if I were telling them stories of the paladins of France, things from far away, with the blood just a colouring, as in the pictures on their carts.

The secretary at the Fascist Party offices treated me as if I had gone to fight the war in Spain on his account, in his name; he displayed pride in the hand I had lost, our town weighed in with my hand in the scales of victory, he said: 'We have written a page of honour'; this was the final sentence of the citation for the medal I had been given, the citation he had had copied by a teacher in ornate handwriting full of scrolls and flourishes and surrounded by fascios and flags in water-colour; it hung, framed, between a fellow-townsman's Holy Sepulchre Fascist's diploma* and the picture of a soldier who had been killed in Abyssinia. Photographs of men who had died in action, diplomas and citations for medals covered the walls of the House of Fascism, and behind the secretary's so-called 'work-desk' stood one of the commandments of the Fascist decalogue, framed: 'Guarding a petrol can means serving the Fatherland', a commandment that was displayed not without reason, for Mussolini could rely on the secretary to guard the can – the petrol he sold afterwards. Almost every day the secretary sent for me; he said the Fatherland would not forget its debt of gratitude towards its finest sons, he was working to remind the Fatherland of its debt to me, he wanted

* Given to all those who had taken part in the inaugural public meeting of militant Fascism in Holy Sepulchre Square, Milan.

the Fatherland to find me a suitable job, but the Fatherland had so many heroic sons to remunerate and was perhaps a little forgetful. The secretary wanted me to tell him stories about the war, he was a fan of General Bergonzoli – 'Electric Whiskers' they called him – as if he were a footballer or a bullfighter. I told him things about Bergonzoli that I had read in the newspapers – I had never seen those whiskers; and then I would tell him of the most inhuman incidents I had witnessed, the stuff that really makes you spit at Fascism; and I told him these things absolutely straight, without showing any anger at all. He listened with mounting enthusiasm. 'Oh yes,' he said, 'the country folk are a nasty breed' – he meant the peasants – 'if you treat them well they bite you. And the sulphur miners too, yes, there are some like you but on the whole they're people who should be handled with a big stick. They're out to get Spain into their own hands ... But the Duce is vigilant – Communism must not be allowed to rear its head on our seas ... '

'In fact', I said, 'there are very few Communists in Spain. Mostly they're Anarchists, Republicans and Socialists.'

'They're all Reds,' said the secretary, 'slaves of Moscow. And the Anarchists are the most dangerous of them all – they're savage beasts.'

One day he sent for me to tell me that the Fatherland had responded to his repeated requests. It had remembered me and offered me the post of a school caretaker, but the Fatherland's school caretakers, that is to say the school caretaker jobs that the Fatherland could dispose of, were only in places where there were secondary and higher schools – elementary school caretakers were not state employed; it was therefore necessary, the secretary regretted, for me to take up a post in a larger town, though with any luck there would be a town close by ...

'No,' I said. 'A town far away would be better – outside Sicily, a really large town.'

'Why?' asked the secretary in surprise.

'I want to see something new,' I said.